The Katydid Effect

Edward R Hackemer

The Katydid Effect

Edward R Hackemer

frustration; Norwegian that she learned from her grandfather. In a few moments, she would have collected her emotions, a smile would curl at her lips, and Annie would get on with the task at hand. Early on, she proved to herself and Alex that she was a resilient, confident and task-driven woman.

In any marriage, as in their new union, disagreements and the unavoidable tiffs agitated Alex and Annie's affinity now and again; from small irritations like leaving dirty clothes on the bathroom floor, to not turning off the headlights when parking the car, or splattering paint onto laundry drying on the line outdoors. They quickly worked through those minor marital squabbles and never went to bed angry at each other.

Annie began her new life on the ranch and quickly learned about equine husbandry. She worked tirelessly with Alex, and helped with the grooming, feeding and cleaning after Sebastian and Cassie. Indeed, when Alexander bought the farm the previous year, he was a novice horseman and heavily relied on the help of his neighbor, Louis Verdune. Their friendship grew steadily, and the two men complemented each other's skills and knowledge. It was a give and take alliance between an experienced mechanic and a knowledgeable equestrian. Their wives also took to each other well and they enjoyed sharing nearly all aspects of life in rural Chumuckla. Annie cherished the newfound friendship and company of their neighbors and had genuine respect for Louis' wife. Hedy was three months pregnant with her second child, managing her household with a dedication and personal strength that Annie admired. A German girl who, two and a half years earlier, married an Air Force GI, Hedwig was still adjusting to life as a new mother and wife in the Florida panhandle. Annie, as a transplant from Wisconsin, was in a very similar place in life. She found a strong new friend in Hedy and often took comfort in her friendship. Starting a fresh life in completely new surroundings, it was occasionally difficult not to feel like a had gotten married the previous June. Annie settled quickly into life on the small ranch, making the transition from the upper Midwest to the Florida panhandle as smooth and pleasant as a barefoot stroll on the pristine white sands of Pensacola Beach. She felt secure and satisfied with Alex and the new life they were molding from their shared dreams, passions, and labor. Annie filled her days on the farm caring for their bred pair of well-minded quarter horses: Sebastian and Cassandra. Cassie, as Annie would call her, was pregnant and would foal in late August or September. With long, devoted hours of work, detailed help and advice from their neighbors, Louis and Hedy, Alex and Annie were building a strong, healthy family: a quarter horse family line.

The past July, Alexander financed, and Louis helped build the two-bay garage at the end of the long drive off Chumuckla Highway. They opened a machine shop and engine repair business. Louis carried his reputation as a reliable, honest mechanic from his old employer outside the Pensacola Naval Air Station. A solid customer base followed, and the two men enjoyed a quick changeover from developing and nurturing to growing and expanding a promising new business.

Annie's adjustment to her new roles, as homemaker and wife seemed as smooth as warm as maple syrup poured over buckwheat pancakes. She took on each new day with the excitement and innocent anticipation of a young girl unwrapping a birthday present. There were moments of frustration to be sure, such as the aggravation of a stopped-up kitchen sink just as the pasta needed to be taken from the stove-top and drained, or the wringer washer rolling, dancing freely across the floor, wildly spewing out suds of *Ivory Flakes* until the plug was forcefully yanked from the electrical outlet. Moreover, when such things occurred simultaneously, Annie would stomp her foot, clench her fists, and blurt out mild Norwegian curse words as an expression of evolution from life within the small city of Appleton, Wisconsin to the rural reality of Santa Rosa County, Florida. It seemed that there could not have been a better beginning.

"I'm Sorry."

Ten months later:
Saturday morning, April 16, 1955
Straight Eight Farm, Chumuckla, Florida

After breakfast, Alex and Annie sat and relaxed comfortably on the wooden front porch swing. A soft, warm spring breeze from the gulf pushed across the porch and gently brushed at Annie's auburn curls. She was sitting close and resting against Alex; his arm was on the back of the bench, over her shoulders. It was springtime in the Florida panhandle and life was grand. The smooth sound of Kay Starr's sultry *Fool Fool Fool* drifted softly from the radio inside the parlor. There was static and the faint crackle of lightning in the background. Dark thunderheads on the far horizon slowly rolled across the sky and brought the promise of a warm spring rain. A few vanishing golden rays of sun forced their cutting swords of light through the thick clouds and allowed pale, watercolor shades of rust and carmine to paint the edges. White cotton curtains pushed outward against the screened porch windows like the billowing petticoats of carefree young dancers.

Alex was moving his foot just enough to put the swing into gentle motion. The weathered wood creaked in mild protest. They sipped at their cups of *A&P* coffee.

"It's going to be another great day, Honey."

"Yes, it is, Alex. Yes, it is."

They cherished these quiet personal moments. Their love grew vast and boundless. Emotionally, physically and spiritually, their lives had woven tightly together since they

4

chairs to the left of the door. A flagstone walkway led from the driveway to the front porch. Native white honeysuckle was twining its way up and around the porch posts on each side of the steps; its spicy sweet fragrance filling the yard. A Carolina wren was busily announcing his presence, bouncing from porch rail to branch and back with his loud chatter. He was making it clear to everyone within earshot that he was a permanent resident.

Ten yards beyond the oak was a sea of knee-high green grass and a path leading to a freshly painted red barn, whitewashed wooden fence and a twenty-foot-tall concrete block silo. Annie noticed two smaller outbuildings standing away from the barn and closer to the house. Annie asked in a nervous, curious tone, "Are any of those buildings an outhouse, Alex?"

His response was reassuring, "There's indoor plumbing, Annie girl, and I even have hot running water ... all the modern stuff."

She was relieved, but immediately justified her question in a bashful, almost embarrassed, tone. "Well, I *have* been in an outhouse before. Just because I'm from Appleton, it doesn't mean that I'm a city girl. I was just wondering, but it's good you have indoor facilities. Outhouses can be scary at night."

Alex reassured his wife yet again, "No need to be scared here. No need. You're going to love it here. I know you are."

Alexander was right. Within days, Annie had adjusted quickly to her new life and surroundings on the homestead. They started their lives together with excitement and untiring enthusiasm. Little by little, one room at a time, the old farmhouse became an expression of their lives. From gingham curtains, end tables and lamps to bed linens and kitchen utensils, it all came together. They were busy establishing their lives with one another, coordinating their work on the farm, and building a future. Annie willingly embraced her new surroundings and began a smooth mansion in *Gone with the Wind* to Uncle Remus' humble cabin in *Song of the South*. Gradually, further down the drive, she could see the roofline of the house she was about to call *home*. Her eyes strained and with one hand on the dashboard, she sat forward on the car seat. Alex looked over to his wife, smiled and gave her a sly wink. She was too busy to notice. Her husband was driving painfully slow.

"I know this car can go faster than this, Alex!"

No sooner than those words left her lips, the house came into full view. Alex stopped the Packard a few yards from the wooden steps of the front porch. Annie sank back into the seat and let out a deep sigh of satisfaction. "This is fantastic. That's all I can say. This is super duper, just great. I know I will love it here." She slid across the seat, pushed against her husband and gave him a passionate kiss.

"I love you, Alexander Throckmorton."

There was a large Live Oak on the east side of the house, with long, low-lying, wide branches, spreading toward the dwelling, as if to surround and protect it. Three mature Southern Magnolias stood on the opposite side, their leathery leaves hanging stiff and still in the gentle breeze. Alex turned the key, and the engine became silent. The Packard sat parked at its destination. Alexander and Maryanne Throckmorton were home. He had his arm around her shoulders as they sat and looked through the windshield at their home. Annie was awash with feelings of joy, love, hope and thoughts of new friends; allowing her aspirations and dreams to fill the Packard. Life was a gift. Love was the wrapper, passion the ribbon. The world was all theirs.

It was a 1920's legacy home, with graying, weathered, white asbestos siding shingles. The wood trim around the home, double-hung windows and screens gave contrast in dark blue enamel. A porch ran the length of the dwelling, with an old oak swing on the right side and two weathered, woven wicker

2

ONE: HOME - STRAIGHT EIGHT FARM

"My Happiness."

Sunday, early afternoon, June 13, 1954
Rural Route 2, Chumuckla, Florida

Married a mere twelve days earlier, Alexander and Maryanne's two-thousand-mile honeymoon road trip was ending. Over the last week and a half, they had spent their days driving south, safely surrounded by American steel formed by American labor: a new *Packard Patrician*. The nights were something else. Sheltered from a thunderstorm in a cheap motel, frightened to the bone in a jail cell, or relaxing in the luxury of a seaside resort, it was a trip they would remember the rest of their lives. It was a trip shadowed by years-old mystery but brightened by personal discovery.

Annie sat up straight and focused her eyes on the road ahead. Her body tingled with anticipation and waves of excitement pulsed through her veins.

"We're getting close, Annie girl. Real close." Alex took the opportunity to tease his wife. He gently touched the brake, slowed, turned the large, cream-colored automobile into the driveway, and stopped. "Here we are ... this is it ... home."

"I'm not seeing anything! Nothing! Come on now, let's get to it. Stop teasing me and drive on in and let me see this place, Alex!" She gave him a playful punch on the upper arm. Alex nodded, grinned, put the car in gear and drove ahead slowly.

The driveway was sand and stone, with tufts of grass and weeds growing down the center berm, gradually turning away beyond a grove of Scrub Pine and knee-high Saw Palmetto palms. Annie felt her heart thumping inside her chest. She had thrilling expectations and her mind raced with images. Her imagination wildly traveled from the Twelve Oaks

1

WHAT'S INSIDE:

ACKNOWLEDGEMENTS:

My proofer: Edny
My editor & pen pal: Letitia
My reader: You
My inspiration: The musicians,
singers, & writers
My gang: The Pirkle Woods
Packard Parkers

Cover photography and design: ©2013 Edward R Hackemer
Photo properties:
Latitude: 34.196457
Longitude: -84.152414
Height above sea level: 1202 feet
Date: August 4, 2005
Location: Castleberry Rd, Cumming, GA, USA

THE FINE PRINT:

Sincere effort has been taken to ensure that this novel contains the straight stuff for 1954 thru 1967. Please realize that most of this story is fictional except the parts that are not. The needle was changed to protect the record and only the record.

This is a novel, therefore most of the story and many of the characters in this book are fictional. Any resemblance in the description or name of any real person, living or dead, is likely to be either coincidental, unintentional or both. Any name specific identification, dialogue, or comments by any specific character either real or fictional, are used only for descriptive purposes.

Any lyrics or music mentioned in this book are the intellectual property of individual copyright holders and are referenced only for descriptive purposes. The reader is strongly encouraged to purchase the music, listen and either tap his or her foot or snap their fingers enthusiastically.

Brand names, products or services are generally shown in *italics*. Whether actual or fictitious, those mentioned in this book are the trademark of their respective owners, past or present, and are used solely for descriptive purposes.

Retail, government, service, or religious institutions mentioned in this book, whether actual, fictitious or fantasy, are not included as an endorsement or criticism of their products or services. They are recounted solely for descriptive purposes.

TITLES BY THIS AUTHOR

Titles are available in Hardcover, Paperback or Kindle® format.
Visit the author's Facebook, Goodreads, or Amazon page.

The Katydid Effect

(Book 2- Throckmorton Family Novels)

~ a novel ~

Edward R Hackemer

Hardcover ISBN: 9798792111028
ISBN-10: 1482669838
ISBN-13: 978-1482669831

fish out of water, isolated and swimming upstream in unknown rivers. Hedy was the steadying force, the helping hand and the port in the storm that Annie occasionally needed. She had that no nonsense, stoic, German sense of humor that meshed with Annie's unabashed opinions and fearless mannerisms. Annie began to think of Hedy as a sister; a sister as close as she and Beth always were.

But, lurking just below the surface was a secret envy, a gentle jealousy and a private, personal longing that Annie kept hidden even from her husband. She longed for the day she could tell Alex, Hedy and the entire world that she too, was pregnant. Annie had a calendar pictured in her mind; a calendar that was fluidly focused nine months into the future. She held her love for Alex as the strongest fixture in her life and she longed to bring forth a child to celebrate, verify and steel their devotion. She felt it deep in her heart, soul, and existence. When she and Alex made love, she surrendered her entire being into their intimacy and all her heart into their combined passion. Alex treasured her sensual fervor, shared her rapture and reveled in their love. He welcomed the idea of an addition to the family and expected that a child would come along but was unaware of Annie's secret calendar.

Three hundred yards down the sand and gravel driveway stood two neatly lettered, large white rural mailboxes. They were fixed atop three old *Buick* crankshafts, welded together and formed as a "T". The first had "Throckmorton" lettered neatly along the top in red, with *"Straight Eight Farm"* and *The Throckmortons* just below. The second box read *"L & H Verdune"*.

About halfway between Chumuckla Highway and their front porch was the machine and engine shop. Then the driveway forked, broke off, curved left, leading toward the horse barn, equipment sheds and on toward Louis and Hedy's place, tucked behind several Florida maples. There were Laurel and

Turkey Oaks along the sides of the drive, clumps of spring-fresh grass, and a few smaller magnolias spreading out and away from the home. A mockingbird was usually sitting atop one of those magnolias, loudly mimicking the countless calls of other species in a clear, distinct melodious tone unmatched anywhere else in nature. The morning was slowly drifting into mid-day.

Alex was still deftly pushing the swing with his foot, moving it in a restful, almost hypnotic sway. The soft, smooth motion perfectly fit their mood. Annie was leaning into him, her head on his shoulder, with her eyes closed. Alex noticed something. The swing's gentle movement slowed to a wobbling stop. Annie opened her eyes to see a large sedan coming up the driveway, leaving a rising trail of dust disappearing behind. She sat up.

"I wonder who that is, Alex? On a Saturday morning? Who could it be?"

"I can't imagine ... we'll find out soon enough, Annie girl."

They looked down the drive to the approaching two-door coupe. In a split second, Annie recognized the woman in the front seat. It was Jovita, the black-haired, bronze-skinned barmaid at *Fernando's Hideaway* in Jacksonville. They had met the previous June, and she answered to *Joey*.

Alex and Annie stood up from the swing. It gently bumped against the backs of their legs. There was an emotional hollowness opening in the center of Alex's chest. He felt butterfly tickles in his stomach and electric prickles on his skull. Annie felt roller coaster nerves. The hair at the nape of Alex's neck tingled. His father, Nicholas, who he had last seen in 1946, was behind the wheel of the car. The big *Oldsmobile* stopped a few yards from the front steps. Small stones under the white-wall tires clicked and settled under the vehicle's weight.

The rumbling V-8 became quiet. The mockingbird's song could no longer be heard. Annie was firmly holding her husband's hand and gently forming a welcoming smile. Alex stood motionless, his eyes steady and without a blink. He did not recognize his emotion. He was unable to present any reasoned, steady reaction. This was unknown territory. He was seeing his father for the first time in nine years and two wars later. Additionally, it was eleven months earlier that he discovered that his father was still alive, and not dead from hostile action as was reported by the Army Air Corps.

The doors of the deep green, *Olds 88* two-door sedan opened. The occupants exited and started toward the steps of the porch. Joey wore a demure, insecure smile and Nicholas, either willingly or not, carried no outward display of emotion. They walked toward the porch hand-in-hand. Joey was wearing a floral print cotton dress, white slouch socks, black-on-white saddle shoes and a small red scarf around her long black hair. Nicholas had a straightforward, serious look with sleek, pressed black trousers and a crisply starched white shirt, sleeves rolled halfway up. He removed his aviator sunglasses and stuck them inside his pocket.

Alex and Annie took two steps toward the end of the porch. As Joey approached, Annie opened her arms and the women shared a short, firm nuzzle. Nicholas walked directly up the steps onto the porch and was the first to extend his arms and hold his son. In an unsteady pitch, he spoke over his son's shoulder, "I'm so happy to see you, Alexander. I have so much to tell. I'm sorry, so, so sorry things turned out so damn tragic and this has taken so damn long. I admit being driven by ignorance."

Alex held his arms around his father without emotion. He was deeply searching for the right words, the right reaction. He wanted to say the right thing, the right way, without unforgiving umbrage, yet still showing his deep disappointment and indignation.

Alex broke the fragile hug and took a half step back. He forced the words from inside, "Glad to see you again, Old Man. This is a surprise I didn't see coming ... not by a long shot. I know we have a truckload of things to chin wag about ... let's go inside. I think we're going to be talking quite a while." With that, he turned and led the way inside to the sitting room. Annie looked over toward her newly discovered father-in-law, gave a slight nod with an impish smile and motioned him inside. Joey followed, then Annie. Her white *Keds* sneakers squeaked with each step as she crossed the shellacked, white pine floors of the hallway.

Alex stood outside the living room entrance with an outstretched arm and welcomed their unexpected guests into the room. "Come on in, find a seat anywhere and make yourselves comfortable. I need to call my partner Louis and let him know I'll be a bit late this morning." His voice had a nervous instability, and he briefly wondered if anyone noticed. He knew they did.

Nicholas stepped inside the room and turned to Alex. "You don't need to do that, son. No need to skip work. We showed up as a real surprise, I know. We can have a quick visit and come back later in the day or ..."

Alex quickly corralled his nerves and interrupted, "You are not going to escape that easily, Nicholas Throckmorton. Not today. Louis and I own the shop. It's Saturday and I can take an hour or two or three off. Now, sit down, you and Joey, and we'll chat and nibble ... or holler and gobble. Whatever. Annie will fix up some coffee and cookies or cake or something. Make yourselves comfortable. I'll be right back." He nodded affirmatively to his wife and walked down the short hall to the kitchen. Annie remained in the center of the room, dressed in barely beige jodhpurs and a white shirt rolled up over her elbows. She gestured with her hands in the direction of the sofa and smiled at their guests as they sat down. It was an old, over-stuffed, church rummage-sale divan with burgundy upholstery and black piping. Annie politely excused herself to put on a pot of coffee, switched off the *Philco* table radio and left the parlor to join her husband in the kitchen.

As Annie entered the kitchen, Alex was just ending his short conversation with his partner Louis and hanging up the *Western Electric* telephone. His thoughts were raging, and his words came out as a torrent, "I've cleared it with Louis and I'm taking the whole day off. At least this morning. Anyway, we'll see how this ends up. It's Saturday ... I think this is going to get interesting, so please make the coffee good and strong ... OK, Annie girl? And how many times have we wondered when this meeting was going to happen? Huh? Now the time has come. Here we are ... all together for the first time. Damn near a year goes by and the Old Man finally makes the trip from Jacksonville ... and after all the mystery and misadventure we experienced last year, now this. Are you ready for this, Annie?"

She took a half step toward Alex, touched her lips to his cheek and held him. "This is good, Alex. Real good. Be nice and no heated words, OK? I'm happy this time has come so let's make the best of it. And now I am looking forward to hearing his story and getting to know your father. So, give him the chance I think he deserves. And Joey, too. We owe this to each other and to them, just as they owe it to us. It's about time, don't you think?"

He kissed his wife softly and gave her a firm, pressing hug. "You're right ... I love you."

"I know, Alex. I know." She broke off their embrace and said, "Now go on in there and get to know your father again.

I'll bring in the coffee and the rest of that coffee cake and some Oreos or something. Go on. And be nice."

He gave his wife a light kiss on the lips and left the kitchen. Anticipating the coming confab, Annie let out a gratified sigh as she stepped to the cupboard for the coffee. She felt the excitement building and sensed a subtle hint of mysterious intrigue. She and Alex strongly suspected that Nicholas was a spy, a spook of sorts. It was the only explanation for a barrel-full of unanswered questions. When it all started, where he had been and what he was doing now were the nagging unknowns. Who, what and wherefore were the big questions that Alex and Annie sought answers to. She and her husband realized they probably would never have full disclosure, but they each deeply wanted, and felt they deserved, an explanation for the missing nine years.

Annie could hear them talking in the front room as she scooped the *Breakfast Blend* coffee into the percolator. Not conversation, but chatter, was finding its way down the hallway and into the kitchen. She reached into the top shelf of the cupboard, brought out the serving platter and set it on the counter-top. Someone must have said something humorous. Joey was giggling faintly in a Latin-laced tone. Annie was curious as to how Joey managed to accentuate her heritage by her laughter. She shrugged her shoulders and cut the coffee cake into five slices. With her hands on her hips, looking at the pieces of cake, Annie decided it was simply not enough. She got three cellophane packs of *Hostess* vanilla cream *Twinkies* from the pantry, opened them and positioned them neatly on the platter between the slices of cake. Annie thought it was a satisfactory solution to a serious shortage of breakfast confections.

Annie lit a *Chesterfield* and took a seat at the kitchen table to wait for the coffee to trickle down. The chrome tubing and plastic upholstered chair released an impolite blat under her weight. Taking a puff on the cigarette, she put an elbow on the grey *Formica* top of the table and watched as the coffee bubbled, burped and perked up and around inside the little hollow glass knob on top of the pot. She blinked her eyes at the burn of the cigarette smoke and strained her ears to pick out some understandable words from the buzz coming up the hallway. She exhaled in exasperation, crushed out the cigarette and knew she could only wait in solitude. Once again, she silently vowed that someday she would quit smoking.

Down the hall, inside the living room, Alex sat at the edge of his seat on a tall-armed, brushed velour Victorian parlor chair. He was leaning forward, with his hands folded between his open knees. Alex quickly became aware that Jovita was the driving force behind this visit. She looked over to Nick often, smiling, nodding to affirm the direction of the small talk, fitting in a *"Si, Nicky."* to nearly every sentence. Jovita was weaving an entertaining tale about yesterday's trip from Jacksonville. She gave detailed descriptions of the thunderstorm outside Madison and their sea bass dinner in Tallahassee. She was talking fluidly, in her spicy Latin accent, trying to fill the uneasy vacuum between estranged father and son.

They left the Florida east coast the day before and spent the night a few miles down the road at a motel outside of Pensacola. Joey's conversation brought back all of the countless motel memories that Alex and Annie had experienced on the past year's trip from Wisconsin.

As he listened to Joey, Alexander's eyes were busy, looking to the olive-skinned beauty and back to his father. He glanced now and again, almost nervously, toward the hallway, awaiting Annie. His emotions were running in every possible direction. He felt anxiety, anticipation, emotional hunger and disappointment, all dancing barefoot on his soul.

He was aware that his palms were sweating; his nervousness was unsettling. Alex looked across to his father again. Nicholas had the complexion and skin tone of an outdoorsman, with veteran wrinkles at the corners of his eyes. His jet-black hair, combed straight back, was graying graciously. His eyes were so dark they appeared as a spit-shined night sky; glistening and reflecting the sparse morning sunrays like a bottomless well; teeming with dark secrets and hidden emotion, deep in the black, remote regions of the unknown.

Alex stood up abruptly and announced, "I'm going to help Annie bring in the coffee and cakes. Be right back." He was outside the front room and down the hallway with a few steps. He was unconsciously seeking Annie's help and needed the comfort of his wife's company. He knew what he wanted to say and what he wanted to ask, but hidden somewhere inside, he felt he was entering a strange, dark room with one hand on the doorknob, pausing and needing encouragement to open the door. He often fed on Annie's courage and unashamed wit.

"Let me give you a hand, Annie. I need you in there. I really need to have you in that room with me."

His wife stood at the table, wiping her hands on a dishtowel. The coffee pot, cups and cake plates sat on a handled, rectangular metal kitchen tray with paper napkins, spoons and forks. Annie folded the towel in one motion and tossed it to the sink. "Grab that tray, Alex. I'll bring the cakes, cream and sugar." It was perfect timing.

"Singing The Blues."

Saturday, mid-day, April 16, 1955

From her work as a waitress, Annie knew it was easier to start, continue and expand a conversation with your hands around a warm coffee cup. Nibbling on bits of baked sweets can fill the uncomfortable moments of silence, while either waiting for a reply or allowing steamy words to cool. The four people in the parlor were about to do just that.

Alex and Annie were the more anxious pair, sitting up straight and near the ends of their chairs. They were hanging on every word, awaiting clarification of past events and all those missing years. They were not to be disappointed. Alexander's father was beginning to tell entwining stories of lost love, heartbreaking misfortune and detailed decades-old wartime and foreign adventures. There was not a lot of exact or date-specific detail, but his stories expressed the loneliness of a man in what certainly was a form of self-imposed exile. While listening to Nicholas, it became clear that he was a man forced to make the best of the circumstance that he had helped create and then, in fact, nurtured. He expressed sadness about the chasm that had opened between himself and Alex. The war made sorrowful separation inevitable, but in later years, he pushed aside his responsibilities for personal convenience. Army Air Corps Captain Nicholas Throckmorton once considered the majority of his decisions to be a direct link to a sense of personal and patriotic duty. As he continued, he became increasingly retrospective, articulate and unforgiving, with his personal assessment of some of the errors he made.

Annie became teary once, twice, and more, and reached over to hold her husband's hand. Alex acknowledged her touch, but kept his gaze fixed on his father. There was an avalanche of words spilling into the room, rolling across his memories, challenging his senses, and testing his loyalties.

Alex listened intently as his father told the story of how he and his mother fell from love's grace and the unfortunate events that followed, by either choice or fate. Discovery abounded over the next hour. Nicholas Throckmorton's melancholy, blues-laden narrative entwined and captivated everyone in the parlor.

It was in 1938 that the marriage of Nicholas and Nora Jean Throckmorton crumbled. Alex's mother steadfastly refused to accept the circumstance of a divorce. It was unthinkable. Nora ascertained that she already sinned by marrying outside of the Catholic faith and would not commit another with a divorce. She would not budge on that issue and took the stand *"Hell or high water"* as Nicholas explained it. He knew better, but in the remote hope that some kind of reconciliation or compromise could come, he joined the Army Air Corps. Assigned to the American Volunteer Group (AVG) in the Orient, he dreamed perhaps his marriage would heal and mend itself by distance. Maybe his absence would make their hearts grow fonder. He said he was truly hopeful and there was indeed some promise in Nora's letters. Time passed and the letters became more infrequent, due to his remote assignment, the war, or the indifference brought by time. Over the period of nearly three years, the AVG evolved into an integral part of the Air Corp's war in the Pacific Theater of Operation. From clandestine trips to and from Rangoon, Guanshi, Hong Kong, Manila, and bombing raids on Japanese airfields in China, the *"kill bounty"* doled out by the Chinese, the bonus pay, and black-market cash added up. He spun tales of tempting danger, daring intrigue, and smuggling precious stones with his Air Corps comrade-in-arms, Robert McElvoy. He glazed over his fighter pilot experience and told of his recruitment by Army Intelligence, which eventually led to photographing Japanese military installations inaccessible to the Air Corps. In 1945, as the war was winding down, he became more involved in the Office of Strategic Services, the OSS. He explained there was no coordination of services and each branch of the military had its own intelligence agency. As things evolved, he took many trips to Manila and spent extensive time in the

Philippine mountain jungles. He explained that he became tired of war, withdrawn and downhearted, longing for home in Michigan, his son and yes, his wife.

The war ended and he mustered out from active duty. Then his tale entered familiar territory: things that Annie and Alex had found out for themselves over the past year. Nicholas told of a night of drinking and carousing in Chicago and meeting a young Cuban barmaid. He stayed in Chicago a week before continuing on to Detroit. Jovita tenaciously hung onto Nicholas' words; her dark eyes sparkling with intense, infinite mystery.

Annie interrupted with her brassy nature. "We already know all that. Alex and I uncovered that last year, when we met your Army buddy McElvoy in North Carolina. Then we drove to Jacksonville, found your Joey at that bar and solved the rest of that complicated little jigsaw puzzle that you left behind, Mister Throckmorton." Alex wasn't in the least bit surprised. Annie was sharply firing on all cylinders.

Her tone was not indignant, but inquisitive, intense, and determined. She was overly anxious for Nicholas to continue his story; reveal the truth and the real reasons he had remained under the radar all those years after the war. And most curiously, why he never tried to reconnect with his wife or son.

Nicholas cleared his throat, made eye contact with his son Alex and daughter-in-law Annie, took a sip of lukewarm coffee and continued, "I apologize … I was drifting away and going off subject. You're right. I'll continue."

All four shifted their bodies on their seats, repositioned their spines, backsides, and settled in for the long haul. Alex made a Twinkie disappear in two bites. Annie lit a Chesterfield and Nicholas continued with his open-ended narrative. Jovita sat with her hands folded on her lap.

Nick explained that when he returned to Detroit in 1946, his wife Nora had grown completely cold toward him. There was no feeling, no emotion, and no desire to make amends. He was overseas for eight years and coming back as a stranger. He too, knew their union was beyond any hope of repair. They agreed to part amicably, go their separate ways, without any squabble or legal filing. Nora felt that the shame of being alone and without a husband was the only viable alternative to the sin of divorce within her Catholic faith.

Nicholas was willing to accept his own personal punishment for the failure of his marriage. He believed his solitude would become his repentance. He thought of returning to Chicago and the young, olive-skinned beauty, but denied himself that option. He accepted his failure as a husband and decided to re-enlist, returning to the home he knew, now known as the Army Air Force. He left Detroit once again, bequeathed several thousand dollars to Alexander for college, a good sum for Nora and left much more in two safe deposit boxes. He thought his new life's direction was clearly laid out before him. He was confident he had made the right decision and was taking care of his familial obligations to the best of his ability.

Nicholas explained that two days later, he bought train tickets for the *Saint Louis Limited* and *Texas Rocket*. After another three days and fifteen hundred miles of railroad track, he had arrived in Texas at Fort Sam Houston Army Air Force Station, where he re-enlisted in the 12th Observation Group. Soon thereafter, he was back in the Orient, flying tactical reconnaissance in P-51 Mustangs. When his plane went down in the Hainan province of China, the Army filed a Missing Airman Report, and he was assumed Killed In Action in the Chinese Civil War, or *War of Liberation* as the Communists preferred to call it.

18

Nicholas lit a cigarette, shifted his weight on the sofa, and went on, "Long story short: three months in Commie confinement let me rationalize that it was all right for my family to consider me lost. I was eventually released to the French in Indochina and finally made my way to Okinawa again. By an act of congress, the Army Air Force became the Air Force and records were conveniently lost. I was erased. My life vanished. I no longer existed. Dead, gone. Lost. Your mother got a paltry sum in life insurance, and you got freedom from worry. I met Jovita, my Joey, in Chicago. Truman got the National Security Act passed, the OSS became something called the CIA and here I am. I'm here, but I'm not. Not in that capacity. Understand?"

Alex muttered, "Judas Priest. We figured as much."

Seconds later, his father responded, "You got that cuss word from your mother, Alexander. She used to say that: Judas Priest. You learned how to swear without swearing. You learned that from your mother. Say what you will, she was a decent person."

There was an air of uncertainty in the room: an unsteady calm, and unsettling quiet. Annie looked around at the others, getting a sense of everyone's demeanor. It was subdued; everyone was withdrawn deep inside his or her soul, in a suspenseful whirl. It didn't last long.

Alex was irritated. He stood, looked down at his father and asked, "Do you even know that she's dead? Your wife Nora? My mother? Do you realize that? Do you care?" His voice labored, straining not to fully break into a nervous crackle.

Annie stood and reached out to her husband. He motioned her away, twitched his shoulders, and prodded his father again, "Well, do you?"

Nicholas sat motionless and looked up at his son. Jovita took his hand. It was an eternity of seconds. He stood and with

Jovita next to him, his voice splintered as he stammered, "I was out of country when you came to Jacksonville last year. I only got back two days ago, and that's the God honest truth, Alexander. As soon as I got back, Joey told me that you and a young lady had been there ... and I knew right then and there that you must have opened those safe deposit boxes in Detroit. And then I immediately checked on your mother. I did, and I called some people. Then I called her sister Marie in Oshkosh, lied, and told her I was a real estate agent. It was only then, during that long-distance telephone call, that I discovered that your mother had died last year. I didn't know, son. I didn't know. I had no way of knowing, and I'm so damn sorry it has boiled down to all these caked-on, burnt, dried, dirty old secrets."

Annie and Alex, Joey and Nicholas stood unmoving, stoic and silent. Outside on the porch, the empty swing discreetly creaked and deftly moaned in the fresh breeze. The Mockingbirds had started their loud chatter again.

Annie glanced at their guests, her husband and quickly around the room. Her eyes danced and she broke the quiet like a sonic boom, "Okey dokey, then. How about another pot of coffee? Anybody?"

Alex nodded. Nicholas answered, "Yeah. Why not? Sounds good to me."

Joey forced a smile. She was the first to sit down, followed by Nicholas. Annie grabbed the enameled coffee pot and left the room for the kitchen. Alex put a match to one of his *Lucky Strikes*, drew the smoke deep inside him and held it. Through pursed lips, he exhaled a gray cloud into the room that rippled, curled and drifted upward toward the tin ceiling tiles. Seconds passed as connected eternities. It was too quiet to ignore.

Alex looked to his father and asked, "How about a couple fingers of bourbon, Old Man? Dad?" Alex could not

20

remember ever calling his father *"Dad;"* he wondered how that happened, and why. It was awkward. It didn't sound or feel right, and he decided that he would never use it again.

Nicholas nodded, took hold of Joey's hand on her lap and watched his son walk across the room to the buffet. Alex brought back a bottle of *Old Crow* and two mismatched glasses.

Shortly, Annie brought the second pot of coffee into the parlor and started to chatter - telling short tales of her childhood, and how she and Alex had met and fell in love. She quickly glazed over their drive south from Wisconsin and told of how she was growing to love her new home. She giggled about the mockingbirds' song and how the birds rudely woke them at five o'clock nearly every morning. Annie worked her magic and allowed her vanilla voice and chipper disposition to cover the room. The tension eased. The knot inside Alexander's chest collapsed, loosened, and became unwound. The morning evaporated smoothly and without notice. It was washed away with conversation, coffee, cake, a couple Twinkies, *Royal Crown* cola, and some bourbon. The earlier stress, anxiety and uneasiness disappeared, but strong undercurrents of doubt and uncertainty still churned inside Alex's mind. Annie too, felt there was much more to Nicholas' tales.

The brass, broad-faced clock on the buffet harshly sounded a loud, impolite two o'clock. They decided to break and meet later for dinner at a local roadhouse a few miles away in Milton.

Alex and Annie stood on the porch and waved to their parting guests as the green sedan drove off and vanished down around the bend in the driveway. She stood next to her husband with her arm around his waist. "That went well, Alex. I am proud of you. You behaved yourself."

21

She paused, turned, and faced her husband. Annie took his hands in hers, looked into his eyes and soul and continued, "And I want you to think about this, Alex ... you just think about it, OK? Think about it ... after a wound heals, Alex, it can hurt all over again when you pull off the *Band Aid*."

"Let Me Go Lover."

Saturday evening, April 16, 1955
Munson Highway, Milton, Florida

Alex drove the Packard onto the blacktop and gravel lot and parked next to his father's forest green Buick. More than a dozen other cars and a few pickup trucks were scattered around. "Looks like the Old Man and Joey beat us here. They found the place all right."

"I didn't have any doubt that your father could find the place, Alex. I bet you there isn't a dive or hash house anywhere he wouldn't be able to find."

It was a long building, with two large picture windows on either side of the door. A weatherworn canvas and aluminum awning stretched fifteen feet outward from the building and over the entryway. Colorful neon signs glowed in the windows, brandishing beer brands and a bright red one, flashing *OPEN.* Large white letters stood along the edge of the roof, spelling out *Do Drop Inn*, lit with floodlights on each end. Large black script announced *Music* and *Dancing* across the whitewashed stucco front of the building.

Alex strode to the passenger side and opened the door for his wife. As they walked to the entrance, Annie had her arm tucked into his; her right hip bumping him with each step. They entered the long, expansive watering hole, stopping just inside. Looking around, their eyes adjusted to the dark and scanned the interior, searching for Nicholas and Jovita. Joey waved an arm and motioned them over to their booth.

Annie and Alex wore blue jeans, Alex with a plaid flannel shirt and Annie a white puff-shouldered blouse and her sienna flat-toe *Acme* boots. They slid into the Naugahyde booth and sat across from Nick and Joey. The thick, plastic upholstery sighed, moaned and crunched with their weight. Although churned around by several slow-moving ceiling fans, the odors inside the roadhouse hung heavily; weighed down with tobacco smoke, stale beer, and the not-so-subtle hint of cheap perfume. It was a world, a universe, by itself ... the din of muffled talk ... loose laughter ... the crack of pool balls ... seductive whispers ... the ding of a *Gottlieb* pinball machine ... and Joan Webber, from within the *Wurlitzer* jukebox, belting out *Let Me Go Lover* in her butter-pecan ice cream voice: smooth, sweet and with a nice little crunch.

Alex took the inside of the bench seat, Annie settled in, slid close to her husband, looked into his eyes and gave him a kiss on the lips. She giggled and announced, "Now I'm ready to rock and roll! Everybody doing OK?" That broke the ice. Annie was good at that.

Joey beamed a smile; Nicholas gave a positive nod and boldly replied, "We're doing fine. Just fine, thanks. And I promise my best behavior."

Alex caught a hint of sarcasm in his father's tone. The juke joint, while it appeared boorish, had the reputation of a place that did not allow any wild shenanigans. Over the big brass cash register behind the bar, a boldly lettered sign announced: *No Fighting. Colt Enforced.*

Alex explained, "This place is owned by the Lee County Sheriff, Gil Conrad, a tough old boy and Marine. It's local knowledge that nobody gets out of order in here, Old Man." Alex spoke just as a waitress arrived at their booth. A buxom young blonde, wearing a red gingham flair skirt, a turquoise apron, black pumps and at least a half dozen red ribbons in her hair.

"Hey, y'all. I'm Millie. What can I get for you folks to wet your whistles? She spoke in a heavy, Gulf Coast, Dixie drawl."

The Alabama state line was only about an hour drive from the Do Drop Inn. Elgin Air Force Base and the Pensacola Naval Air Station were the driving economic factors in the Florida panhandle. The abundance of employment drew families and individuals from miles away to work in or around the military installations. It was a booming area.

Alex and his father ordered a pitcher of beer from Millie. With a roll of her tongue, Joey asked for a *Cuba Libre*. After Joey's translation, Annie said she would enjoy a rum and cola also. Nicholas asked for a menu and Millie quickly, politely replied, "We ain't got no menu. We got two things. We serve fried Blackwater River catfish, with hush puppies and collard greens. Or you can get a big old burger with fries. That's it. That's all we have, and we do them both pretty damn good."

Annie interjected, "Sounds pretty plain and simple, doesn't it, Alex?"

Alex knew Annie would ask for the burger. He was correct.

Millie brought the drinks, took their dinner order and crossed the floor to the kitchen window. She belted out, "Three cats and a cow, Charlie!" It was a brash and bold beginning to the evening. Annie was enjoying herself and Joey seemed genuinely fascinated with the honky-tonk. Joey explained that after tending bar in Chicago and working at her family's place in Jacksonville that she was no stranger to barrooms, but this was an entirely different experience for her. A couple was bouncing on the dance floor to Carl Smith's *Loose Talk,* a country tune with an unlikely Caribbean bongo beat. Joey was tapping her foot, amused at it all. The tension everyone felt earlier in the day had quickly melted away. The beer, rum and a couple shots of bourbon greased the rusty wheels

24

of conversation. Annie and Jovita were already getting on like best friends, complete with some quiet whispers and an occasional giggle. After dinner, the Do Drop Inn began to fill with the Saturday night crowd, becoming immensely more active and clamorous with music and chatter.

A meaningful, heartfelt moment came as Alex and his father vowed to rebuild and retain a strong personal connection. Both men withdrew from the booth, stood and shared a firm handshake and bear hug. Alex's antagonism toward his father began to fade. He began to understand his father's explanations and what drove him to commit to a life path of self-exile and solitude. Alex understood but withheld complete absolution. For eight years, he believed his father had become a casualty of war in the Pacific. Annie hoped that the chasm between father and son had all but vanished, leaving only a shallow ditch; to be filled in later, over time, with continued contact and a strengthening bond.

When the men returned to their seats, Nicholas leaned across the table and spoke in a determined, steady, clear, unmistakable tone. "When I got back from Cuba on Thursday and Joey told me that you and your wife were there last June … well, I was not just surprised, but emotionally ravaged. At first, I denied myself any sentiment … any feelings at all. The next day I cried. I broke down, Alexander. I was destroyed. It was the first time I cried since I was a kid … back in 1927. I hit a brick wall of reality at a hundred miles an hour. I know I scared the hell out of Joey. She never saw me fall apart before. Ever. We agreed then and there, that it was absolutely necessary to make the trip out here to find you ... and try to set things straight between us … between you and me ... between father and son."

He lit a cigarette and drank a half glass of beer in two gulps. His eyes seemed to focus outside, and beyond the roadhouse. His voice sounded like it was coming from the depths of some underground cavern, echoing emotions both shallow and deep.

"For years, Alexander, I went out of my way to get out of the way. I was living the *pretend I never happened* life. There is only me to blame. I played the role of the intentional orphan. How I acted and what I did was cruel to my wife Nora … your mother … and you.

"But you, your mother and Detroit were a long time ago. I was a long time ago. But … now you and I are together again … and I'm here. And so are you. And your wonderful wife. And my Joey. You can't find lost time or lost opportunity and pick it up off the sidewalk and put it back in your pocket, Alex. Once time is gone, it's gone forever. It simply washes away unappreciated … down the gutter and into the sewer."

He paused, downed the remaining bourbon in his glass, and took a breath.

"I can't expect you to look up to me, so I have to ask if you could look down to me … and recognize that I am damn sorry about how I helped create this mess. I will try my very best to work up to you and your wife. And Joey. You may think I have an iron heart ... I don't. But I was damn selfish. I am asking for patience and forgiveness, Alexander."

Annie's hands were clasped around Alex's; just as they were ten months ago back in Appleton, Wisconsin. Joey held onto Nicholas' lower arm. Father and son's eyes were steadily fixed on one another.

Nick went on, "I'm tired ... worn out. They say there's a silver lining somewhere inside every cloud. I don't know about that … I never saw one when I was flying around. But I do know that I'm quitting the field work and I'm putting in for an administrative position … a desk job. I have enough seniority with the Agency. I am sick and tired of sleeping in jungles, chasing ghosts and dodging dysentery.

"And sick of sleeping with one eye open in a back-alley hotel room, looking and waiting for shadows under the door, or listening for the distinctive click of the safety on a 25-caliber *Beretta*. Being pals with bought-and-paid-for *generalissimos*, mobsters with deep government connections, and the whole ball of wax. The whole thing stinks. It stinks like the month-old sheets of a Yucatan whorehouse."

His words found home. Everyone listened. Joey had never heard this tone before. She rapidly blinked her eyes. Nicholas' words about that brothel in Mexico made her skin crawl.

Annie felt Nicholas was giving them witness to a revelation and an intimate awakening, like some kind of roadside evangelical Christian revival. The hair on the back of Annie's neck prickled. She wondered if more was on the way.

Alex was attentive, unsure, but hopeful, and he strained to understand his father's emotional intonations. He briefly wondered what could have driven his father to tears back in 1927. It was an unexpected announcement, coming out of the heavens above like a booming clap of thunder.

Nicholas' voice was steady as he made the ardent statement, "I'm done. Stick a fork in my ass and turn me over. Cooked. Well done. Take me out of the oven. Done ... over done."

All ears had been pinned to Nicholas' spoken words. He had kept everyone's unwavering attention. As soon as he finished, Nicholas waved his arm through the haze of smoke and caught the waitress' eye. It was like a signal that things could return to normalcy.

Inside the booth, the noise inside the bar came back on. Chatter, music, laughter and playful mayhem returned on high. Their waitress Millie slid across the floor without effort and arrived with a mile-wide smile. Nicholas ordered another full round. The four at the table remained silent, sipping at the melted ice in their glass, smoking cigarettes, and looking around the bar room. When Millie returned and delivered the fresh round of drinks, the brief intermission was over. Nicholas cleared his throat and squashed his cigarette into the metal ashtray. He wasn't finished talking. Annie and Alex weren't surprised, but it appeared that Joey did not expect a continuation of his tale. He had never before exposed his inner self to her in such a bare-boned, skeletal manner.

"What do you say, Alex? Ready to give me … your father another chance … ready to start over … ready to forgive me?"

His emotional question surprised Annie and pushed through Alex's soul. His voice broke and pitched like cracking, breaking china, the sound of shattering porcelain. Jovita looked at him wide-eyed, wondering what more could her Nicky have to say.

The men moved outside the booth, stood and hugged one more time; firm, hard, and strong. Two souls came together again, holding close for thirty seconds what was lost for eight years. When they sat back down, each was drained of pent emotion.

"And one more thing ..."

Annie and Joey looked at each other, their thoughts racing, imagining what could be next. Alex anticipated another booming, thunderous clap, the flood of the century, or some other earth-shaking revelation. Certainly, an up-against-the-wall moment was coming.

"Right here and now, I am asking this young lady, Jovita Maria Vasquello, to marry me. To become my wife." He turned to his left and took her hands.

Joey beamed. "Si, si, Nicky!" They kissed, their lips locked for several moments, their bodies pressing and pushing tightly, awkwardly, together on the bench seat. The *Naugahyde* upholstered seat moaned in futile protest. Annie was surprised. She smiled, overwhelmed by their spontaneous euphoria. Alex was incredulous. It was like a script from the nighttime *One Man's Family* radio soap opera … unnecessarily dramatic and just barely believable.

Nicholas and Jovita broke their cuddle, reveling in the momentary celebration. Annie stepped right into *No Man's Land*. "Are you Catholic, Joey?"

"No. Metodista. Methodist."

"Don't."

Sunday morning, April 17, 1955
Straight Eight Farm, Chumuckla, Florida

Annie and Alex awoke early, took a shower and slid under the cool sheets again. Rays of morning light pierced through the bamboo blinds and danced across the white cotton bedspread as a sunshine chorus line. An easy breeze pushed the window blinds just enough to allow the sunrise waltz to gleam on.

Her head resting on his arm and against his chest, Annie was lying as close as possible to Alex. He turned, faced her, drifted a hand down her belly, stopped with his palm on her mons Venus, and gave his wife a soul-deep kiss. She pushed against him, held tight, pressed her thighs around his hand and purred thorough contentment. He kissed her again, whispered it was time to get out of bed and reluctantly, delicately broke their morning snuggle.

Alex walked to the closet, took out a white shirt and khakis, and pulled on his boots over bare feet.

Annie noticed, "Socks, Alex. Socks. It's Sunday."

He opened the dresser drawer, brought out a pair, and tossed them onto the bed. "Yeah .... Argyle socks inside boots and Sunday sermons. Sounds like a Pat Boone song title. I'll put on that pair, right after I let the horses out to paddock and pasture, Annie. And maybe I'll even trade the boots for wing-tips, OK?"

Annie slid her naked form out from under the bed sheet, across, and out of bed. As her husband grinned and ogled, Annie crossed the room to her husband, and gave him a little kiss on the cheek. "You're teasing me, Alex … it's nearly seven and your father said they would be here around ten. So, you go to the stables, tend to Sebastian and Cassandra, and I'll fix up some breakfast. Go on."

Alex cracked, "Yes, ma'am!", turned on a heel, and was on his way to the barn. He so enjoyed his life on the farm, he told Annie time and time again that he would not trade places with anyone, anywhere on Earth. Alex was vastly content in his world ... and his love.

At the Dutch door, the stallion pushed against Alex's hand and arm, snorted a *good morning* to his keeper and shook his head vigorously. He was a horse of extremely good mind, calm natured and steady for such a young breeder. 'Doc' Sam Adams, the equine veterinarian in Munson, held a very high opinion on Sebastian, and admired the young horse on his visits. Alex remembers Doc telling him, "You got yourself a good one here, Alexander."

In the next stall, Cassie whinnied and tapped a forelimb on the elm floorboards. Alex opened each door, clicked his cheek and gave each of his roan charges a gentle smack on the rump as they exited to the yard. He turned and watched as they nosed one another, Sebastian leading the way with his high-foot amble and Cassandra behind. Alex stood watching them and relished in the sight. As he walked back to the house, he turned his head now and again to catch another look at the pair.

Alexander kicked off his boots on the porch, peeked into the kitchen at Annie and walked to the bedroom where he dutifully put on his socks and slipped into his *Teddy Boy* gray suede loafers. He then necessarily stopped to wash his hands. If he dared to skip it, Annie would be sure to know. He often teased her, saying she had some sort of radar early warning system and discovered early on that it was always best to do it right the first time.

"I fixed up some ham and eggs, Alex. And I knocked out some *Bisquick* biscuits ... ready in two minutes ... just like it says on the box." Annie turned on her feet like a dancer, reached for the coffee pot and brought it over to the table just as her husband sat down. "Perfect timing, Alex. We're a team, we are!"

After breakfast, Alex did the dishes, as he often did on weekends. He enjoyed it: the washing, scrubbing, drying, sorting, and stacking. The likely motivation was the whole routine of setting things in order, clean, neat, and in their proper location. As an added incentive, the window over the kitchen sink had a view of the paddock and lower pasture. He could watch the horses and daydream while washing and drying the ironstone dinnerware.

The distinctive, precocious, clattering ring of the ivory wall phone disrupted the morning quiet. Alex flipped the dishtowel over his shoulder. He spoke the concise greeting, "Good morning." It was Louis, his partner, neighbor and friend, being understandably inquisitive about Alexander's visitors.

Annie walked into the kitchen clipping on her faux pearl earrings, just as Alex was ending the brief conversation, "Yep, will do. See you tomorrow morning."

"That was Louis?" Annie asked, flipping her subtle auburn locks back into place. She was wearing a fully pleated plaid skirt and short-sleeved white, embroidered eyelet peasant blouse.

"Yeah. He was curious how things were going. I said *'OK'* and I'd fill him in on all the sordid details tomorrow."

"There's nothing bad, Alex."

"I know. Just a figure of speech, Hon. All in all, I think it's all worked out pretty damn well. I mean, I can almost completely forgive my father ... I'm working on it ... why don't we have a cup of coffee out on the porch? What do you say?"

"Super duper." Annie reached into the cabinet and grabbed the two heavy *Buffalo China* cups she kept from Maxine's diner back in Appleton. She filled them with black coffee and followed her husband outside to the porch swing. Her pumps clicked across the pine floorboards.

"You know what I've been thinking, Alex? Joey can't be more than four or five years older than you and me, if that. And she's about to become your stepmother, for goodness sake."

Alex carefully took his cup of coffee from Annie and cautiously sat down on the bench swing. "Joey will be my father's wife, Annie. She's not going to be anything else. And, yeah ... It just proves the point: *The apple doesn't fall far from the tree.*"

"What do you mean?"

He played the smart-aleck, and repeated himself, "Just that: *the apple doesn't fall far from the tree.* The son fell in love with a good-looking waitress and the father fell for a good-looking barmaid."

"You hit the nail on the head with that one. You're frightening me, Alex!"

"Don't be scared, Annie girl! You can be sure that I'm not going anywhere. You're stuck with me, Honey. Kisses don't lie."

"I know, Alex ... I've noticed."

"Problems."

Sunday morning, April 17, 1955

It was almost ten o'clock, just as expected, when the dark green sedan came into view. Annie and Alex walked from the porch to meet them as Nicholas parked. Jovita exited the car carrying a paper sack. She had a shining smile and walked with an arresting spring in her step. She wore it well: black pumps, a crisp, close-fitting, pale-yellow skirt, wide black belt and beige brushed rayon sweater that complimented her figure. Following Annie into the house, Joey mentioned they stopped at a breakfast bakery in Pensacola, and she had pastries in the bag: a mixed dozen of fried apple and peach pies. With perfect, unrehearsed timing, the women's heels tip-tapped in unison across the wood floor of the porch and into the home.

The men remained alongside the car. Alex, his arms folded across his chest, asked his father, "What's that, Old Man, a '50 *Buick Rocket*?"

"It's a '51. Haven't driven it much ... been parked most of the time, in a skinny, dark, little alley garage behind the bar back in Jacksonville. I'm good at that ... buying cars and keeping them parked in a garage. And I really don't know why I bought this one ... me being out of the country so much and all. But like I said, all that's going to end before too long."

So began a detailed mechanical conversation about engines, transmissions, power, comfort and handling. The men walked slowly, made their way to the carport on the far side of the house, and to the Packard parked there. Nicholas admired the Patrician and expressed his sincere appreciation of the vehicle. Alexander told his father he actually bought it in Milwaukee, and explained that his old Chevy went belly-up in Cincinnati during his unexpected trip north to Oshkosh the year before: the trip to see his ailing mother, and her funeral. That created a brief, awkward silence. Alex interjected, "Let's go inside to Annie and Joey and have some hot coffee."

They found themselves in the parlor again, individually adding to the family confabulation in unique ways. Annie still had buckets full of colloquial Wisconsin ornaments to embroider the talk. Joey painted her colorful Latin lilt delicately on the canvas of conversation. It was her uniquely personal and enchanting contribution. Her voice was smooth and soothing, like the music of gentle rain drops. Nicholas was direct, off-the-cuff, and pragmatic in his speech. He was experienced at that, creating descriptions and explanations without any impetuous undertones. If one could put his stories to paper, they would read like technical journals. Nevertheless, during the brief interaction of yesterday and the details of today, he demonstrated that while he was not without emotion, he was a man who could willingly tuck it away, hidden and undisturbed. To clarify and punctuate his persona, he accentuated it perfectly when he told Alex: "I did love your mother, Alex. Very much. But it didn't go beyond respect. Sadly, not for Nora either. The love shriveled up"

A bit more relaxed than the day before, Nicholas spoke every word with distinctive clarity and a tone that was methodical. His explanations and opinions came across as sincere and as life lessons learned. He expected that someday, someone from his past would enter the cloak-and-dagger life he was living. This time, when he came home from Cuba and Joey told him of Alex and Annie's mysterious visit, he knew his life was coming to a crossroad. His return to Jacksonville and the woman he loved had given him the news that dramatically changed his situation, his attitude and his outlook on life. His son, along with the woman he was with, had discovered his whereabouts and his secret life. It came as a relief; a burden lifted, and it cleared the pathway for new beginnings.

Stories of Nicholas' past, from nearly thirty years ago, were unfolded and presented candidly and without remorse. Everyone listened with ears tuned only to his steady, but occasional, raspy and gruff voice. His tale started when he left Buffalo, New York in August of 1927, as a young man of seventeen, two years before the onset of The Great Depression. He broke away from a family fractured by bootleg Canadian whiskey, tuberculosis, tragedy and all the problems lurking in the dark corridors of sleazy, off-Broadway burlesque houses. He found it necessary to forego his tedious, muscle-wracking employment at Russell-Miller Milling. The wheat, rye, and oat flour made his entire existence seem as dry and meaningless as the white dust around him. It sifted and ground its way into his clothes, hair, and humanity. Nicholas explained that one August morning in 1927, instead of taking the Broadway streetcar down to the mill, he crossed the bridge to Canada on foot, and caught a ride to Detroit with his thumb. He only had a dollar and some change in his pocket, but good fortune traveled with him. Soon after his arrival, he found steady employment at a tool and die works. He met a beautiful young woman named Nora working a lunch wagon on the sidewalks of Gratiot Avenue; she was just sixteen. When October came around, he turned eighteen and they were married. He spoke bluntly, "We were still very wet behind the ears. Both of us. And you were born in May, Alexander. You can figure out the rest. Do the math."

Annie could not resist the temptation and had something to add. "Did you hear that, Alex? Your father fell in love with a waitress, too. Well, almost a waitress. A lunch girl. Talk about the apple not falling far from the tree." She turned and winked at her husband, then directed her words to Nicholas, "I was a waitress in a diner when Alex and I met." Annie continued, "See that? Like father, like son. You know what I mean. It's not a bad thing, just an interesting coincidence, right Alex?" She and Alex had spoken of this axiom just the day before. Alex was aware of the irony and certain that Annie knew that he knew. Alex considered Annie's brassy sense of ironic humor to be one of his private and personal treasures.

Nicholas acknowledged Annie's comment, "You're absolutely correct, Annie. *The acorn doesn't fall far from the oak* is another way to say it. And there's nothing wrong with that ... usually."

The off-topic comments were a brief and satisfying break. The fried pies went down easily and were half-gone, prompting Annie to put on another pot of A&P Breakfast Blend. Everyone welcomed the opportunity to stretch stiff legs, walk out to the porch, have a smoke, or make a bathroom visit. The day was sparkling clear; the spring sun was warming the world and glistening on fresh foliage.

Refreshed, they ambled their way back inside the living room. Annie was the first to rekindle the chatter. She told how she and Alex met inside Maxine's Roadside Rest, their whirlwind romance; and that her sister Beth had called it a *Wisconsin tornado*. When she spun the tale of Alex's marriage proposal under the streetlight and how he guessed her correct ring size, Joey sighed and gave doe eyes to Nicholas. "Nicky promised me a diamond, right Nicky?"

"Yes, milady. I sure did. And you're going to get one." He leaned in and shared a gentle kiss with her.

It seemed that everyone took turns at life stories; equally frank and forthright. Nicholas listened very closely to Alexander's recounting of his Navy days before his assignment to the *USS Valley Forge*. Much of the content of that conversation was new to Annie as well. Upon joining the Navy in 1947, he went to the Bainbridge Training Center outside of Baltimore, then the joint services aircraft mechanic school in Ypsilanti, Michigan and on to Norman, Oklahoma. Once he was aboard the aircraft carrier, his days and nights were busy, completing two Korean deployments from December 1950 to late July 1953. He told tales of heavy seas, blinding rain and even snowball fights on the carrier deck. By chance, in September 1951, the command offered him Temporary Shore Duty at Fleet Activities, Sasebo, Japan. He hesitated at first, wondering if volunteering for anything in the military was a good idea. As it turned out, it was good duty: office and administrative work. He spent nearly a year at Sasebo before returning to the Valley Forge. Alexander was honorably discharged from the Navy in late February 1954 at the Pensacola Naval Station with the rank of Petty Officer First Class. He then repeated his father's earlier statement word-for-word, "And you know the rest."

Annie asked, "Is that were you got that black shoulder bag, Alex? That leather satchel of yours with *'USN'* and the eagle symbol on it? I wondered about that, I mean, I thought that you were an airplane mechanic."

Alexander stood, stretched his frame, and withdrew into his thoughts for a few seconds. Korea was not only far away, but long ago. He answered, "That's exactly where I got it. I did a little inter-office courier work on the base for a short time, between the United Nations Operational Headquarters and the US Naval Command. We put that shoulder bag to good use last year, didn't we, Annie?" He saw an opportunity to change the course of conversation away from Korea. He stretched again and walked over to the buffet cabinet. "Can I induce anyone to join me with a glass of bourbon?"

The others got up from their seats and accepted the libation invitation. Alex poured the Old Crow into the empty coffee cups and suggested they could sit outside and enjoy the fresh air on the porch. It was a welcome suggestion. Alex brought the bottle. The women took seats on the swing; Alex and his father each took a wicker chair and moved them to sit close. Everyone was eager to continue. They wanted more: more information, more dreams, more emotion, and even more truths. There was an impatience to move the conversation ahead, a desire to reveal the unknown and a curiosity-driven willingness to oblige.

Nicholas was direct, "Tell me about last year, Alex ... your trip up to Wisconsin and all. And you spent six years in the Navy with no tattoo to show for it? At least, none that I have seen!"

Alex was unsure how the last part of that question was intended. He jerked up his eyebrows, looked to Annie, and barely shrugged his shoulders. "Well, I never really got drunk enough to get one, I guess. To me, tattoo ink is nothing more than a jazzed-up, burned-on livestock brand. And I knew some sailors that carried a lot of regret when they couldn't put a face to the name they got tattooed on their arm just the night before." Alex felt he had made his point.

Nicholas acknowledged his son's response with a nod and added, "Makes good sense, that does. Pictures and names burned onto your arm can't hold a candle to the memories that somebody burned into your brain. Or onto your soul."

Alex acknowledged his father's reply and began to detail the events of the previous year, starting with the phone call he received from his mother's sister, Marie. He detailed his trip north to Wisconsin, the breakdown of his Chevy, the bus trip to Milwaukee and the final leg of his journey to Oshkosh in a new Packard. Although Nicholas had phoned Marie just Thursday, when he returned home to Jacksonville, he did not reveal his identity. He was unaware that Nora died of rapidly spreading cancer. He also did not know that Alexander had traveled to and arrived in Oshkosh after her passing. Alex explained that his mother did not know what was inside those Bank of Detroit safe deposit boxes. When Alex and his mother left Detroit for Oshkosh in 1946, she never mentioned them to her son. The contents remained unknown to her. In fact, Nora had left the keys to those boxes, her Will and $5000 of Nicholas' cash in the custody of her lawyer.

Nicholas bit his lower lip. "The contents of those boxes were for you and your mother, Alex. It's sad that she never used any of it. It's a testament to how she felt about me and our marriage, I guess. The dirt washes out, floats to the top as soap scum, and the truth gets exposed in the end. It always works out that way. Always." Nicholas' mood was reflective and subdued. "You and Annie have the contents of the boxes, don't you? The cash? It was meant to be that way."

"Yes, we do. Quite a bit of it still. Most all of it," Alex answered. "But I need to know one thing that still bothers Annie and me. The beer coasters with the addresses, the dog tags, the Chinese money, and the cash ... I understand. Annie and I got all that stuff figured out last year. But what about that Smith and Wesson 38 revolver? What was going on with that? That was a service weapon."

"Nothing really. At the time I stuck it in there, I didn't know what I was doing. I guess I didn't even trust myself with it. I knew your mother and I were over. I just met Joey three days before. I was lost, homesick without a home, falling out of love, then maybe falling in love, and totally confused. I was lost, Alex. It was probably a blessing in disguise that I put my service weapon in that box. Lord knows what I could have ended up doing with it. In retrospect, maybe I should have gone right back to Chicago and Jovita. But what would that accomplish? Your mother wouldn't divorce me. I ended up drinking myself into a frog-fighting, knee-crawling drunken stupor and re-enlisted. And here I am. Ten years later. Here *we* are. I'm just damn lucky that this woman believed in me. Joey did me good. She stuck with me. And she wasn't actually *with me*. That's tricky, isn't it? And that takes some guts. We kept in touch with the occasional letter. Unpredictable, quick in-and-out visits lasting a day or two. That was it."

He finished the whiskey in his coffee cup and held it out for Alex to refill. He took another swallow and started again. "I'm no saint, Alexander. Far from it. I met a British field officer outside Hong Kong during the war. She was a big-busted dame, built like a brick shithouse, not afraid of anything, or stepping on toes. She told me: *If whiskey kills you ... and whoring is illegal ... then we're all dying young ... and love's a damn sin.* At the time, that made sense to me."

"And where do Joey and I go now? Where am I supposed to go from here? I am going to quit the fieldwork with the *Company*. I'm done with the spooks. I am not going to continue traveling down a road that disappears into some distant jungle, a sleazy hotel room, mud hut or mountainside cave. You know what, Alex? Annie? This woman here, my Joey, she put down roots in my mind. And they go right through my brain, to my heart, and into my feet. And I am going to plant myself down and not go anywhere, anytime, anymore. Alexander, all I am doing in this job is spinning my wheels in muck. The only thing that gets accomplished is the crap ends up spread around. Like a big green *John Deere* manure spreader. Everybody and everything gets shitty. One day you are smoking cigars and drinking rum at a table with *el Presidente* ... and couple of days later, you are arranging the release of his biggest enemy and two dozen of his cohorts, from a rotten, remote island prison. I mean, what the hell is in focus in that photograph? And it's getting fuzzier with every day that passes. It's not the same anymore. There's a new kind of warfare out there now, Alex. It's not bombs, tanks, or fighter planes. Nowadays, it's rag-tag revolutionaries with Russian guns and hand grenades in shopping baskets ... and Molotov cocktails in the hands of angry mobs, teenagers, women and even kids. The world is changing. And nothing we do is going to stop all of it. We can only put out the big fires."

Nicholas spoke as a man who had just accepted his fate. He knew that someday, someone from his past could enter the secret world he was living in. His return to Jacksonville just a few days earlier had delivered the news that dramatically changed his life and his life view. The wife he left behind in 1946 was dead. His son and daughter-in-law discovered him and his secret life with a woman fifteen years his junior. His existence on Planet Earth became altered forever. Things would never be the same. They couldn't be.

Joey straightened herself on the porch swing. "Nicky, light me a cigarette, OK? Now it's my turn to tell stories and tall tales." It seemed she wanted to change the subject. She was clever. She interrupted for the sake of stopping the clock. She was sly enough to ask for, and got, a *time out*. After a very short sip of whiskey and a puff on a *Phillip Morris*, she started to speak in her Latin-laced lilt once again. Her voice was light, modest and unassuming.

"I come to America in 1945, after the war with my aunt Agnes. Uncle Simon, he was a translator for the American Army in the Philippine for a year. He then moved to Chicago after the fighting stopped, and then I come. My mother Carilla, and my father, Fernando, were in Cuba and stayed on the sugar plantation for months before they come to America. They could not leave immediately."

Like a kid carrying a secret, Nicholas had a wry smile, nodded and gave Joey a wink. She continued, "Then I met my Nicky when I was at university in Chicago, and I knew I was in love."

Annie put her arm around Joey and gave her a gentle hug, "And here you are, Joey. You're one of the family already, by golly. You just need to get married and you're in; in like Flynn." She giggled and added, "In like Throckmorton."

With her clever, well-timed interruption, and without another word, Annie called a cease-fire and the busy non-stop talk ended. The soul-searching and fact-finding exercise was over. Alex suspected Nicholas knew what Annie just did. And it did not matter. What needed to be said, was said. What was to be discovered, was. Alex and Annie didn't suspect it, but some secrets were still secrets.

Annie needed to put her point across once more. She wanted to make sure the discussion was over. She boldly re-enacted the announcement that Jimmy Durante makes at the end of his television show, *"Good night Mrs. Calabash, wherever you are."*

Nicholas looked at his wristwatch. "Good God. It's nearly three o'clock. We need to get on down the road. I want to get a good night's rest and get an early start tomorrow. I'm going to have a busy week. A real busy week. Our lives are changing, Joey, sweetheart."

Alex walked up to his father and extended his hand. "Thanks, Old Man. We learned a lot. Both of us. A helluva lot. And let's not let this happen again, all right? I mean, we need to keep in touch. No more eight-year-long interruptions."

Nicholas stood and shook hands with his son. Annie gave Joey a brief hug, grabbed the coffee pot, two of the cups and disappeared inside the house. Alexander took a step and hugged Joey. "It was really nice getting to know you, Jovita."

For some unknown reason, Joey was teary-eyed. "Si, Alexander. Si. You have a nice home and a beautiful wife; a wonderful woman."

Annie came back out onto the porch with an *Eversharp* ballpoint pen and a small, black address book. "Nobody is going to leave without sharing their telephone number. We need to give *Southern Bell* the business! What I mean is ... we got telephones and we need to use them. That's why they made them in the first place! This getting together stuff after eight years has just got to end right here and now." Annie could crack the ice in more than one way. Nicholas wrote his name, address, and telephone number in the book for Annie. She nodded and gave him a sincere 'thank you'.

A couple hugs and a few minutes later, Alex and Annie stood side by side, waved and watched the Olds 88 leave their driveway for the second time in as many days.

"Well ... that's over ... we had quite a day, Annie, didn't we?" He moved the wicker chairs back to where they were and sat on the swing, one arm across the back. Annie sat next to him, as close as she could.

"I think it went darn well, all in all. Your father came clean. He uncovered a lot of his mysterious background, right down to his job with the OSS or CIA or whatever it is. I don't think he's hiding anything else, do you?"

Alex started to rock his foot slowly again and forced the swing into a smooth, gentle motion. He slid his arm off the back of the swing and around Annie's shoulders. She leaned into him. He was relaxed for the first time all day.

"It seems that the Old Man told us everything. He told us a lot, anyhow. I think it went really well, all in all; like you said. It's all out in the open, now. And that's a good thing. I think he really meant it about settling down. I think so. I really hope so."

"I think you should forgive his shortcomings, Alex. He may have deserted you and your mother for the Army, but he always provided a home and income, didn't he?"

"Food in the pantry, four walls and a roof don't always make a house a home, Annie girl."

Nicholas and Jovita were married without frill or fanfare on April 25, 1955, inside the Birmingham Avenue chapel at the Jacksonville Naval Air Station. When he heard the news a week later, Alexander felt like he had been shut out in the cold until Annie reminded him that couples have a right to keep their intimate moments to themselves. For whatever reason, Nick and Joey had kept their wedding private.

TWO: 1960 – A NEW DECADE

"Dream Lover."

Four years, eight months later:
Mid afternoon, Monday, December 28, 1959

Four and a half years had passed since Alexander's father left his position as 'Accounts Specialist' at *Caribbean Aircraft Exports*. With the seniority and work history he had with the Company, he was able to transfer from the International Sales division to the Southern District Headquarters. He began working close to home, just outside the gates of Jacksonville Naval Air Station and well within walking distance of Joey's bar.

After their reconnection, father, son and their wives stayed in touch. Visits, telephone calls and overnight stays were plentiful, pleasant, and rewarding. Nicholas, Alex, Annie and Joey became closer and rebuilt a strong family bond from the maelstrom of empty years. When Christmastime 1959 rolled around on the calendar, two toddlers had entered the fold: Nicholas and Jovita's children, four-year-old Roberta, and her two-year-old brother, Hector.

Annie had spent a busy morning in and around Pensacola. Christmas was over and New Year's Eve was knocking at the door; 1960 was only three days away. Her combined purchases of a half dozen T-bone steaks, five pounds of ground chuck, and two dozen hot dogs at Federal Meat Market totaled nearly twenty dollars. Next came the dutiful stop at the *Piggly Wiggly* where she purchased not just groceries, snacks and condiments, but also a case of twenty-four mixed *Nu-Grape* sodas, and a bag of charcoal. The spacious trunk of the Packard became nearly full on her way home. She made another stop at the ABT package store for two cases of *Viking* lager and fifths of rum, vodka and bourbon. As in previous years, this New Year's party was planned with Nicholas, Jovita, their neighbors, shop employees, their farm hand Renaldo, and his wife Teresa. Over the last four years, the New Year barbeque soiree had developed into a tradition. Annie enjoyed the busy excitement of preparations and the anticipation of good times that come with good company and successful planning. From the days of her childhood, the words *"company's coming"* meant happy get-togethers, friendship, love and precious memories. Nicholas, Jovita, and their children Roberta and Hector, were expected to arrive on Wednesday for their holiday visit and stay through New Year's Day. Annie anxiously awaited everyone's arrival, especially the youngsters.

Alexander and Louis had left the farm at dawn, in Alex's Chevrolet pickup, towing a *Country Boy* horse trailer behind. The previous summer, at an auction and tack show outside of Mobile, Alex arranged the purchase of a two-and-a-half-year-old filly; a Racing Quarter, which would be in season during the summer or fall. Sired by a black Steel Dust stallion and a Bay dam of good mind, Alexander was eager to get the young horse home. Their destination was Itta Bena, Mississippi, a small rural town just north of Yazoo City. Annie laughed at those names and accused Alex of pulling her leg and teasing her. He could only satisfy her curiosity and prove his innocence by showing her the towns on an *Esso* roadmap. The men planned to be back on Thursday, the day of the New Year's Eve party.

Annie was ardently looking forward to their return despite her full day of errands in Pensacola, shopping and an appointment in Milton. She had experienced perhaps the most exciting day since she and Alexander were married back in June 1954, in Mount Clemens, Michigan.

Annie was champing at the bit, eager to share her news. As soon as she got home, she called her friend and neighbor,

Hedy and invited her for coffee, cake and chatter. Hedy would be bringing her two children along, so Annie realized that she needed more than just coffee. She took the cheese Danish she bought at the supermarket out of the bag, placed it on an ironstone platter, and sliced it into six pieces. Coffee was on the stove. She opened a package of *Oreos*, put about a dozen on a saucer and poured two glasses of milk. Annie was excited and impatiently awaited her friend. With butterflies in her belly, stars in her eyes and joy in her heart, she was on cloud nine.

Clarence, their coonhound interrupted the mid-day calm when he brayed loudly from inside the paddock. He had announced the arrival of a visitor. Seconds later, the doorbell sounded. Annie did not expect her neighbor and her children quite so soon. As she started walking down the hall from the kitchen, she could see it was Henry, the mailman at the front door.

Henry was an effervescent man, and always seemed to be in a jubilant mood, "Hello, Missus Annie Throckmorton! Today I have a registered letter for you ... for your husband really, but you can sign." He held a manila envelope, and other pieces of mail, all rubber-banded together in one hand. He offered a ballpoint pen and signature pad to Annie in the other.

"Sign right there, Missus Annie. Right there in the book, on the next open line."

She signed the book and handed the pen back to the mailman. Annie spoke as she fingered through the bundled mail, "Thank you, Henry! And have a Happy New Year!"

"Yes, ma'am. Same back at ya'll."

Along with week-old whiskers and in dire need of a haircut, Henry, a big man, smelled like an ashtray. The first two fingers of his right hand were stained nicotine brown from countless packs of king-size *Pall Mall*. Clarence, the hound found it necessary to howl a few more times before the mailman had squeezed himself back inside his beat-up Ford *Country Squire* station wagon. Henry started down the driveway and out to the rest of his own, secure, *Post Office Department* world. He was sprawled across the right side of the front seat, left arm extended, hand on the steering wheel and left foot on the accelerator. He was proud of his twenty-plus years of accident-free mail delivery and given the opportunity, Henry would gladly take the time to show his mail patrons the safe driving pin he was awarded.

Annie brushed back her wind-tousled hair, turned and started back toward the house. She pulled at the tight rubber band around the mail bundle as she walked. It snapped, broke, and stung as it hit her cheek. Annoyed, she grimaced, blinked and looked curiously at the envelope that had required her signature. It was from Alex's aunt Marie in Oshkosh, Wisconsin. The other mail was the usual fare: a power bill from *Peninsula Gas and Electric*, a late Christmas card from her mother in Vermont, and January's issue of *Good Housekeeping*. She put the mail into the top drawer of the hall desk but kept the card from her mother. She slid her finger under the flap, opened it, barely noticed the snowy rural scene on the outside and read the generalized message inside: *"Merry Christmas and Happy New Year."* Underneath, neatly printed by hand in the turquoise ink of a fountain pen, were the words: *"Love, Walter and Irene."* Annie's mother did not call on the telephone. Annie tried to connect about every other month and wrote letters in between. But her letters were never answered.

She reached back inside the desk drawer, took a piece of *Scotch Cellophane Tape* from the plastic dispenser, and stuck the Christmas card from Vermont onto the parlor door jamb. She glanced around at all the other cards taped onto the doorway molding. There were so many: dozens of them, from people that she actually spoke with and saw occasionally.

Walking back down the hall, she collected two wilted leaves and a tattered bract off the poinsettia sitting next to their wedding portrait on the buffet. In the kitchen, Annie took the coffee pot off the burner and let the brew rest. She gazed at the clock, brushed at her blouse, and walked to the bathroom to touch up her lipstick and tidy her hair before Hedy came by. Looking in the mirror and primping, she was humming and caught herself smiling. A tune she heard on the car radio that morning would not leave her mind. The song causing the tonal torment was *Dream Lover* by Bobby Darin.

In ten minutes, Clarence sounded off again, but not as loudly or as long, the Bluetick recognizing Hedy and her two boys, Thomas and Benjamin. Annie was beaming and opened the door for her friend and confidant. The children ran ahead of their mother, and noisily bounced up the porch steps.

"Easy boys, easy! Please! No rough-housing." At the sound of their mother's voice, the youngsters slowed and stopped short of the doorway. It was almost a military command. Hedwig Verdune still carried a heavy German accent.

"Come on in, Hedy. Come right into the kitchen because I have coffee at the ready, and a Danish pastry. And I have cookies and milk, too, boys!" In a flash, the brothers had once again passed Annie and their mother, and were inside the kitchen, sitting and waiting at the table.

"What's going on, Annie? You must have some news, I think. The way you are smiling, it looks like you're hiding something big!" Hedy nudged her friend with a playful elbow. "Come on, now. Open the mustard jar! And bring out the sauerkraut and wurst!"

Annie set the coffee cake on the table and filled the coffee cups. The women sat next to one another, across from the boys. Hedy squeezed the little half-pint can of *Borden* condensed milk over her cup. She handed it to Annie who did likewise. The milky concoction squirted out of a little hole punched in the top of the thin metal can and into their coffee. With perfectly timed swirls of their spoons, their chat session was about to commence. Hedy's sons were twisting the Oreos apart, dipping one half in their milk and scraping the cream filling off the other with their front teeth. Both had close-cropped crew cuts that were short all around, stiff and sticking straight up.

Annie lowered her voice just enough to pique the curiosity of the children, but not loud enough for them to pick up every word. Boys of five and three don't pay too much attention to adults so soon after Christmas has come and gone, anyhow.

"Well, Hedy ... finally. I've got one in the oven! Not that we haven't been trying for goodness sake! Finally! Five years of *practice makes perfect*, that's what it has to be. The doctor is pretty sure that I am in the family way, but he took a test that will tell for sure, and he said he should have the results back from Pensacola for me tomorrow, or Wednesday, at the latest." Hedwig beamed with happiness for her friend and leaned in to give Annie a hug.

Across the table, the two brothers looked at one another in bewilderment. Complete with telltale black crumbs around his lips and a milk mustache, Benjamin interrupted, "You said that you have more cookies in the oven, Miss Annie?"

"Loose Talk."

Thursday afternoon, December 31, 1959, New Year's Eve

Annie, Hedy, and Teresa had worked since early morning with the preparations for the night's festivities. The success of the machine shop had made the annual New Year's Eve get-together special. The shop was doing extremely well, with repeat customers and a five-year renewal of contract work for Naval Air Station, Pensacola. Two new mechanics had been hired to keep up with the increased workload, enabling Louis to become shop foreman and manager. Alexander was then able to shift the focus of his work at the shop to improving and expanding the business and tending to the daily operations of the horse ranch. Annie, using her experience at Atlas Paper back in Appleton, also started to work part time on accounting for the engine and machine shop.

The increased success of the shop, hiring of help, the continued good fortune the farm and quarter horse breeding, made the New Year party exceptional. There was good reason to celebrate. And, of course, there was the biggest reason of all; the very special news Annie got from her doctor on Monday. She was waiting in earnest to tell her husband and could barely contain her excitement. For years, Annie had worked to restrain her anxiety, and hoped that any day could be the day she became pregnant. Magazine articles, medical advice, thermometers and extra pillows brought no result. In addition, a dog-eared, illustrated hardcover book with full-page color illustrations detailing countless coital positions brought no result other than minor chaffing and muscle strain. The months came and went, the years slipped by, and all without the fruition of her deepest, inner dream to conceive a child.

Occasionally over the past three months, she would feel light-headed and just slightly nauseous. After missing her last two monthly cycles, and now a month overdue, Annie made the doctor appointment. She mentioned nothing to Alex or anyone else, fearing the news would not be as she hoped. On Monday, three days earlier, Doctor Isaac Heinemann gave her the news she so longed for. In addition, today, her husband was coming home with yet another addition to the farm. Her nerves would not steady, a plight Annie found strange and uncomfortable. She could not remember ever before being so much on edge. Hanging multi-colored crepe-paper streamers from the ceiling moldings and blowing up balloons was not helping to calm her.

All morning she awaited her husband's signal: that he and Louis had arrived and were coming down the driveway. She knew her husband would announce their return by sounding the pickup's horn with two short burps followed by a longer one. He started doing that right after they moved in; she did not know why and never asked. Alex did it, it worked, and she did not mind. She was intently waiting for it now.

The living room furniture sat pushed up against the walls along with the braided rug, rolled up and standing tucked in a corner. The white pine floorboards lay exposed and ready for dancing feet. Two twenty-gallon galvanized tubs of ice sat out on the porch, one fully stocked with Viking lager, the other with assorted bottles of cola, orange, grape and cream soda. The buffet cabinet became a makeshift bar, with mixers, rum, bourbon, and vodka.

An obnoxious, twelve-inch mirror ball hung from the center of the living room ceiling. On an impulse, Alex had ordered it from the *Montgomery Ward* Christmas Catalog three years earlier. He brought it home from the catalog store and presented it to Annie as a celebration in its own right. He had sold their first-bred (Sebastian and Cassandra's colt) at an auction in Daphne, Alabama, across the bay from Mobile. Annie light heartedly insisted that it was the last piece of whimsy he could purchase without her consent. She needled him for months about that mirror ball and each New Year's Eve since, it has hung in the middle of the living room. During any party, Alex would praise its aesthetic value and on New Year's Day, Annie would quietly pack it away. The preposterous globe and all its divergent, shameless reflections became a playful tradition that prompted loose talk and laughs.

Sitting along one wall by itself, was an *Admiral* television and stereo record player in a walnut console. A stack of long-play phonograph records sat atop an end table, with an impressive pile of 45 rpm singles on the floor. Alex had joined the *Columbia Record Club* a few years prior, thus enabling him and Annie to build up quite a record collection. Music filled their lives. It was a passion joyfully shared. Their taste ran the full spectrum from Bix Beiderbecke's jazz to Hank Williams' country, hillbilly laments.

Outside, just beyond the porch steps stood a new charcoal barbeque grill from *Sears Roebuck*. Annie knew her husband would be spending a good deal of his evening out there cooking the steaks and finding room for hot dogs and hamburgers wherever possible. The women set up two card tables with *Chinet* paper plates, a half dozen steak knives, plastic forks, spoons and condiments on the porch. It was a warm morning and it turned out to be a very pleasant afternoon to set up the party, inside and out.

Annie announced a hopeful forecast, "The weatherman on the TV news said it's supposed to be a pretty nice night, about fifty-five, sixty or so. That's good. No wind or rain, so we won't be stuck indoors."

It's hard to resist a cynical comment about weather forecasting and Hedy readily took the opportunity, "The weatherman doesn't know what's going on until he sticks his arm out the window. And then, if it's dark out, or he's wearing a long-sleeve shirt, you still can't believe him!"

Teresa's Johnny, and Hedy's Ben and Tom would be underfoot occasionally, but all three boys got along while playing together. They had toy trucks made of pressed tin and little rubber cars. Johnny used his hands to scoop gravel like a steam shovel, the brothers made roads in the dirt, piled stones on the trucks, knocked them around, and started all over again. Of course, they took the opportunity to ask for, and drink a cold cream soda. They spoke in unison, "Thank you, Miss Annie!"

When it was time for everyone to take a break, Annie opened three lagers. Hedy and Teresa sat on the swing, squeezed over and made room for Annie. It was the right time and the right mood. In the background, they could barely hear Carl Smith's *Loose Talk* on the table radio in the parlor. Three women, best friends, dressed in cotton housedresses, hairdos unkempt, smiling and drinking beer. It was a perfect afternoon.

Two or three sips of beer mixed smoothly with some chatter about the new plot on *The Edge of Night*. Abruptly, Annie's agonizing wait came to and end with three beeps. The sound of a horn signaled someone was coming up the driveway. Alex's dark blue '55 pickup, pulling the horse trailer, came into view. Louis waved an arm out the passenger window. The women stood, Annie and Hedy waved back and ran off the porch to meet them.

The boys turned their heads to look and went back to their road construction. With three swallows, Teresa finished her bottle of beer like a teamster, and set the empty into the case on her way off the porch. She took her little Johnny by the hand and started down the walkway away from the house. "See you later!" she called to Annie and Hedy.

The truck stopped and both doors opened. The men got out and held their wives. Annie put her arms up and across Alex's back, with her hands on his shoulders. She pressed herself to him and gave her husband a soft, meaningful kiss. He kissed back and sensed his wife's elation. She backed away and held his hands in hers.

"I got news! Big news! We're having a baby, Alex."

Never before had Alex seen his wife's eyes glisten and gleam with such glittering emotion. Her words waltzed across his mind. He paused before he spoke.

"Annie, this is Heaven on Earth. That's what this is. Plain and simple." He took his wife into his arms again.

They held each other; really held each other.

"The Tennessee Stud."

Thursday, late afternoon, December 31, 1959

Poko Coko, a pretty chestnut with white stockings, was the newest addition to the ranch. The filly was in the paddock, becoming acquainted with Sebastian, a seventeen-hand tall Tennessee stallion Alex acquired in 1954. Alex was hoping for a smooth introduction of his new addition. It turned out to be just that. The stud was a good-natured breeder, in his own surroundings, and confident. Renaldo was working them both. The rest of the herd was not far off in the pasture.

"Break up a bale of Alfalfa for them, Renaldo. It looks like they're hitting it off all right. And ... you are coming up to the house with Teresa and little Johnny for the party tonight, aren't you?"

"Si, patrón. We will be coming. Thank you, boss."

Alex nodded, touched a finger to the brim of his beaver-belly Stetson and started to walk toward the house. Annie was sitting on the porch swing, waiting for him.

It had been two years since Renaldo began working on Straight Eight Farm: his first steady employment with a single employer. After years of seasonal, migrant farm work in central Florida and South Georgia, he emigrated from Puerto Rico and married. Prior to 1957, Vidalia onion, watermelon, and strawberry farms with hot sun, driving rainstorms, and hard labor were the only elements of life he and his new bride knew. They stumbled upon their future by way of a curious twist of fate. Teresa and her husband crossed paths with Alex and Annie by pure chance. Reynaldo was standing on the edge of a berry field, on the shoulder of a dirt road in Sopchoppy, Florida. His young wife sat beside him straining, trying to hold back her pain. Her husband frantically waved his straw hat, high in the air, at a cream yellow Packard Patrician as it passed. Alexander braked and stopped.

Renaldo asked for help and got it. Alex and Annie, heading home after a horse and tack auction, gave him and his pregnant wife a ride back to Tallahassee Memorial Hospital. That ride in the back seat of Alexander's car was the beginning of a better life for him, Teresa, and the new life she was carrying.   A month later, he was working on the Throckmorton ranch. In his native Puerto Rico, he grew up around horses at *El Comandante* thoroughbred track in Canovanas, where two generations of his family lived and worked. His exposure to horses and his work with them were reason enough for Alex to offer him employment. Annie admired the devotion he and his wife shared for the animals. Renaldo was gracious and eagerly accepted the steady work. It was not more than a month later that Alexander arranged for *Florida Sectional Homes* to build a modest, two-bedroom, wood frame house on the property. Placed on a concrete slab beyond the paddock and outbuildings, and between two spreading Florida Maple trees, it was assembled in two days. It was a new home and a new beginning for a new family. When lives touch, souls touch; life expands, and kinship grows. A respectful friendship was born of serendipity, trust and gainful employment.

Annie watched as her husband walked up the porch steps and sat down next to her. The seasoned oak swing creaked with his weight.

"The new filly is getting acquainted with her new home, Alex?"

"Yep. She's doing fine. I think we got another good one. Sebastian nosed her, and she's doing fine, and I know she's going to fit right in." He reached over and put his hand on his wife's belly. "How long you been keeping this secret, Annie girl?"

"It wasn't a secret, I just wanted to make sure, that's all. It's been a couple months since my cycle, so I called Doc Heinemann for a check up. I went there Monday and he said that I was probably pregnant, but he took a test anyway."

"They have a test for that? Is that the rabbit thing I heard folks talk and joke about?"

"This was news to me, Alex, and it's interesting, I think. They don't use rabbits anymore; it's too involved and gets expensive with all the rabbits ... I was flabbergasted! They use frogs now!" Annie lowered her voice, and leaned into Alex, as if someone was listening around the corner, or in the doorway.

"I had to pee, and the doctor kept a sample to send to a laboratory, down there in Pensacola, and they inject the pee into a frog. Now get this ... if the frog produces eggs in a day, I'm pregnant. Well, that was Monday. Doctor Heinemann called Wednesday. The frog agrees with the doctor ... I'm pregnant!"

"Frogs? Really? Are you kidding me, Annie girl?"

"Nope. Frogs. No kidding. He told me the test name, but I cannot remember it. They use just one frog. Can you believe all this new stuff they keep coming up with?"

"Annie! Can you imagine if they start using frogs to test our mares? I don't think I'd want to try to catch horse piss."

She thought a moment, looked at Alex incredulously, wrinkled her nose, and giggled. She then playfully punched him in the upper arm. "Wise guy!"

He put his arm around her. "You got to admit it, Annie. That would be funny ... catching horse piss."

They sat in brief silence, the swing moving slightly, as a few Blue Jays squawked out an argument over fallen acorns.

"Enough about horse pee and the jokes, Alex. I think we're all ready for tonight. I'm going to shower and get dressed and you can check around and see if we missed anything. We need more ice on the beer and soda. Alrighty then?"

They stood, and Alex playfully gave Annie's fundament a pat. "Yes, dear."

"Auld Lang Syne."

Thursday evening, December 31, 1959

Two hours earlier, a magnificent orange marmalade sunset had promised a gorgeous evening. It came to fruition. The weather was perfect: gentle breezes, warm air, and a clear starlit sky. Night flies and moths danced around the bare light bulbs that ran along the electric cord from the porch to the Live Oak. Nicholas and Jovita, with their children were the first to arrive. The first time they had visited Alex and Annie, back in 1955, they stayed at the *Wee Tuck You Inn*, about five miles down the road in Milton. It became a predictable tradition, and a standing joke that added an extra bit of fun when two-year-old Hector tried to pronounce it.

Annie and Alex greeted them as soon as they got out of the Oldsmobile. After a flurry of quick hugs between adults and children, Annie made her announcement. A smile came across Nicholas' face and Joey gave Annie a bear hug. After father and son shared a hearty handshake, the six o'clock newscast was over and life returned to normal. The expectant parents shared a quick and questioning glance. They had envisioned a little more fanfare than the fluffy cotton candy, and marshmallow soft congratulations they just experienced.

As more guests arrived, there were folks milling around the yard, standing on the porch, or seated on the wicker, canvas chairs or swing. Nicholas, Louis, and Renaldo stood close to the barbeque, trying to avoid the smoke and talking over the music flowing from the house. Alex stood poking and turning all the various meats on the grill. Tiny crimson sparks danced up and away, escaping the glowing lumps of charcoal and dripping fat. A Perez Prado record was on the parlor stereo, sending the passionate trumpet bleats and Latin sound of *Cherry Pink And Apple Blossom White* out to the yard. Annie, Jovita and Teresa stood on the porch swaying subtly, involuntarily, and almost instinctively to the music.

Between Thanksgiving and Christmas, Annie bought a bold emerald green, fitted sheath dress, with a swooping neckline, half-sleeves and embroidered bodice just for this party. As she stepped into it, reached around and grasped the zipper, her nerves jumped, and she bit her lower lip. She let out a sigh of relief; it still fit … but only just. Over the last few years, when the opportunity to dress up came around, Annie jumped at the chance. Rewarding as it was, life on the ranch was a variance from what she knew in Appleton. That night's New Year get-together turned out to be so very special. Annie was radiant; the dress proved to be worth all of the twenty-two dollars she spent. She carried herself well, with confidence, her auburn hair falling in cushy curls at her shoulders. She wore black pumps, a faux pearl necklace, bracelet, and earrings.

Joey's black hair fell just to the back of her neck, held in place with a scarlet headband. She dressed in a white skirt with a flair hemline, red blouse, red heels, and wide black belt. Teresa was dressed in a rose and black print swing dress with three-quarter sleeves. Standing together, the women looked wonderful.

All five children, two girls and three boys, aged four, three, and two, sat on the floor in the parlor. A set of *Lincoln Logs*, green rubber infantrymen, *Tinker Toys*, a paperboard dollhouse, vinyl dolls and *Pik-Up-Stix* were keeping their attention. Things were going well on the pine floorboards.

Jeffrey and James Brownlee along with James' wife Carla, and Jeffrey's date Sally arrived next. They were surveying the lay of the land, mingling and checking out their surroundings. This was their first "company picnic": their first invitation to any such employer-employee party. The men were brothers, hired last year as mechanics and machinists. Uncertain of what to expect, they started toward the barbeque. Alex and Louis approached them, shook their hands, and welcomed them. Annie came over, took Carla and Sally under her wing and walked back to the porch. Carla was a tall blonde, wearing a light pink, combed cotton hobble dress with a knee length hemline and a black corselet belt. Her poodle skirt, ankle socks and saddle shoes betrayed Sally's young age. A bottle of beer, a glass of sangria, a cola, and a shared laugh tempered the mood and melted all the ice.

The steaks, hotdogs and burgers made it to buns or platters, serving trays, and over to the two picnic tables stuck together just beyond the porch steps. Macaroni, tuna, and potato salad, three bean casserole, and sweet potato pie shared center stage. It was a bumping boggle of bodies, a bevy of arms and elbows, and a bungle of plastic cutlery and paper plates. Everything was going just as planned. There was a Ricky Nelson long playing record on the Admiral console. Laughter, chatter, and clinking glasses stirred the night into a dusky party stew spiced with light-hearted fun and camaraderie. Nobody broke away from the others; everyone interacted, with no solo or paired-off separate performers. There was a gender divide; however, the women occupied one of the two picnic tables. At one point, Jovita and Teresa were caught up in memories of their homelands, mixing English and Spanish. Joey listened with keen interest as Teresa told of her youth in San Juan, her life as a migrant farm worker and meeting her future husband Renaldo in a Florida strawberry field. Joey, true to form, played her cards close to her chest, and kept the details of her family's life in Cuba to herself. Perhaps it was the presence of children, or the mixed company of people who just met, but there was no rowdy, bawdy, or drink-driven behavior. Indoors, outdoors and back again, people mixed and interwove. The gaudy mirror ball was a stark *objet d' art* conversation starter for the adults and a source of wonder for the children.

Alex and Annie took opportunity as it presented itself, and danced often, on the porch, or in the parlor. When Paul Anka suggested *Put Your Head On My Shoulder*, Annie found Alex and did just that. It was acutely obvious that they were extremely happy and still very much in love.

A new decade was approaching, and it was only a few hours away. There was a sense of inevitability; that a new, modern age was coming. Memories of World War II had turned cold and the Korean Conflict had ended with a bloodstained whimper. The year 1960 was peeking around the corner with big bright eyes and winking the subtle promises of all the happy days just around the corner. The entire world was tempting them with things to come and adventures to be experienced. 1960 was beckoning and teasing them with transistor radios in pastel colors, countless new plastic gadgets, aluminum drink ware and thing-a-ma-jigs and fashions in synthetic fabrics. Everyone and everything was traveling in faster cars, bigger trucks and on new expressways. Speed-of-sound airplanes, rockets and the United Nations were bringing a once-dangerous, war-torn world closer together. The Cold War was just political talk, and maybe the Russians were not the heartless, one-eyed monsters they were reported to be. It was the best of times.

At eleven-thirty, Alex stopped the record player and tuned the television to CBS Channel 5. Guy Lombardo and his band were performing their annual live New Year's Eve broadcast from The *Roosevelt Hotel* in New York City. The women in sequined gowns, the men in black tuxedos, whether holding champagne glasses or noisemakers, all awaited the band's signature tune. Everyone in the parlor at the Straight Eight Farm did also. As midnight neared, the noise in the room quieted. Even the children, tired, half-asleep, and bewildered, not knowing what to expect, awaited the stroke of midnight. It was magical. When everyone exclaimed *"Happy New Year!"* the youngsters looked around excitedly, and those who could, did their very best to repeat the words as they heard them. Everybody was happy. Some applauded, some kissed and some just watched. The kids wondered what had just happened.

Under the guidance of Mr. Lombardo, his *Royal Canadians* played *Auld Lang Syne*. Alex and Annie shared a moment they would forever remember. A new year, a new decade and the new life Annie carried within her sparkled in the center of their universe, just like that flippant mirror ball hanging above their heads, smack-dab in the middle of the room.

When the song ended and the shuffling and dancing stopped, some gave acknowledgement with applause. The party was over, another year began automatically, and no further action from humanity was required. Time smoothly passed by without any human help. The next day the sun would come up and another page of the calendar would flip without any further fanfare whatsoever.

Parents milled about collecting their children and any of their toys. The leftover food was covered in sheets of *Cut-Rite* wax paper and put on the floorboards of either an Oldsmobile, *DeSoto* or *Nash*. Alexander and Louis shook hands with Jeffrey and James, thanked them for coming, gave each a fifty-dollar holiday check and thanked them again. The two brothers expressed their appreciation and took the time to thank Annie and Hedy, saying they hoped their employment would last long into the future. Sally and James' wife, Carla, graciously encouraged the men into the beige Nash Rambler, and were able to drive off in a few minutes. With a honk of the horn and waving an arm out the window, Carla and Sally had them on the way home. Annie waved back, and told Alex, "They're nice people. Good people, Alex. We got some good people working for us. I like Carla; actually, she's a very pleasant person. She just looks a little brassy with that bleached blonde hair. Sally's still a kid, but she's a good kid."

Nicholas, Joey and their two children were the next to pack up to leave. Nicholas put a three-quarter empty bottle of *Jim Beam* and a half-full jug of Puerto Rican rum in the trunk. He gave Annie a bear hug, wished her Happy New Year again and once more congratulated her on her pregnancy. There were kisses on the cheek, soft-spoken wishes and brief hugs from Jovita before she got into the car. The children, Roberta and Hector were sound asleep, already sprawled out across the back seat, covered and tucked in a blanket. Nicholas placed his left hand on his adult son's shoulder and gave a firm handshake with the right. Alex stepped in close and said, "Happy New Year, Old Man. Thanks for coming. Those kids of yours are growing up fast, aren't they?"

Nicholas gave a subtle nod in agreement. "Kids grow up and are gone before you know it. Take it from me, Alex, I know. I learned the hard way. Joey and I are so happy for you and your Annie. Soon you will have a family of your very own. I know you both have waited for this."

He told his son they would stop back in again tomorrow, between breakfast and lunch. They would enjoy a quieter, more private visit on their way back to Jacksonville. Alex's father slid behind the wheel of the Oldsmobile. He turned the key and started down the drive. The taillights of the emerald-green Rocket 88 faded quickly into the darkness, cloaked behind the dust kicked up by the tires.

Renaldo was holding his son Johnny in his arms. He spoke softly. "Good night, patrón, thank you. See you tomorrow, Alexander."

His wife Teresa gave Annie a brief one-armed hug, holding onto a canvas bag of leftover burgers, hotdogs and salad. "Buenos noches, goodnight, Annie. We had a nice time. Very nice. We all thank you," she spoke graciously. Teresa, Johnny and husband Renaldo started their short walk down the driveway that led to the security of their home.

It was necessary for Hedy to lead her sons Tom and Ben by the hand, all the way from the parlor and into the back seat of the DeSoto. Annie followed close behind on the way from the house. The boys did not want to leave, but were barely awake, fighting sleep with each step. Once inside the car, they fell into each other, oblivious to the world. Hedwig covered them tenderly with the plaid woolen blanket from the rear window deck. Louis and Alex stood waiting next to the car. Annie hugged her friend. "Good night, Hedy. Thanks for all your help."

After a drink, two, or three, Hedy's German accent became stronger. She spoke with more affirmation and certitude. Drink enhanced her solid, stoic, no bull, cut-and-dried German attitude and thick Stuttgart accent.

"Ja, Annie. It was nice. No silly stuff. We all had a good time, we sure did. And you are welcome. We worked together and had a good time." She gave Annie a peck on the cheek and another to Alex before she maneuvered herself into the front seat of the car. Inside, she reached into her purse, brought out a *Winston* and lit it. "Take me home, Louis, *mein schatz*. Me and the kids want to go to bed."

Louis and Alexander shook hands. "Good night, Alex. Good night, my partner and friend. Thank you, we did a good job, last year. It was a nice party to start a new year."

"And thank you, too, Louis. I'm sure I'll see you tomorrow. Good night, buddy."

Annie walked over to her husband and put an arm around his waist. Louis got in and started the DeSoto. It was perhaps four hundred yards to their front door. Alexander reminded him, "Drive carefully now, Louis. You have a long driveway! Good night, Hedy."

Annie and Alex watched Louis' DeSoto travel round the bend, down the driveway and onward to his home. They turned and walked back toward the house. Alex unplugged the extension cord for the string of light bulbs that hung over the picnic tables and barbeque. The heavy smell of the charcoal fire still hung in the night air. Quiet returned to their home. They were alone and the party was over. He had his arm around Annie's waist as they walked onto the porch.

"How about we split a beer, Annie girl? Like we used to?"

"Sure." Annie reached into the galvanized tub and brought out an icy cold bottle. An opener was tied to the tub handle by a string. The top came off with a flick of her wrist; a *snap* and a *whoosh*. "Let's put on that Sinatra record, Alex. Turn it down low. Put it on side two, Hon."

Inside the living room, the full-screen test pattern was on the 21-inch, black-and-white television. At the top center was the head of an Indian Chief, adorned in a full-feathered headdress, with large black numbers, one through nine, in a big circle. Starting in the center, kaleidoscope patterns of straight lines spread outwards. The only sound was a low-level, constant, electronic *beeeep* coming from the front panel. Alex turned the television off and raised the hinged lid on the stereo side of the console.

Alex found the Sinatra vinyl, placed it on the turntable and gently set the needle down. He heard Annie's heels tap-tap-tapping on the pine floor and watched her every step as she walked over to the sofa. "You look terrific tonight, Annie. Extra terrific tonight." He undid his necktie, pulled it through his collar and tossed it on the crooked pile of records. Alex pushed the ottoman away from the wall with his foot and shoved it in front of the sofa. They sat relaxed, with legs outstretched on the hassock and tasted the Viking lager. Annie leaned into her husband, sighed and put her head on his shoulder.

"It was a good night, Alex. Good party all around. I think everyone had a good time. Nobody got all goofy or anything, and that was nice. The kids all behaved; couldn't have been better. It was one darn good party. It really was, don't you think?"

"Yeah, Annie girl, it was. We had plenty of food ... salads ... cold plates ... everything. And it was all good."

"Except for Teresa's macaroni and cheese."

"Really? It tasted all right to me."

"Nope. You cannot call it macaroni and cheese when it's macaroni and *Velveeta*. I mean, good golly, I'm from Wisconsin, Alex. Velveeta is just not cheese. It's cheese-flavored *Crisco* shortening!"

Alex just nodded, knowing not to argue. Something else was going on. Sinatra was inviting them to the center of the room with his gentle rendition and smooth intonations of *What's New?*. "How about one last dance, Annie?"

They held each other, shuffling their feet slowly, in an almost inseparable clutch. Alex nuzzled his cheek into Annie's chestnut curls. He put one arm around her waist and the other across her shoulders. She was holding him close, with both arms. He was not going anywhere. She moved a hand down to his buttocks, pressed and pushed her hips into him. They were feigning dance moves across the floor; vertically entwined, passionately connected with footwork constrained, yet fueled by horizontal, physical desire.

Alex stood motionless and slowly bent at the waist. In a long, smooth motion, he slid his hand down her leg and stopped at the hemline of her dress. In a gentle, deliberate progression, he moved his hand up Annie's leg and stopped at the garter snap, halfway up her thigh. With a gentle squeeze, and firm, kneading fingers, he whispered, "I want to eat you up tonight, Annie. I want to taste every delicious bit."

She kissed him, the fingers of her left hand playing through the hair on the back of his head and the other still pressing into his buttocks. Her body tickled all over and released a tremble of desire. There was a silky, yielding, sigh, a surrender to the coming rapture. "Take little bites, Alex. Tidbits ... nibbles. Make it last. Long ... sweet ... solid. Like a *Sugar Daddy* bar ... or a big *Tootsie Roll*."

"Rocket 88."

Friday morning, January 1, 1960, New Year's Day

They got up early, showered, went back to bed and performed an encore of last night's libidinous New Year celebration. It was now just past nine, and they sat at opposite sides of the kitchen table. Annie was holding the heavy, white china mug between both hands, her elbows on the table and looking steadily into her husband's eyes, without a blink. Between sips, she gently blew across the hot coffee. Her opulent, baby blue bathrobe had oversized, brushed cuffs and a wide, plush collar. She had it marginally open at the top, cautiously suggestive. Alex was in a red plaid flannel shirt, jeans and white socks.

He stabbed the last two bits of home fries with his fork, wiped them in the broken egg yolk, and his breakfast was gone. The fork landed on the plate with metallic chatter. He picked up the glass, finished his orange juice, and looked across the table, locking eyes with his wife. A gentle smile curled up the ends of her lips. Her left foot, covered in a fuzzy pink bedroom slipper, slowly worked its way up his calf, just beyond the knee, onto his thigh. Alex reached down, pushed the slipper off, and held her foot. When Annie's other foot joined in, Alex began to rub and massage both of them.

"The Old Man, Joey and the kids are going to be here before too long, Annie."

She had her eyes closed and still held the coffee in her hands. The foot massage was working wonderfully. "Whether you realize it or not, you are a man of many special talents, Mister Throckmorton. You rub me the right way … the right way." She wiggled her toes.

He continued to massage her feet. It calmed him and created a reflective mood. "We've come a long way since last year. The business has really taken off, we developed a strong, wonderful herd and now we have a little one on the way. I meant a baby ... a people baby ... a baby *"us"*. Not a colt or foal. A baby. We're blessed, Annie. We enjoy good friends, great employees, and good times. We have a lot to be thankful for, the two of us."

She sat relaxed, thinking, and dreaming. She smiled wide, opened her eyes, pulled her feet back, stood and walked around the table to her husband. Annie put a hand on his shoulder, brought her head down and kissed him.

"I love you, Alex." He stood. They held one another and kissed again. "I'm going to get dressed and get this place cleaned up as best I can."

"And I'll come back inside to help in a minute, Honey. First, I'll put Poko and Sebastian out to pasture with the rest of the herd. They adjusted real well yesterday afternoon and evening."

On the porch, Alex pulled on his boots and looked around the yard. It was apparent that Renaldo was out of bed already; there were no telltale signs that a party had taken place. The last two remnants of the New Year celebration were the picnic tables; obviously a two-man job. It was another unusually warm and humid day. The morning air hung thick and damp. There was unmistakable evidence of heavy dew and earlier fog.

As he approached the barn, he could hear the radio playing. Walking inside, he knew he would hear his stable master greet him. He called out, "Good morning, my friend!"

"Good morning, Mister Alex! A lovely morning! The little one, Poko, she's out in pasture with the others. I was not sure about Sebastian, so he is still inside, patrón."

"Thank you, Renaldo. Thank you. I'll set him out. Thank you." Over the French door of the stall, Sebastian snorted a greeting, head-bobbed and gave Alex a nicker as he approached. The horse lifted and dropped a foreleg on the elm floorboards, letting Alex know he was ready to join the rest of the herd out in pasture.

The stallion was eager, left his stall and waited at the paddock gate. As soon as Alex unlatched and opened it, Sebastian set off in an ambling gait.

On his way back to the house, a thought came to Alex, an ironic coincidence; the seven-year-old stud had a growing family also. Alex too, had a spring in his step and knew it was related to the news his wife had yesterday. He bounded up the porch steps two at a time, opened the screen door and announced, "I'm back, Annie. We can put the house back together." Inside, Alex used the bootjack to pull off his brushed *Acme* work boots. There were two things Annie insisted upon: clean hands and no boots in the house.

They made quick work of the party cleanup. Alex ran a damp mop over the parlor floor, laid the braided rug back down and pushed the furniture back in place. Annie squared away the kitchen and Alex used the mop over the entryway and hall floors.

A little after ten o'clock, Nicholas and Jovita arrived with their children, Roberta and Hector. Alex was putting the mop and bucket away in the front closet when the driveway gravel crunched under the weight of the Olds 88, announcing their approach. He called down the hall to his wife, "Perfect timing, Annie. We got company."

"What's New?"

Friday, mid-day, January 1, 1960

Since they reconnected in 1955, Alex and his father had regular visits, both in Pensacola and in Jacksonville. Annie and Jovita treated each other as good friends, and that seemed to work perfectly. Alex also thought of Joey as a friend. Considering her age, notwithstanding her marriage with his father, he could not think of the Latin beauty as his stepmother.

There was a seventeen-year hole in the father-son connection between Alexander and Nicholas. Between Nicholas' 1938 enlistment into the Army Air Corps and their meeting in 1955, there were only a handful of days in 1946 when they were actually together. Now, they have plenty of things to talk about, old and new. Annie and Jovita formed a friendly, personal friendship over the last four years, and shared many life stories. There was talk of the children, Roberta and Hector, running a household, shopping, and doctors. They even worked in discussions of plot twists in their favorite soap opera, *The Guiding Light*.

Nicholas and Alexander had two different and distinctive types of connection. There was the once non-existent, strained and broken family bond, full of holes and empty years. That bond had been carefully, but tenuously, repaired. The other seemed to be more of a friendly companionship and male camaraderie, loosely tied together by military service, genetics and curiosity. Their conversations covered the scope of Nicholas' children, old Army and Navy anecdotes, "war stories," or politics. Many of his father's tales intrigued Alex - at the very least, the parts he was willing to talk about. Many were incomplete or inconsequential. Most of them bordered on the ribald or comical. Annie, and even Jovita, would often learn little tidbits, things they never knew about Alexander or Nicholas Throckmorton.

Alex and his father often spoke in private and would go off to the other side of the room, somewhere out of earshot. During this visit, they wandered out to the yard and sat at one of the picnic tables with a bottle of Old Crow. Annie and Joey remained in the parlor with coffee, cake and the children. With a glass of bourbon and a day-old toast to the New Year, Alex and Nicholas started to share stories once again. His father began to detail an interesting evening at the *Hotel Nacional* in Havana seven years earlier. He began his narration about a table packed elbow-to-elbow with politicians, military personnel, aides-de-camp, and *el Presidente* himself, Fulgencio Batista. Meyer Lansky, the mobster who ran Havana's gambling empire and the entire Cuban drug trade, sat alongside the dictator. Nicholas said the story was completely based on second-hand information and he was not there. His father disavowed personal knowledge, but it was not difficult for Alex to picture his father at the table. When Nicholas related tales from his past, he often claimed innocence by disconnection, absence or anonymity. He described the scene in detail, down to the table decorations, white linen tablecloths, the bottles of *Havana Club* rum and the hand rolled cigars at every place setting.

Nicholas continued, "There was a floorshow, a huge song-and-dance deal, with *Ginger Rogers*, an all-out extravaganza like a Hollywood musical for the dignitaries and big-wheels. It was clearly a victory celebration. Batista's government just squashed a band of rebels and repelled an attack by the forces behind *Fidel Castro* at the Moncada Barracks in Santiago. It was late July 1953. After the show, Lansky expelled a lung-full of cigar smoke, coughed and laughed. He declared, *'That broad can wiggle her ass, but she can't sing a goddamned note.'* Batista looked across the table, and called Lansky a *culo pomposo*, which translates as 'pompous ass' in Spanish." Nicholas laughed from deep within his chest and continued, "Nobody dared to translate, so the mobster was unaware of the wise-crack insult. Batista didn't know it then, but that attack on Castro was the beginning of the end for him, forcing him to eventually go into exile in Portugal. And Lansky ... well ... he had to leave Cuba before the revolution went full bore and hell, now he literally owns Las Vegas, so I guess things worked out for him anyway. He's living it up, running the whole damn show out there in the desert. And now, I bet you that he has plenty of big-busted babes around who know how to shake their sweet little ass *and* sing."

Alex looked incredulously at his father. Both men took a drink of their bourbon. "It's true, Alex. No bullshit. It happened. It happened just like that." Alex was amused and chuckled briefly. Nicholas nodded in agreement and looked at his watch. "Hey, Alex ... me, Joey, and the kids need to hit the road. It's a seven-hour drive, or a little more, back to

Jacksonville across US 90. The kids get restless in the back seat, even with their comic books and *Tootsie Toys*. And Joey, well, she usually sleeps." He leaned close to his son and whispered, "Me, I get damn bored with the road and my ass gets sore. Driving ain't nothing like flying."

Both men maneuvered off the picnic table benches. Alex grabbed the bourbon and the two glasses, and they started back to the house. "We had a good time, a good visit, Old Man. Thanks for coming down again."

Nicholas agreed. Alex started, "Annie and I will drive over sometime this summer, I imagine. We can spend a couple days or so and stay up in Fernandina Beach at the *Atlantic Resort* again. We enjoyed that place up there. We think of it as the place where we spent our honeymoon. It's a nice place right there on the beach."

His father was silent, nodded and walked inside. Alex sat on the swing and set the two glasses and bottle down on the floor. He could see some of the horses out in the pasture. Inside the barn, he saw Renaldo pitching fresh straw in the stalls. He had the swing slowly rocking. The talk he had with his father stirred some memories, but still, he wondered whatever happened to his childhood. He couldn't remember much: a *Detroit Tigers* baseball game, a speed boat race and a visit to an Army airfield. It was so long ago; he could not get a distinct picture. Everything was a blur. Alexander wondered how so many years and so many memories could have simply disappeared. He was lost in the fog of the forgotten past.

Hector and Roberta sprung from inside the house, the screen door banged shut and Jovita called out, asking them to slow down. The children were down the steps, into the yard and inside the Oldsmobile before their mother and father made it out of the house. It was all over in a flash. The children were already waiting in the car when Nicholas gave Annie a hug and shook hands with his son. Joey gave hugs to Annie and Alex alike, complete with an unemotional peck on the cheek. The green Olds was down and out of the driveway in mere minutes.

Annie and Alex watched as the car disappeared around the bend, down the driveway and out of sight. They stood together, holding hands. "That was just like a big wind, Alex. In and out before you know it. No permanent damage, just smudged lipstick, a messed up hair-do and some dirty dishes. Like that Bob Crosby song, *Big Noise Blew In From Winnetka*. It blew in and blew right out again."

That got a chuckle from Alex. "Let's sit awhile, Sweetheart. It's time to relax." They sat on the swing for several minutes, not saying a word, looking out at their world. "Did you notice the Old Man didn't get worked up about our baby news? Not last night, not today either. You would think he would be real excited and all jazzed up about becoming a grandfather. Sometimes I think his thoughts take him far away ... far away from the people directly around him. Maybe deep down, he thrives on isolation ... on being alone. Or maybe he's stuck in the past ... with people and places he's been."

Annie added, "Your father didn't say anything special to me about being pregnant, only that bland congratulation. It was as if he had something else on his mind. But Joey gave congratulations, in a way. Maybe it's hard for her to say it English, but the only thing she said was: *that's very nice, Annie. I think you will be happy.*"

"Tell you what, Annie girl. I'm happy. I'm so happy for both of us. And our baby. This baby is going to have a full-time father. I promise that with all my heart and soul. I promise."

Annie leaned into him and placed a little peck on his cheek. "I know, Alex. I know." The only sounds were a noisy Blue Jay and a persistent Mockingbird.

Annie became reflective and said, "You know, maybe I shouldn't say this, but sometimes I wonder about Joey. I mean, I think there's something there that just don't mix. Last night, at the party, she and Teresa were talking about their childhood. Joey didn't offer much. You know, it's like the fat that floats to the top on leftover stew in the *Frigidaire*. Why would a beautiful girl, maybe twenty-some years old, a college student working in a bar, fall in love with, and carry the candle for an Army pilot in his mid-thirties? And in Chicago of all places. I have trouble putting their relationship into perspective. I always did."

Alex was surprised at this line of conversation. "My goodness, Annie. You and I met, fell in love and were married in only a week, for goodness sake."

"Yeah, but that's just it, Alex. We got married. Joey waited what, another four or five years? Goodness gracious, Alex. Five years hanging around waiting for someone you met in a bar and knew for only a few days? There is something about that wheel of cheese that just doesn't roll right."

Alex gave it a moment of thought, and said, "I admit it. You're right. We don't know everything about their connection ... far from it. We probably will never know. Maybe the Old Man connected with her more often over the years and hasn't told us. We just don't know. And according to him, he thought he was still married, and didn't know my mother had passed away in '54. We should just come right out and ask him sometime." Alex kept his curiosity to himself and did not mention it, but he was intrigued. Annie's line of thought and the direction of her conversation had piqued his interest. Her comments cast a shadow of doubt and Alex was captured. Annie had his full attention.

"And think about this, Alex. Did you ever notice how sometimes she completely loses that Cuban accent? All of a sudden it can disappear. I mean one sentence can be loaded with all kinds of Spanish overtones and words and stuff and the next sentence is perfect English. What's up with that? I can't figure that out. I mean, I still talk like I'm from Wisconsin, don't you know."

The weathered wood swing was stirring their thoughts in its unique, gentle, to and fro motion. Alex picked up a glass and the Old Crow. He offered Annie a drink. She just shook her head and he poured two fingers into the glass for himself.

Annie was on a roll. She started again, "And how about this ... her family. We have never seen her mother and father in Jacksonville, have we? She never introduced them to us or even tried when we were there. And she has always been vague about her family ... ever notice? She's never told us about her life growing up on that so-called sugar cane plantation in Cuba. And that aunt and uncle she supposedly has back in Chicago, the ones that she came to America with. Nobody knows if they exist. Nobody. I mean, I never met your aunt in Oshkosh, but I know she exists. She sent ..."

She hit a brick wall. Annie stopped in mid-sentence and did not finish her thought. In a flash, like a lightning strike, Annie remembered the registered envelope she had signed for on Monday; the one from Alex's aunt in Oshkosh. She flushed from embarrassment and immediately apologized.

"Gosh, I'm sorry, Alex! I forgot! You got some mail from your Aunt Marie on Monday ... in a big manila envelope. With the party and all, and the guests, our new filly, and the news from my doctor, I just plain forgot. I'll go get it. I'm so sorry." She was up, off the swing, and back out on the porch with the big envelope in a matter of seconds.

Annie handed him the piece of mail, sat back down on the swing and apologized again. "Forgive me, Alex. I got

76

carried away with all that chatter about Joey. I didn't mean anything by it. I was just gossiping away, that's all. Forget what I said ... Joey's a good person."

He spoke as he studied the piece of mail. "Forget it, Honey. No big deal." He turned the envelope around, looking at both sides. "Registered mail ... must be important. Hope everything's all right. Maybe it's just a big Christmas card and maybe a note or calendar or something."

Alex took his pocketknife and cut the flap of the envelope. Annie watched wide-eyed, with her hands folded on her lap.

"Fever."

Friday afternoon, January 1, 1960.

Alex pulled the contents of the brown envelope out and set them onto the swing seat between them.

There was a Christmas card and a short, separate hand-written letter from his aunt Marie. He glanced at it quickly, his gaze rapidly moving over his aunt's script. Her note was a brief, direct apology for not forwarding the contents earlier, followed by some banal details of the latest family news. He did not fully finish reading his aunt's letter before he passed it to Annie.

Alex's aunt had forwarded a long white business-size envelope, post marked November 25th, from an attorney in Rochester, New York, and addressed to him; simply *"Alexander Throckmorton, New York Avenue, Oshkosh, Wisc."* It had some indiscernible pencil marks on the outside, along with *"not Route 2"*, and *"unknown"*. He examined it, turning it over and back again. His thoughts were racing. He could not remember ever knowing anyone from Rochester. He flipped it over, and over, again.

Annie was watching closely. "I guess the only way you're going to find out what's inside is to open it, Alex."

"It's got me baffled. I have no idea ... it looks like this envelope was all over Oshkosh before they delivered it to my aunt's house ... it was mailed more than two months ago. Somebody, some Post Office worker, must have remembered my mother's married name: Nora Throckmorton. I bet that's why it was eventually delivered to my Aunt Marie at the old family home on New York Avenue."

He looked into Annie's green eyes. She smiled and shrugged her shoulders. "Let's see what this is all about, Annie. I don't know anybody in Rochester."

"Do it, Alex. Do it! Open up the gosh darn thing!" She nudged her husband with her elbow.

He put his pocketknife to work again - slipped the blade under the flap and slit along the top of the envelope. The letter inside was typewritten on thick, ivory cotton bond. Alex unfolded it, creased it open and held it between them. They read it together, their eyes moving methodically across the lines.

November 24, 1959

Reginald G. Meriwether

Attorney At Law
25 Main Street East
Rochester 3, New York

Alexander Throckmorton
General Delivery (New York Avenue), Oshkosh, Wisconsin

Dear Mr. Throckmorton,
Let me begin by wishing that this correspondence has successfully
found its way to you.
I am representing Miss Katherine A. Dobbs, of Brighton, New
York, with the preliminary preparations for a timely settlement of
her estate. Miss Dobbs has named you as a beneficiary of her
estate; including, but not limited to, custodian of a modest Totten
trust. Miss Dobbs has asked me to stress that this is a matter of
significant importance and personal in nature. She expresses her
deepest hope that you give it your sincere consideration in lieu of
a protracted probate with the courts of Monroe County and New
York State.
You may contact me by telephone either at my office (CApital-
4610) or at my home on weekends or evenings (MOnroe-3226).
Sincerely,

Reginald G. Meriwether, Esq.

Alex sat motionless, looked out across the yard toward the pasture and without a word, passed the letter to Annie. Although she had just read along with him, she again studied every word closely. Curiously, she could feel her pulse at her temples. In an instant, the name *Katherine Dobbs* became etched into her mind and soul. She sensed that it would remain forever and that somehow, her entire life was about to change. Alex did not say one word. Annie was patiently awaiting an explanation. She watched as he once again allowed his gaze to became frozen somewhere out in the pasture with the horses. She decided to give him more time, and carefully folded the letter and held onto it, still curiously watching her husband.

The universe had been jolted to a motionless standstill. Time stopped. Nervous and impatient, Annie could wait no longer. The words finally came out, "We all got our secrets, but who is this Katherine Dobbs person, Alex?"

He was still looking beyond the pasture. He answered in a distant, steady tone, almost matter-of-fact, "Lieutenant Junior Grade Katy Dobbs. I served with her in Korea. We knew each other well. Very well." He lost his stare and looked over to his wife. "Let me see that letter again, Annie."

She unfolded it and handed it to her husband. "You really knew her well? Really well? Like knowing someone *in love* well?"

He didn't answer. His eyes quickly ran across the letter again and he began to read aloud, "It says here: *"preliminary preparations for a timely settlement of her estate"*. And down here it says: *"Miss Dobbs has asked me to stress this matter..."* That sentence sounds to me like she's not dead, Annie. And the lawyer calls her *Miss* Dobbs. That means she's not married. And if she's not dead, why the Will? And if she's not married, why contact me? What's all this, do you think?"

"First, I think you better call that lawyer, Alex. Then I think you better fully explain your familiarity with this *Katy* woman to me and why you never mentioned her before." Annie gathered the contents of the manila envelope and put them back inside. Alex held onto the lawyer's letter. Together, they stood from the swing and started for the screen door. It was getting cloudy, with dark, heavy, coal-gray skies. A change in the weather was coming. The wind was picking up.

Inside, Annie sat at the kitchen table. Alex stood holding the letter and spoke with two operators before he was connected to the attorney at his Rochester residence. Alex then sat next to his wife; the coiled telephone cord stretched to its limit. Annie rested her arms on the table, with folded hands. She had listened closely and intently, trying to understand the conversation while hearing only one side of it. Alex had a troubled look, a deep pensive expression that transformed to sadness when he acknowledged the lawyer's message that Katherine Dobbs was now deceased.

He put his hand over the mouthpiece and whispered to Annie, "She's dead." It was a short conversation, with segments of silence, as Alex had nothing to add and could only listen. He only nodded and exhibited varied emotions as the attorney spoke. Alex thanked him, said he would be in touch again and would call him soon. He stood and hung up the wall telephone. He had lost color and his complexion became ashen.

"Let's go sit in the parlor, Annie. There is a lot to tell."

Annie picked up all the papers, followed her husband back into the front room and sat next to him on the sofa. It wasn't like Alex to act so seriously. She knew this would be an important and lengthy talk. Annie wasn't apprehensive of what she might hear, but voraciously curious. Alexander never spoke to Annie about any personal love interests in his past. He never mentioned that he carried a torch for anyone, anytime, anywhere. This Katherine Dobbs woman must have been someone special.

They sat close; Annie set her hand over his. Alex took a breath, exhaled and began to speak. He had gathered himself.

"I never expected to hear from Katy after she left Korea. We met when I was on *TDY* … Temporary Duty with the United Nations unit in Sasebo, Japan. Katy was an officer in the Information Service. We were seeing each other, against Navy regulations, for almost a full year. She was an officer, Lieutenant Junior Grade, and I was enlisted personnel, a Petty Officer Second Class. Regulations stated that fraternizing was a strict no-no. But it went on … obviously … and not just between us, me and Katy, I mean. Believe me, it was not uncommon. But that's not what this was about. Our liaison started in the office … sending, transmitting, recording and even hand-carrying messages to other UN commands, the British, Australians, and the various US forces, Army, Marines, Air Force, and Navy. Paperwork mostly. We ended up getting intimate. It started after a typhoon knocked out the main power and telephone lines; it was *Super Typhoon Ruth*, if I remember right. We were stranded, sort of, in the dark with no electricity for three full days. And it started … the intimate stuff. From then on, it was a comfort-based affair; neither of us ever talked about any permanent commitment. We never crossed that bridge. We never entered that territory. We never mentioned it. We were together about … not quite a year … I think … ten months or so."

He leaned back into the sofa and looked over to his wife. He wasn't certain what Annie's reaction would be. She looked into his eyes. Alex did not detect any seismic activity or pending volcanic eruption. There was no evidence of an emotional tidal wave. She still held his hand in hers and gave him all her attention.

Seconds passed before Alexander continued, "There was a flu outbreak, a serious one. Katy got really sick with a fever and was hospitalized for over a week. I cannot remember exactly how long it was. Following her sickness, right afterwards, she got a new set of orders. It was late 1952 when she was transferred back Stateside. It was unexpected, to be sure, I was taken aback. I realized we never made any long-range pledges, and we did not promise anything to each other. But Katy left, kind of unannounced and definitely all of a sudden. So, I was hurt I guess. Pretty bad. And it ended just like that. I had a hole in my heart big enough to swallow me whole. The Navy and Katy put the kibosh on our affair and me. No more. It was kaput ... over ... ended. Then, my temporary assignment came to an end a couple weeks later. I went back aboard the Valley Forge, sailed to San Diego, through the Panama Canal, to Pensacola, and mustered out of the Navy. By then it was 1954 ... I got the news about my mother ... went to Oshkosh ... met you ... and well ... you know the rest."

They shared deep, intimate glances. Annie shifted her hips, settled into the couch and eased taut muscles. Alex was still sitting on the edge of the sofa, with his back straight. He folded his hands, leaned forward, with his elbows resting on his thighs, chin on fists, and deep in thought..

Annie asked, "Did the attorney say anything else about the estate? What are you required to do, or what is expected of you, I mean, being named as a beneficiary and that custodian thing?"

Alex sat up straight, and settled into the sofa again. He began, "Well, he told me that Katy specifically asked that I be present ... and I should try to come up there ... and bring my birth certificate or a *Photostat Xerox* copy for identification.

He was sort of vague and didn't reveal anything ... just that is very personal, and intimate in nature. He asked if I was married ... and I said I was ... and that I should ask you to come along ... and maybe make a vacation out of it and visit Niagara Falls while we're there. I guess that would be OK, even in the winter. But it gets cold up in New York during January, you know that. Wisconsin cold."

"Tell me about her, Alex. Where was she from? What did she look like? Tell me all about Katy Dobbs."

"Well, I know she grew up in Syracuse, New York and she was adopted right at birth and raised as an only child. She talked about journalism and photography and graduated from *Cornell* ... with some type of degree in design, if I remember right. This may be about money, or maybe Katy has some new business adventure, or something. Who knows?"

Again, seconds passed before he continued, "Back then, I got the impression that her family had money, but she never said anything about it. She enlisted in the Navy and was awarded a Lieutenant's commission. She ended up working as an Information Officer in Navy Communications. That's about all I know ... that's all there is to tell."

"What did she look like? You didn't answer that question ... and tell me the kind of person she was." Annie's curiosity was working overtime and teasing her imagination.

Alex was reflective, pensive; his gaze drifted again, out and beyond the parlor windows. "Well, Annie, she was about your height, about your build, with short hair. She was a brunette ... a real dark brown. She kept it short, with curls, sort of like *Natalie Wood* in that movie *Rebel Without A Cause*, but shorter. Blue eyes ... bottomless, sky-blue eyes ... she had a very soft voice ... she was a gentle person ... cared about people and couldn't wait for the war to end ... she wanted to work for *Life* magazine, or *Allied Signal*, like her grandfather. Sometimes she would write short stories about

84

people and places ... and take pictures of the people she met. I asked her if she ever wrote about me, and she told me she didn't. I just wasn't that interesting, I suppose, or for some reason I wasn't important enough. I can't imagine why she stuck me in her will."

Annie was quiet. She was satisfied. She knew enough. "How about we head for the *Pink Pig*, and get a beer and a pulled pork sandwich, or something? What do you say?"

He spoke the words, "I guess we could do that." His reply was sterile, emotionless. He was thinking of a woman who once held a piece of his heart and a love that might have been. At that particular moment, his thoughts were an ocean away, eight years and ten thousand miles ago. There was a distant rumble of thunder.

"Primrose Lane."

Friday evening, January 1, 1960

The rain began to fall on the way to the restaurant. "The band starts at nine, so we have about two hours of relative silence, Annie."

"I think we will be back home by then, Alex."

Alex ordered a short rack of ribs, a basket of French fries, and a bottle of Viking lager. Annie opted for sweet tea, and said, "I remember an article in *Redbook*, written by some doctor that said women in the family way should be careful about drinking alcohol. The article said, *'what the mother does, the baby does.'* That made sense to me. And I'm happy we're not smoking anymore. And besides, thirty cents a pack adds up."

The waitress brought their entire order in one trip. She balanced everything on a round tray, holding it over her right shoulder, and in one motion, set it smoothly on the table.

They were seated in a small booth, away from the bar and along the wall in good company with a *Seeburg* jukebox. A big fat silhouette of a pig, formed with pink neon lights, beer signage, a single incandescent bulb hanging above a pool table and weak, florescent ceiling fixtures gave the juke joint all the dim light required. Customers occupied six booths, and a dozen or more individuals sat at the bar. It was a mixed crowd; couples neatly dressed, single men in work clothes, an unshaven fellow in ragged coveralls and a disheveled woman with a wrinkled, red crepe dress; possibly a left-over from last night's party. Alex held the opinion that New Year's Eve was oftentimes nothing more than a *Ted Mack Amateur Hour*: there is no special skill required to make a fool of yourself.

He whispered privately to his wife, "There's quite a cross-section of people in here tonight. I think we ought to start driving a little farther down the road, nearer Pensacola."

Annie had a salty Mona Lisa smile. "Yeah. People of our caliber should frequent the high-class dives more often. We wouldn't want the neighbors to catch us in a cheap beer joint like this. We need to keep up our appearances, get classy and steer clear of these honky-tonk dumps ... now ... pass me them ribs."

Alex grinned. "You're a jewel, Annie."

There was not much conversation during their meal. They picked at the fries and ribs, gazed at each other, looked around the room and shared a smile or a nod. Combined, today's letter and telephone call with the attorney had dumped buckets of information at their feet. There was a lot to mop up, wring out and put in perspective. The manila envelope from his aunt tipped over a barrelful of emotion, spilling out forgotten feelings and creating countless questions. Alex was once again searching for answers lost in his past. Six years ago, the mystery involved his father. This time around, it entailed a puzzle from a past love affair. He looked across the table into his wife's green eyes. "I am sorry you had to get caught up in this, Annie. I really am."

"I am not caught up in anything, Alex. You are my husband. We are in this together, and everybody has a private history. Everybody. We all have a secret or two that we keep."

She put the straw to her lips, took a sip of the iced tea and wiped her fingers on a napkin. With her arms on the table, and folded hands, she took a breath and exhaled. She did not wish her husband any further anguish over a past love and decided to tell him a story that she had kept hidden for nearly a decade.

"When I graduated from Appleton High in 1950, I fully expected to be married within a year and raising a flock of kids. I had a steady boyfriend, Arnie Ericson, a very redheaded, freckle-faced kid, all through junior high and right up to graduation. His father owned Ericson Furniture and Fixtures right there on Oneida Street. After graduation, he started accounting school at Rasmussen and got his draft notice a week later. Well, Alex, we almost got married right then and there. I wanted to claim him as my own. I was ready to become his wife and start having babies. But he convinced me, despite my objections, to wait. I was in love at the time, rock solid love. My world crashed and burned when he got on that *Trailways* bus for Milwaukee. He left me standing there and broken hearted in a cloud of diesel exhaust."

Her voice wavered with emotion, "My dreams were smashed. Ten months later, I found out that Arnie was gone. I mean, gone for good. Ripped from his family, and me ... lost in Korea. And I did not allow myself to get close to any other man until the day you walked into Maxine's, wearing your hat and that white silk scarf of yours."

She wiped a tear with the back of her hand. "So, it's like I said, Alex. We are in this together. We'll make our plans, you arrange it with Louis and Renaldo, and we'll go to Rochester and get all this settled, over, and done with. And it's just like you say all the time, Alex: *plain and simple*. Now, wipe your hands on your napkin and dance with me."

He slid out of the booth, stood and gave his hand to his wife. Paul Anka's voice fell over the gin joint with the smoothness of a silk sheet. *You Are My Destiny* smoothly drifted from the sixteen-inch speaker of the big Seeburg jukebox. They held each another close and danced slowly across the gray and white tile floor. Alex put his cheek into Annie's auburn curls. "I love you, Annie girl."

She looked up and answered softly, "You make it all worth while, Alex. My whole life. You make everything worth while."

He held her around the waist. She had her arms up along his back and her hands on his shoulders. Their feet barely moved. After Paul Anka, they shuffled their way into, through, past, and beyond Jerry Wallace and *Primrose Lane* before they sat back into the booth, side by side. Alex ordered another round of beer and iced tea.

"Do you think you're able, I mean, do you think there would be any problem with you taking the trip to New York, Annie?"

"Goodness gracious, of course not. I am not a wilted daisy for goodness sake. I am absolutely going with you. I'm pregnant, not incapacitated. But if it makes you feel better, I'll telephone Doctor Heinemann first thing tomorrow morning and double-check with him. He's in the office on Saturday mornings and does his house-calls in the afternoon."

That was it, end of the discussion. Annie would go to New York. Their trip to Rochester was now in the planning stages. They talked about the possibilities of rail, automobile and air travel. The reality of limited flights from secondary airports and all the dying, bankrupt railroads left their 1954 Patrician as the logical choice.

Alex finished the last swallow of beer and set the empty bottle on the table with a distinctive thud. His thoughts were scurrying across his mind's eye, hurriedly sorting and pre-planning the trip. He decided to check and re-pack the wheel bearings and change the oil in the differential and crankcase. With a new set of tires and a mere forty thousand miles, Alex was positive the Packard would make the trip north without difficulty.

"We'll figure all this out over the weekend, Annie. And I'll call that attorney and let him know when we are going to leave. And maybe I can find out some more details about this whole thing."

Annie's elbow nudged her husband, and chuckled, "We are long overdue for a road-trip anyway."

There always is a certain excitement, a curious impatience and heightened anticipation awaiting any form of travel. Some outwardly dread it, some openly welcome it, but all acknowledge its culmination. To the accomplished traveler, not only is getting there half the fun, reaching your destination can be a positive life experience.

They could hear the rain outside. Alex got up from the booth, helped Annie with her jacket and turned up the collar for her. A mid-winter thunderstorm in the Florida panhandle means a quick change in the weather.

The raindrops were as large as quarters; unrelenting, striking, and bouncing off the hood, windshield and roof all the way back to the house. Annie sat close to her husband, looking down the road into the blackness ahead. The headlights pierced the darkness and turned the raindrops into countless falling, sparkling rhinestones. The dim ivory glow of the instrument panel was the only light inside the Packard.

When he parked the Patrician under the carport, he leaned over and gave Annie a gentle kiss. "It's good to be home, Honey."

"Yeah. We'll watch some TV and go to bed early."

"A Lover's Question."

Saturday, January 2, 1960

They didn't get much sleep on New Year's night. A steady rain lasted well into the early morning hours, pelting the windows, filling the gutters and gushing into the downspouts. Cooler, more seasonable temperatures moved in. The rain, rumbles of thunder, gusts of wind, and thoughts of far away and long ago made restful sleep impossible. And there was that stinging, pesky, rock in their shoes that did not allow them peaceful slumber. Attempting to be as considerate as possible, trying to lie still, endeavoring to push persistent thoughts back into the darkness, and covering uncertainty under the blanket of troubled sleep, their combined best efforts failed. A restless bed partner begets a restless bed partner. There is just no way to ignore that fidgeting human form in bed next to you.

Saturday, at the first subdued light of morning, Alexander was in the kitchen, cutting up left over boiled potatoes in the frying pan. Home fries, eggs, bacon and buttered toast were his regular weekend culinary contribution. A full pot of fresh-perked coffee sat resting on the stovetop when Annie walked into the kitchen wearing her plush bathrobe and fuzzy pink slippers. Breakfast passed with talk of travel plans and preparations for the trip. They did not mention their sleepless night. Annie told her husband she would call her sister and perhaps her mother and give them her baby news.

Alex spent the morning in the stables and paddock with the new filly, letting Poko become better acquainted with him and her surroundings. He advised Renaldo that he and Annie would be traveling to New York State and that they would be gone just about a week.

Annie cleared the breakfast dishes, brewed a fresh pot of coffee and poured a cup. Anxious to spread her good news, she telephoned her sister in Green Bay. Beth and Bobby Olsen already had a three-year old daughter, Rebecca, a two-year old son, George, and another child due in March. They talked for the better part of a half hour about Christmas and New Year's celebrations and all about her pregnancy. Annie also told her sister about their impending trip to New York and explained only that Alex was named as an heir and Executor for a friend he knew during his time in the Navy. Even with two toddlers underfoot, Beth was able to have a meaningful conversation with Annie. Miles apart, the bond between them was as strong as it was when they shared their upstairs apartment back in Appleton.

Against her better judgment, Annie reluctantly called her mother in Putney, Vermont. When she told Beth she was going to make the telephone call, her sister sighed and commented, "Bless you, Annie." Neither Annie nor her sister were ever able to qualify their mother's acute, sometimes caustic, criticisms or her stinging, almost brutish, remarks. There were times when Irene Hendriks' comments could be so sour, they would pucker a preacher's lips. Yet away from home and out of familial earshot, she was the epitome of social perfection. Those outside of her immediate family considered Irene to be an outgoing, friendly, kind and charitable person. Annie and Beth were in agreement that their mother Irene was walking, talking, proof that two different people can occupy one body.

After the usual cordial greetings, chatter about the Christmas just past, the general back-and-forth health questions and answers, Annie cheerfully gave her mother the news, "We're going to have a baby, Mama. I found out Monday. I'm due in late June or early July." Annie's toes curled inside her slippers. She was awaiting the inevitable: one of her mother's terse, stinging remarks.

On this particular day and during this particular conversation, Irene's response did not alter from the norm or waiver from the anticipated. "I was beginning to wonder if there was something wrong with you or even that man of yours. Does he have real bullets in his gun? Have you been doing it right? I mean, you've been married for what, five, six years? Are things normal in the bedroom or what? Your baby sister got married and had a little one, and another one in no time at all. And she's pregnant again; a baby machine, your sister is. Your sister Beth and her Bobby must really be in love."

Annie sat back in the kitchen chair and took a sip of her lukewarm coffee. "Well, Mama, we got a new horse on Thursday, too. A filly. That makes five now."

"Are you absolutely sure you're pregnant, Maryanne?"

Annie took a deep breath. "I've got to go, Mama. Alex needs me outside. I'll call again when I get the chance. Or you can call me. Bye-bye, Mama." She did not mention that she and Alex were driving to New York and did not think of it until after she had hung up. Annie considered that when it comes to her mother, some stones are better left unturned, and some dogs better left asleep.

She stood, shook her head in obvious frustration and looked out beyond the barn, to the pasture. Naming each of the horses to herself, she counted all five and realized she miscounted. They now have six. She could see that Poko was working in the paddock with Alexander. She shook her head in disgust and carefully bit her bottom lip, knowing her mother didn't care if they have five, six, or twenty horses. All things considered, her telephone call with her mother went all right. It could have been much worse. Sometimes it

92

seemed that Irene relished bad news, whether that of her family or complete strangers. At least there were no unsettling surprises or disturbing bits of news this time - none that her mother mentioned. If there were any, Irene would certainly have let her know, without hesitation. Annie remembered the Christmas of 1941, before her father had left to fight in the World War. Her father, Herb, took her and Beth to see Santa at *Zahm's Emporium* in downtown Appleton. Her mother Irene was not with them, for some reason unknown to this day. Her father explained it in a way she never did fully understand. Herbert Dahl told his daughters *'your mother has her own cross to bear ... and it's heavy.'*

Annie looked at the kitchen clock and put herself in motion. She changed into her housedress, did the dishes and called Doctor Heinemann as she promised Alex. He gave Annie the news she wanted to hear and confirmed that she was indeed able to take the trip without any problem or worry this early in pregnancy. The doctor added he did not anticipate any issues during the entire term, considering her over-all health and the fact she was not experiencing any harsh symptoms of morning sickness.

When she ended the conversation, it was nearly noon. Her husband would be coming in for lunch. Annie busied herself in the kitchen and made up three fried bologna and cheddar sandwiches. The phone call with her mother was like so many in the past; after a time, the stinging words fell away, like rain drops off a duck's back.

During lunch, Annie told her husband about her backwards phone call with her mother and that Doc Heinemann gave her the "OK" to travel.

"It's strange, Annie. I mean, when we told my Old Man and Joey, they seemed sort of bored and the whole conversation was ... mundane ... yeah, that's the word. Mundane.

Emotionless. It seems that some other folks are simply not as excited about our baby news as we are."

During lunch, they worked out some of the preparations for Rochester. The road trip was coming together. Later that afternoon, Annie brought Hedy and her children along for a shopping trip to Pensacola. A winter coat was something she did not have in her closet, and a definite necessity north of the Mason Dixon Line. Two pairs of slacks, a sweater, crew socks and a woolen scarf were among the items Annie returned home with. Thinking ahead, she made sure her selection of slacks had the new elastic waistbands.

Alex telephoned the mechanics, Jeff and Jim, and offered them Sunday overtime to help get the Packard road-ready. They readily accepted. He decided it would also be a good investment to replace the spark plugs, points, condenser, distributor cap, and ignition harness. New fan and generator belts, heater hoses, and antifreeze were added too. Cold weather can wreak havoc on a vehicle, and it was much better to err on the side of precaution.

Saturday evening, Alex called Reginald Meriwether, the attorney, at home and let him know that he and Annie would begin their trip to Rochester on Monday, and if things went well, they would see him on Thursday. Alex pressed him for more details about Katherine Dobbs' testament to no avail. The lawyer informed him that she had passed away on December 23, a full month after he sent the incompletely addressed letter to Alexander in Oshkosh. She had succumbed from cancer, *'spider cancer'* he called it, that originated within her breast, spread to her bones, and throughout her body. He told Alex that Miss Dobbs sincerely wished that the letter would find him. Alex asked what a *totten trust* was, and again, there were no details given by the lawyer. He ended their conversation with, "I look forward to meeting you and your wife, Mister Throckmorton, and to the favorable resolution of the specific proprietary and privy matters set forth by Miss Dobbs."

Alex hung up the wall phone and sat down at the kitchen table next to his wife. "For the life of me, I cannot figure out why lawyers have to speak Latin, smoke cigars, and dance the Tango around your questions. I just don't get it."

"Lawyers are like undertakers, Alex. They make your skin crawl, but sooner or later, you need one."

They slept much better that night. Sunday, they finished packing for their trip to Rochester and said good-bye to Louis, Hedy, Renaldo and Teresa.

Alex and Annie would begin their trip north to New York State before sunrise on Monday.

THREE: SOME KODAK MOMENTS

"Too Much."

Three and a half days later:
Wednesday, January 6, 1960,
Erie, Pennsylvania

They arrived in Erie just after noon on the third day. It had been a half dozen years since either of them had felt the cold that a Northern winter brings, and January's chill did nothing to warm their nervous thoughts or absolve the mystery behind Katherine Dobbs' appointment of Alexander as Executor of her estate.

At the junction of US Route 19 and US Route 20, Alex spotted the restaurant and motel they were looking for, situated adjacent to one another. The buildings were neat, clean, and attractive and sat on well-landscaped property with ample parking in an adjacent lighted asphalt lot. Both establishments shared the same architecture and color scheme: turquoise cupolas mounted atop a shining, bright, tile roof the color of orange sherbet. The names were lit in neon along the rooftops: *Howard Johnson's Restaurant* and the *Lamplighter Motel*. This was the second *Ho-Jo* combination they found on this trip. The first one outside of Cincinnati, impressed them as a well-run motel; neat, clean and efficient. When they checked out, the desk clerk gave them a pleasant surprise when he offered to make a reservation for them at their next destination. They accepted.

Automobile travel underwent some significant changes since their last long-range road trip in 1954. Freeways, interstates, or limited access highways were springing up alongside the old two-lane thoroughfares. The route north that Alex planned for this trip was being altered monthly, weekly and in fact, daily. The roadmaps Alex got at service stations were outdated when he received them. New highway construction ran parallel to many of the old roads, and it was everywhere. There were new bypasses around the large cities and long, straight stretches of four-lane highway cut through the countryside. Hilltops and mountainsides were bulldozed, graded, or dynamited away to make room for the sprawling, endless, new ribbons of concrete and asphalt. Small family-owned motels were disappearing and giving way to much larger, higher capacity motor lodges. Franchised fast-food outlets and national chains of restaurants replaced countless roadside diners and small truck stops. Large neon signs or floodlights, blazing the words *Motel, Eat,* and *Gas* were erected roadside, and stuck high in the air, lighting up the night sky for miles around, and beckoning travelers and their wallets. Because of the new roadways, their trip was easier than expected, despite the detours and changing traffic patterns. They found Kentucky and Tennessee the most troublesome, with poorly marked traffic changes, or none at all. US Route 119 would disappear into a dirt and gravel cow-path and magically arise again twenty miles later as Interstate 75.

They traveled thirteen hundred miles in three days. When they arrived in Erie, it was foggy, just about thirty-five degrees, with ice pellets and light, freezing drizzle. The winds were coming straight out of the North, right over Lake Erie. It was the sort of damp, cold weather that chills deep into the bone. Annie told her husband it was *hot cocoa and cheddar cheese* weather. He agreed, and added he simply calls it *cold and miserable.*

They checked into the Howard Johnson's and Alex parked the Packard directly in front of their room. They shared a sense of relief and satisfaction about their trip so far. Things were going well, with no mechanical, weather, or other unforeseen delay. It was mid-afternoon and they were safe in a pleasant motel with a family style restaurant right next door. Their destination was less than two hundred miles away. The desk clerk explained that the road ahead, the New York State Thruway, was a direct route of new, smooth, divided four-lane pavement. Tonight, they could relax. That afternoon, Alexander had telephoned the attorney in Rochester and left a message with his secretary that they expected to be there the next day, Thursday, around mid-day. Tonight, they could relax.

Inside the restaurant, the variety of items on the menu impressed Annie. "You would never, ever, have this much to choose from at Maxine's back in Appleton, Alex. I mean everything from roast turkey, meatloaf, spaghetti and meatballs, all the way down to a hotdog. And goodness, twenty-eight flavors of ice cream!" The single criticism Annie had for the restaurant was the sea-foam teal uniforms and orange aprons the waitresses wore. "There's nothing that compares to a snappy, pin-stripe, white cotton seersucker dress with puffy sleeves, Alex."

Alex feigned deep thought for a second, wrinkling his forehead. Then he commented, "I recall you wearing one of those seersucker outfits a few years back," and gave his wife a wry grin.

Alex had the *tender-sweet* fried clams, French fries, coleslaw, and green beans plate once again, as he did in Cincinnati. He laid claim to a new personal favorite for $1.60.

During dinner, Alex and Annie's small talk somehow drifted to nostalgic reminiscing of things and events of years past. Away from home and the everyday, common and objectively familiar surroundings, personal thoughts and conversations can ramble and drift back to the fond memories of times past. That night was such a night. Perhaps it was triggered by their current state of affairs. They were undeniably involved in a time-travel of sorts, directly tied to Alexander's personal experiences in the Navy.

After their meals, they walked from the dining room to the *Shadow Box* cocktail lounge. Alex rationalized their decision by exposing the alternative, "It's Wednesday, and the only thing on television is *Ozzie and Harriet* or *I've Got a Secret*. And those are probably re-runs anyhow."

They found a private nook in a corner set away from the bar. The lounge was dimly lit, with recessed ceiling lights, and it took a minute for their eyes to adjust. Little cellophane and tinfoil stars were spread across the dark ceiling tiles. The make-believe night sky sent Annie's thoughts wandering. "I'm happy we decided to drive rather than fly, Alex. I heard on the news there was another crash yesterday; a plane from New York to Miami."

"Flying is safe and it's going to get safer as time passes, Annie. The TV newscasts make such a big deal of any accident just because there are so many lives involved at one time. Fact is, I checked into the possibility, but there were just too many stops involved taking a plane to Rochester, or even Buffalo, from Pensacola. It would have taken us nearly two days, five airports and connections, and would have ended up costing just as much as driving. And we don't know anyone up there to drive us around when we did finally get there, so we would need to get one of those *Hertz* rental cars, too."

"We really should stop and visit Niagara Falls, Alex. I mean, we're going to be right there."

"Yeah, there you go. And we're taking our time driving up, and we're not hassled with any timetable or schedule, even on our way back home."

Alex sipped on a neat *Old Fitzgerald* Kentucky bourbon and Annie sat nursing a root beer float. They spoke of nothing in particular. The subject matter covered everything from their trip so far; the restaurant decor, the customers around them, and the winter weather. No one can predict the direction of discrete conversation between two adults, especially a couple with intimate knowledge of one another. Maybe it was the uncertainty behind the reason for this trip; the unknown consequences of actions taken by a person no longer connected to either of them. The topics of Rochester or Katherine Dobbs never came up. The shadow of the unknown can be unsettling. One circumstance that did arise was childhood birthdays.

Alex remembered his tenth birthday was a big disappointment. He explained that the issue was not the gift itself, but the discovery of what it was. His father said the ten-year mark was a significant milestone because his age could no longer be counted as a single digit. The anticipation grew as the day approached. He explained, "Sometime during the day, I was thinking that maybe the Old Man was out buying my present. I was wondering, wishing and hoping. I cannot remember exactly what I wanted. But I do remember daydreaming and looking out the classroom window. Eleven Mile Road was right outside the school, and on the way to our house on East 2nd Street in Mount Clemens. Then I saw it. The Old Man's grey Ford coupe with the trunk half-way open and going right past the school in plain sight. Sticking out from under the trunk lid, I could see the bicycle wheels. Man, I was excited. The teacher hollered at me, but it didn't matter. I was getting a bicycle for my birthday. I knew it, I saw it. Then I was wondering what color it was."

Annie was sitting straight up and listening intently.

"When I got home, we had supper. I must have wiggled and squirmed and wiggled some more, in a nervous, anxious fit. I remember right after supper, me, my mother, and the Old Man walked down the basement steps. I knew what was down there. I was sure of it. And then I wondered how I could fake surprise. I got worried. The surprise was over. It was then I got disappointed. Oh, I got the bike, all right. It was a shiny red one. New paint and new tires. I can still smell it. I cried, not because I was happy, but because by accident, and no real fault of my own, I knew it all ahead of time. I never told my parents about that. I don't know why, but I always thought that if my parents knew, they would never again try to surprise me. The Old Man signed up for the Army Air Corps a month or so later. That was 1938. I did not see him again until 1946 ... after the war ... then it was only two days ... you know the rest. My tenth birthday was one helluva birthday."

"Life's a dance, Alex. Sometimes your toes get stepped on." Annie's deflection worked. She threw a perfect curve ball. They shared a quiet laugh.

"I got a doll one Christmas. I wanted one with *real hair*, because all I ever had was ones with no hair, either bald-headed babies or ones with hair molded right into their little vinyl heads. I probably was about six or seven, because I don't think Beth was in school yet. I don't remember the exact year. Anyway, Santa brought me my dolly with the real hair. It was real red, sort of like mine was when I was little. I came home from school some time after Christmas vacation and found my doll, Bessie, with the worst, god-awful haircut ever. It was all chopped off. My sister got hold of a pair of scissors, and Beth did a job on her, I'll tell you. I was a total wreck. Mama gave Beth a hard spanking. She cried and I cried. I cried until my eyes hurt and felt sorry for my sister, too, not just myself, or my dolly Bessie. My daddy took me to the store to buy a new one and said I could pick out any doll I wanted. Well, I got one without hair. I got one with the hairdo sort of molded right onto the doll's head, you know, and colored light brown a little bit."

Annie shifted her hips and posture. She had a gentle smile. "Well, when we got out to the car, Daddy asked how come I didn't get one with hair. I was honest and told him it was because I didn't want Beth to get in trouble anymore. I remember Daddy hugged me. I had that doll for years and I called her Bessie too, just like the one my sister chopped the hair off. I never had a doll with hair again. I think Bessie finally was thrown out when Mama and Walter sold the house and moved to Vermont."

In a far corner, a jukebox was turned down low, playing Elvis' *Don't*. The subject shifted again. "You remember that concert, Alex, the one we went to in Pensacola? That was one of the very best, fun, happy times of my life."

"I sure do, Annie girl." Alex paused and let his thoughts drift back to the Elvis concert. "That really was a good time." There was another short pause before he asked, "Would you like another root beer?"

"No, thanks. But I think I might try a little dish of one of those twenty-eight flavors of ice cream they brag about here. Now that I know I'm pregnant, I can blame all my hunger pangs and cravings on my condition and get away with it, can't I?"

"I think you've earned it. The cravings, I mean."

On her next time around, with a smile and a pleasant '*thank you*', the cocktail waitress took Annie's order for a dish of *Elberta Peach* ice cream and one more bourbon for Alex. Another Elvis song came up on the jukebox, *Too Much*.

"Do you remember when that concert was, Alex?"

"It was before Elvis went in the Army, so it must have been in '56 or '57. I think he's due to get discharged early this year. Yeah, I saw something on the news about it. He's coming home from Germany this spring. Now that I'm thinking about it, Annie, it was 1956, in the winter, when we saw him in Pensacola at the Municipal Auditorium. It was in the afternoon, a matinee. That was a good show. A great show. I remember the tickets cost a buck seventy-five apiece."

Annie's eyes were focused somewhere beyond the lounge. "You know, there is just no describing how that man performs on stage. You see him on the television, and there's just no comparison. He really moves around on stage and puts his entire soul into the performance, I think. There was an electricity at that concert, Alex. I think everybody felt it. I know I did."

"He's electric, all right. He's good at what he does. No doubt about it. He'll sell a lot of records as long as he stays out of baby blue Cadillacs and little airplanes."

"You're talking about how Hank Williams, Buddy Holly and the Big Bopper ended up dying so early?"

"Yeah, and Richie Valens. The road and music come together to make a hard life, Annie. Think about it. Together, hard living and hard travelling make for a helluva life: giving your time and talent to people you will never know. Singing to people who are either drunk, don't care, don't understand what the song means, or even like your music to begin with."

"I guess it takes a special kind of person to do that for a living. I suppose Elvis really loves his music; you know. And them concerts, he sings the same songs over and over again; he really must love to be onstage and do what he does. All the crowd noise, and all the girls screaming and hollering … it was still a fantastic time, Alex. I will remember Elvis Presley on that stage for the rest of my life."

"Think of all the unlimited styles of music there are in the world, Annie. Jazz has piano, Latin has trumpets, castanets and bongos, and those folk singers in Greenwich Village have their six-string guitars, mouth-harps and tone-deaf raspy voices. I don't know how he does it, Annie. I mean all good rock and roll has a horn, a clarinet or saxophone, something. All of it. Except Elvis. No horn. Just like cowboy music needs a steel guitar or a *Gibson Resonator*, rock and roll needs a horn. Maybe Elvis is more cowboy than rock and roll."

"Well, you can't call *Jailhouse Rock* cowboy music. It doesn't matter, Alex. Whatever Elvis is, he's got it. He's got it." Their eyes met. The music talk ended. The mood was somehow changed. A velvet smooth blanket of total contentment, warmth and emotional tenderness covered them.

He spoke first. "Annie, I am so proud of you. Your strength has encouraged me, and your love has completely surrounded me, since the day we met. I am so happy now ... so happy for both of us ... and so happy we're going to be parents. You are my *port in the storm*, yes ... yes, you are. You have always been there, cheerfully, faithfully, lovingly, and with stars in your eyes to boot."

She put her hand firmly on his knee. "Good golly, Alex. You put those stars in my eyes in the first place. I feel like I'm walking right on the moon. And I am pretty darn happy myself, in case you ain't noticed yet."

He spun the last of the bourbon around the bottom of the glass and stared into the amber whirlpool. He spoke tenderly. "No argument there, Annie girl. I know we're both happy. Very happy. How about we go back to our room and get some shuteye?" They slid out of the booth and walked close, tightly and instep, with Alex's arm around Annie's shoulder.

She bumped her hip into his. "Super, Alex. Let's go get some."

"I Wonder Why."

Thursday, January 7, 1960
Henrietta, New York

They checked out of the Lamplighter close to 6:00 AM, then had hotcakes, sausage, juice and coffee at the restaurant's breakfast counter. There was not another Howard Johnson Motor Lodge near their destination in Rochester, but the desk clerk readily assisted them in finding accommodations in Rochester at a *Holiday Inn*; he offered, "Pleased to be of assistance, folks." They were on their way and on the road early. The weather was a carbon copy of the day before; temperatures at or just above freezing, gray skies, snow pellets, fog and drizzle.

From Stateline, Pennsylvania, they drove to Ripley, New York and found themselves on the *New York State Thruway*, Interstate 90: one of the first divided superhighways to be completed in the United States. Alexander was handed his fare ticket at the Ripley tollbooth. In a glance, he discovered the cost to Rochester, about one hundred and fifty miles down the road, was a dollar eighty-five, payable at exit. The road was in excellent condition, smooth, sanded and salted, with dry as well as wet sections. The drive from the State line to Rochester was under three hours, effecting an eleven o'clock arrival at the Henrietta interchange. The Holiday Inn where they had reservations was within sight as they pulled away from the tollbooth. There were a handful of gas stations and restaurants immediately off the exit, nearby, on Erie Station and Henrietta Road. Without a word between them, they shared the same subdued excitement. Before the afternoon would end, they would know precisely how their visit to the attorney would affect their lives.

Alex pulled the Packard into a *Mobil* station with a hand-written sign standing at the entrance, 32¢ Gallon. He looked over at Annie and smiled. "This is just like the old days, when we were driving south out of Michigan right after we were married, looking for gas stations and motels. But it was quite a bit warmer then, wasn't it?" The attendant stood waiting at the driver-side door. Alex rolled the window down, "Fill it up, pal. Thank you." He quickly rolled it back up again and stepped out of the car. He stood at the back of the car with the gas jockey, trying to avoid the damp, cold wind. He stood with his back to the wind and got directions to East Main Street and a recommendation where he and Annie could have a decent lunch. His car was covered in the dried white splash of road salt, and looked like it had been dipped into a bath of confectioner's sugar.

The service station attendant was a gruff-looking, middle-aged fellow, wearing a red plaid hat with black furry earflaps waving freely in the breeze. His brown denim work overalls were covered with countless oil and grease stains. "This here Packard's in good shape; I can tell it's a southern car. Part of a disappearing breed, your Packard is; just like *Edsel, Hudson, Kaiser, Nash* and *DeSoto*. They're all gone. Damn shame they don't make them anymore. Take care of this one, sir. She's a dandy." As the service station attendant spoke, he bobbed his head in agreement and self-confirmation.

Alex nodded, talking as he walked around to the car door. "Yeah, I will. It's a good car. It's always been good to me. When you turn the key, and she starts, and she's ready to go down the road, you got the world by the ass … reliability. Can't ask for anything better than that, can you?"

"No, I suppose not. A lot of the cars now, well, I think they just shove them down the assembly line too darn fast, is all. You got a dandy here, no rust from all this lousy road salt. Make sure you wash this off when you get the chance. It eats right through the steel like a mad rat through a burlap sack. You got a real gem here, sir. Take care of it, all right?"

"I grew up in Detroit, but they never used salt on the roads, not back then anyway. Cinders, sand, and crushed slag is what they used mostly. But you have to admit, the salt and sand mix sure keeps the highway drivable. All the way from the state line, the road was clear and either wet or dry. But I guess that's what the tolls are for, right?" There wasn't an answer, and Alex didn't really expect one. He was busy enough opening the door and getting behind the wheel. The attendant checked the oil and took the time to wipe off the hood ornament. The chrome cormorant gleamed as new. He then squeegeed the windshield and rear window, tapped the rear fender, and waved as Alex put the car in gear. As he drove off, Alex looked into the rear-view mirror at the attendant and nodded. It was the first time a gas jockey ever cleaned up the Packard's hood ornament. He acknowledged the fellow's gesture and announced, "It's lunch time, Annie."

A quarter mile down the road, he parked at the *Olympic* restaurant. Inside, they shed their winter coats and took the time to refresh and relax. Annie took a paper napkin, reached down, and wiped the melted snow off her black pumps. They were making an unconscious effort to stall the pending revelations by enjoying a leisurely-paced lunch. The drizzle and fog dissipated outside of Buffalo, leaving a low, gray blanket of winter clouds hanging over the slowly melting snow. Not only did it feel cold and damp, it looked like it. The snowbanks and piles alongside the roads and parking lots were dank shades of brown and black. The restaurant floor was wet with the snowmelt from shoes and boots. They finished their lunches with their bellies warmed from coffee, soup and open-faced meatloaf and gravy sandwiches.

Annie excused herself from the table, "I'm going to fix my lipstick and fuss with my hair, Alex. I'll be right back."

When the waitress brought the check, Alex asked her for directions again to East Main Street and she verified the same details given by the fellow back at the service station. Their destination was perhaps fifteen or twenty minutes away, New York Route 33, Main Street, Rochester.

Annie returned and sipped at her coffee. "You know, Alex, this is just like living life all over again. What do they call it, *déjà vu*? A carbon copy of the past. Like we have been here before, you know. This is just like living it over again; manila envelopes, lawyers and the mystery about your father's safe-deposit boxes. Ain't it, though?"

It was déjà vu all right, except this was much more personal for Alex. This time around, the mystery concerned him directly, and the interaction between him and a former lover in Sasebo, Japan, back in 1952. It troubled him much more than the questions that swirled around his father's unknown past. This time it was personal: very personal and even more mysterious. It had everything to do with him, but he had no knowledge of why. He let out a deep breath. Annie watched him and was keenly aware of his emotional discomfort. She quickly tried to lighten the moment. "But good golly, we're going to find out real soon. Just down the road, we'll find all the answers. This ain't nowhere near the nervous adventures we endured back in 1954. We don't have to drive two thousand miles to get the answers this time."

Alex looked across the table at his wife and let out a short laugh. "Annie, we just drove damn near two thousand miles in three days."

They both realized that this trip and their trip six years earlier were nearly alike. They were driving toward a predetermined destination with undetermined consequences. Annie recognized her error and giggled. "You got me, Alex. You got me good. I just didn't think about how far we've driven already."

He finished his coffee, reached into his pant pocket and laid a dollar in change on the table. He helped Annie with her coat, a knee length, dark green tailored wool, with rabbit cuffs and collar. She brushed her hand over his sport jacket.

"You look snappy in that coat, Annie. Very nice. This will be your first face-to-face experience with an attorney, won't it?"

"Yes."

"Well, Honey, get ready. This could end up being our very own episode of the *Ed Sullivan Show*. Just like mister Ed says: *A really big show*."

"Katy, too."

Thursday, midday, January 7, 1960

There was parking directly in front of 25 Main Street East. Alex put the transmission in park, set the hand brake, took a quick glance over to his wife and did a little head bob. "Here we are, Annie girl." He exited the car, walked to the curb and opened the door for Annie. Together, they took the three steps up to the heavy wood door and wiped their shoes on the woven coconut fiber mat. Alex's knock was not answered. After another knock, and a thirty second wait, he grasped the brass handle, pressed the thumb latch, and stepped inside, holding the door open for his wife.

Beyond the grey fieldstone floor of the foyer was an anteroom. An oriental rug covered most of the wood floor, with a three-seat divan and four tall-back Queen Ann parlor chairs spaced around the room. A door opened as Annie and Alex were about to sit down. They remained standing.

Another door opened, and bulky woman wearing a deep purple dress greeted them. Her hair was pulled back in a tight bun and was as black as India ink. She said simply, "Good afternoon."

She wore a necklace and matching bracelet of large, crimson red beads, white flats, and black cotton stockings. She stood with one hand on the doorknob, feigning a smile, and smelling of cigarettes. She looked like the Queen of Hearts of *Alice in Wonderland*.

Alexander spoke. "Good afternoon. We are Mister and Missus Throckmorton. I believe that we are expected."

"Indeed, you are. Come into the office, have a seat, and make yourselves comfortable. Mister Meriwether will be right with you."

Annie and Alex followed her into the next room, and heeding the large woman's gesture, they sat in two upholstered leather armchairs directly in front of a large, polished cherry desk. Behind the desk was a very tall, very plush, dark brown, buttoned, leather executive chair. The wall directly behind the desk was full of books, bound in brown leather, embossed with gold and titled in red lettering. The other walls were paneled ceiling to floor in dark hardwood and adorned with diplomas, certificates and a large reproduction of Gainsborough's *Blue Boy* oil portrait. Two long lamps with green glass shades spanned the front of the desk. A thick Persian carpet covered the office floor, with an intricate pattern of carmine, gold, sienna, and the deepest, darkest, red. Two long windows were completely covered in deep maroon, velvet draperies. Hanging in the far corner, next to a modest, narrow door, was a yellow canary bouncing nervously within its bright brass cage. There were occasional, nervous *tweets, chirps, twits and peeps* as the bird jumped from one perch to another.

They were seated perhaps two or three minutes when the bird jumped frantically and began to protest in shrill chatter, startled by the opening of the door.

With a floundering gait, a large man walked directly toward Alex and Annie. It was undoubtedly the attorney. His big feet, adorned with dark brown wing-tip oxfords, were pointing outward, mimicking a duck. He walked toward them, with a wad of papers packed up under one arm. He was

110

a big man, of very rotund build, a round reddish face, full pink lips and thinning gray hair. He wore small, gold-framed, wire spectacles stuck near the end of his round, red nose, a white shirt much too small, a skinny black tie and worn, shiny black slacks. His suit jacket was wide open, his barrel chest and ample belly pushing outward, testing the buttons on his vest. He stuck out his free hand as he came nearer. Alex and Annie stood.

"I'm glad you could come. Welcome, Mister and Missus Throckmorton. I am Reginald Meriwether, as you must have assumed." His handshake was damp, warm and unsettling. "Sit back down, get comfortable, and we will get started. We should be able to finish this up directly, provided no unforeseen issues or rock-solid roadblocks arise."

He wobbled his way behind the desk, set the stack of papers directly in front of him, and worked his body into the chair. A long, steady whoosh of air escaped the leather upholstery. He immediately pulled a pack of *Phillip Morris* out of his shirt pocket and lit one with the silver-plated desktop *Ronson* lighter. He filled his lungs, sat back in the chair and slowly exhaled. He held his eyes shut for perhaps three seconds.

With the cigarette between his lips, he fumbled with the papers in front of him. "Here it is. This is the reason we are here today. I think perhaps that I should read this aloud to you, both of you. Then you may peruse the document for yourselves and ask any questions before we go any further. I think it's a very workable plan. Do we agree?" Ash fell from the cigarette bouncing at the side of his mouth.

Alex and Annie nodded their heads in agreement. They could do nothing else and had no idea what to expect. The lawyer put the cigarette at rest on the rim of a large crystal ashtray, already nearly full of butts. He ruffled the papers and positioned them directly in front of him on the desk. For some unknown reason, the canary protested loudly and noisily. The barrister opened a desk drawer, took out a worn denim shirt and got up from his imposing chair. He walked to the birdcage, covered it and wobbled back to his seat. The bird became quiet.

He cleared his throat and began again, "This is a letter written by Katherine Ann Dobbs to you, Alexander. It's in her own words, for the most part. She wrote and signed it in November 1959, last year, predating her death by about one month. I believe I mentioned during our telephone call, that she passed peacefully in December after a long battle with cancer that had originated in her breast, and despite extensive radium treatments, the disease spread to the bone and beyond. Her letter explains in detail the reason she asked me to help find you and have you present for this reading. It is part and parcel of her Last Will and Testament."

Constrained within the confines of the paneled office, his voice resonated with pontifical authority. Annie believed she could be listening to a fastidious English Literature professor prepare for an extended reading of selected works by John Keats.

He coughed and cleared his throat once more and spoke in a droning, monotone voice. However, he pronounced every word distinctively and precisely. "I shall begin ... "

And begin he did ...

Dearest Alexander,

I hope with all my being, and pray to the Lord above, that this letter finds you, or finds someone who can.

First, let me say that I hope the world has treated you well. Since the time when we parted, I have always sincerely wished the best for you and your loved ones, past, present, and future.

I realize that when I left you behind in Japan, it was sudden, unplanned and very impersonal on my part. I know I hurt you and for that, I am eternally sorry, and hope you have forgiven me. My reassignment, rather, departure from military service, was not intentional. While it was beyond my control, it was due to my decisions, and ultimately, my behavior. It was not my desire to leave Japan; however, there were circumstances that you did not know about. I selfishly did not wish you to know the gravity of my situation. I take full responsibility for the decisions I made. I anguished over it for hours, days, weeks, months, and indeed, years. My heart now deeply aches knowing the choice I made was selfish, heartless and uncaring.

You remember my illness, my hospitalization, the weakness, fever and the influenza epidemic. It was then that everything changed. You visited me often, for hours, and I will never forget your kindness and caring. I felt blessed with your company. The days I spent in Sasebo Naval Hospital were not a pleasant experience, but your company made them endurable.

The day I was to be transferred out of the Hospital, my doctor, a Lieutenant Commander whose name I cannot remember, informed me that of all the tests they took, one of them showed it was possible that I was pregnant. I was still having monthlies and I thought I was simply experiencing bloat and nausea from the flu.

I was transferred to Yokosuka Naval Hospital, Tokyo, where they confirmed the results. I found myself subjected to an emotional storm I would never again encounter. I was the proverbial hot potato. The Navy could not just blame my hospitalization on the flu. They documented it and declared that I had "sickness not in the line of duty."

By that time, your Temporary Duty had ended, and you were back aboard the Valley Forge. Right or wrong, in 1951, President Truman had signed an Executive Order directing that pregnant servicewomen would be summarily discharged. My fate was sealed. The life in my womb changed the course of my life. My Navy career was over. I was to become a mother. That was one decision I could not, and would not, alter. I was concerned only about the life I was carrying. Although you and I took the necessary precautions, I now know that nothing, but nothing, is completely infallible.

I am sorry, Alexander. Looking back, I am ashamed. My decision not to inform you must now seem cold, cruel and unforgivable. But you and I never seriously considered life together after our time in Sasebo. We were honest with each other then. We both agreed that our feelings ended at the barrack walls or dormitory perimeter. And please understand, Alexander, I agreed with that one hundred percent. In retrospect, I wanted it that way. Me. I was the one. I. and I alone placed that condition on our relationship. Right, wrong, or indifferent, it was my decision.

We parted, and we parted as we said we would. Goodbye, good luck and God bless you. I am sorry, Alexander. I did love you. When I left the Navy in December 1952, I made a mistake by not informing you of my pregnancy. Please forgive me.

Fate has cast its mysterious cloak over us, Alexander. However, it does not need to smother, or suffocate the hopes and dreams of the innocent. It does not need to block out all light and bring cold, cruel darkness. It can be a warming, generous and secure blanket. It can be a gentle covering of forgiveness and love.

As I write this, I am dying. I expect I am gone, if not totally incapacitated and you are reading this in the company of my attorney. I have no family, Alexander. Only our twin daughters.

Please understand and forgive my selfishness. I pray you have the heart to love our daughters, Sarah Elizabeth and Karen Ann. I know you have the soul.

God bless you, Alexander.

Katherine Dobbs

Reginald G. Meriwether, Esq.

Sworn this day:

November 20, 1959

Reginald G. Meriwether, Esq.

Edna Hicks

Annie was holding Alex's hands in hers. She looked into his eyes, deep into his being. There was a silence in the room as big and empty as the Grand Canyon.

Alex looked to the attorney and broke the quiet. "Can we look at that, I mean, both of us and read through it for ourselves?"

Reginald Meriwether stood, came out from behind the desk and handed the three pages to Alex. "Absolutely. Look it over. Take your time and look it over. Take whatever time you may need." He then walked back toward the door, his weight teetering side to side and left the room closing the door soundly behind him.

Alex and Annie realized that together, they had reached the edge. They looked at one another, eager to proceed, yet cautiously leery of the next step. They began to study the letter in silence, turning one page, then back to the other, forward and back again. It was two, four, six or more minutes before Alex turned in the chair, looked deep into his wife's eyes and said, "I did not know any of this, Annie."

"Well, that's the whole point, Alex. Katy just told you, after her death. Fair or not, it's done with. Right or wrong, that's just the way it is. There is nothing either of us can do about the past. The only thing we can change is the future by taking action in the present. We will go forward with your twin daughters, and we will love them, and nurture them, and we will give them a good home. We have the means; we have the home and we have the love. We will love them as your children. We will love them as our children. I love you, Alex, and I can love your children just as deeply. I do not need to give birth to someone as a precondition of love. I love you and I will love your children. Straight up and honestly. No doubt. No doubt whatsoever."

She stood, her eyes tearing. Alex rose from his chair and held his wife as never before. If souls could transfer from body to body, from being to being, share life blood, exchange living essence, partake in every breath and transfer the deepest emotion, Alex and Annie were doing so at that very moment. Their embrace was so filled with emotion, they trembled. They became one. Alexander's eyes also began to tear.

"I love you, Honey. Thank you. We can do this. I can do this with you by my side."

"Yes, you can, Alex. We will. We will do this together."

Their kiss forever bound their promise. They were aware of this new commitment to the very centers of their hearts.

They sat down and a calming sense of relief covered them. Annie was holding the letter on her lap, her hands on top. They briefly looked around the room again before setting their attention back to the large, imposing piece of dark cherry furniture in front of them.

Right on cue, almost as if he were watching, the attorney opened the door, sauntered back into the office and eased his substantial form back into his big chair behind his huge desk. He cleared his throat. "Well, I imagine that together you have decided on the course of action you will take from here forward?"

They answered in unison, "Yes, we have."

Annie added, "We will take custody of the children and love them as our own. From this day on."

"Good. That's settled. I was nearly certain that would be your decision, and I assured Miss Dobbs that you, Alexander, would assume parental custody if I could be successful in locating you. And the fact that you, Missus Throckmorton, are onboard with your husband's resolution, is all the better. Miss Dobbs seemed very encouraged with my optimism; her nervousness was put to rest by my positive attitude. When I first met her, she was a troubled soul, full of nervous uncertainty and self-doubt. As time went on, however, she became much more positive. She was truly encouraged by my confidence. I was happy about that. I reaffirmed that I would locate you and reassured Miss Dobbs of that. She recalled that you once mentioned that New York Avenue in Oshkosh, Wisconsin was where your mother lived. So, I tried that address and if all else failed, I could locate your last domicile with your military record. However, that could have taken quite a bit longer and would have involved a good deal of paperwork, so I am pleased that things have worked out."

He lit a fresh cigarette, filled his lungs, looked to the ceiling and exhaled, pushing his lower jaw forward. "Now. I will explain matters as simply and forthright as I can. If you have any questions, please make a note and I will answer them after I run through the probable outline of events."

He picked up a pocket-sized spiral notepad and pencil, reached across the desk and offered them to Alex. Annie quickly stood, took a half step toward the desk and accepted the pad and pencil.

Reginald Meriwether continued, "With the helpful cooperation of the Monroe County Department of Child Protection and Placement, the children are in the temporary custody of a long-time, personal friend of Miss Dobbs: Missus Emily Rutherford. The sisters are staying with the Rutherford family, who live in Brighton, a suburb of the city of Rochester. The people at Child Protection and Placement have been very helpful and understanding of this delicate situation. Miss Dobbs named the Rutherfords as the ultimate Custodial Guardians if you, Alexander, could not be located. Now, with the successful contact and consent of Mister Throckmorton, we should be able to resolve everything quickly and before the weekend. The children have been in a safe family environment with the Rutherfords since the final hospitalization of Katherine. The fact that you are named as the father on their birth certificates, Alexander, and you are accepting the responsibility of parenthood, makes this matter much simpler to finalize."

"Wait a minute ... I'm listed as the father on the birth certificates?"

The lawyer shuffled the papers in front of him, and held up two documents, showing them to Alex. "Yes, right there. You are the father, are you not? In addition, you either signed the Affidavit of Paternity, or gave written authorization to Miss Dobbs. She gave birth on June 21, 1953, to Sarah Elizabeth and Karen Ann Dobbs at Syracuse General Hospital. You were aware that you were named as the father of the twins, were you not?"

Annie and Alex abruptly exchanged a quick, puzzled, questioning, glance. "No, I was not aware. This whole affair has been news to me and my wife. The last time I saw Katy was December 1952, in Japan and I was not aware of her pregnancy."

The attorney's two large eyes opened wide. He looked over the top of his eyeglasses and across the desk to Alex. The whites of his bulging eyes were so full of tiny red veins they looked like road maps. He glanced back down to the birth certificates, and up again at Alex. "This could drastically change things, Mister Throckmorton. Several new options have suddenly presented themselves to you and, frankly, to the estate of Miss Dobbs and to the children themselves. Some of these options could be cumbrous, troubling, difficult and with far-reaching consequences. Not the least of which is the custody and care of two innocent children. You need to realize that their legitimacy would be erased in toto."

Alex felt his insides turn upside down and sideways. The skin on the back of his neck crept. He could feel his heartbeat within his chest. Annie moved forward on the chair and leaned her frame toward the lawyer. "Explain, please, Mister Meriwether. What do you mean, exactly?"

The attorney waved the back of his pudgy hand in Annie's general direction, ignored her question and looked to Alex with wide eyes. The tone of his voice was a pitch higher and seemed nervous. "Are you not the father of these children?"

Annie sat wide-eyed, embarrassed, annoyed and incredulous.

"Katy and I were intimate; I am not denying that. We were open and honest with each other. I trusted her then and I trust the decisions she made with the children, whatever she may have done. I cannot understand why Katy would have purposely deceived anyone."

"Do you doubt your parenthood at all? Is it possible that you are not the father?"

"Katy stated that I was the father, and I have no reason to doubt that. She was not a deceitful person. The Navy gave her a discharge based on the pregnancy. The birth date of the children coincides with our intimacy in Japan. Like I said, I cannot believe she would intentionally deceive me or anyone else. It would serve no purpose. No purpose whatsoever."

The lawyer crushed out his cigarette in the large crystal ashtray already full of butts, and immediately lit another. He drew deeply and held the gray smoke inside his round chest before he spoke. "To be frank, Mister and Missus Throckmorton, Alexander's name on the birth certificates, regardless of the circumstance of their placement thereupon, makes it simpler to expedite these proceedings. If your name on those documents does not present an issue at this time, with either you or your wife, we can continue under the assumption that the parentage is bona fide as listed on these two birth certificates. New York, like most states and medical institutions, issue birth certificates permitting the declaration of fatherhood by either a Certificate of Marriage, or a Statement of Parenthood by the birth father. Both of these particular certificates indicate that a signed Statement of Parenthood was presented by the father. This, in and of itself, considering your unique status, is the preferable affirmation of parenthood. If a Certificate of Marriage had been used, it would indeed present a monumental problem in this particular case. Therefore, you could say, we dodged a high-caliber legal bullet with that one. Please understand that my singular obligation is to Miss Dobbs' estate and legal representation for probate. Be aware that, once you accept the outcome of these proceedings, based on those birth documents and the sworn statements of Miss Dobbs and her Testament, there is no recourse. Your subsequent acceptance of terms of settlement and as Executor will be the determining factors for defensibility. If you are personally content with the confirmation of the children's parentage, we can continue. Beyond that, our discussions within this room are held moot. You must be absolutely certain of your position on this issue. Do you understand, Alexander?"

Annie turned to her husband. "Do you have any reason to believe Katherine would be dishonest, Alex?"

"No, Annie, I do not. I am the father. If Katy said so, it's true. There is no reason on Earth why she would lie. I knew her well enough to be one hundred percent confident about that. I am sure of it."

Annie turned her attention to the attorney. "Maybe my opinion doesn't matter to you, sir. But please, don't go waving your hand at me anymore; no more. Maybe my opinion isn't important to you, but I believe in my husband, so do not dismiss me. I stand with him, and we will stand together for the children."

Reginald Meriwether leaned back in his gigantic office chair. A long ash fell from his Phillip Morris onto the papers on the desk. He took a final drag, crushed it out, stood, and spoke. "Please, do not take any offense, Missus Throckmorton. I represent the estate of Miss Dobbs. I meant no disrespect to either you, your husband, or your opinions. I am sorry if my actions implied any disrespect." He cleared his throat, forced a cough and continued, "Very good. It's time for lunch. That was productive, so let's take an hour, and be back here at, what?" He looked at his wristwatch. "It's one-thirty. Come back at two-thirty and we will finish this. There is a good delicatessen and coffee shop just down the block. They make a decent lunch. It passes my test and take a look at me! I enjoy a good meal."

Alex stood and offered his hand to Annie as she rose from her chair. He put his arm around her and spoke directly to the lawyer, "See you back here in an hour." Annie sidestepped toward the desk and set the notepad and pencil down. She didn't use either one.

Outside in the foyer, they put on their coats and took the steps down to the sidewalk.

"We had lunch already, didn't we?"

"Yeah, but I could use a break, Annie. How about you?"

"Yes. I could use a break too, I suppose. I just got a truckload of information dumped on me that I did not see coming. Neither of us did."

"Sixteen Reasons."

Thursday afternoon, January 7, 1960

They walked past the deli and sandwich shop that the attorney suggested, stopping instead half a block down, at a corner diner and ice cream parlor. A large wooden sign with the moniker *'Sixteen Reasons'* hung above the door. Once inside, a large menu on the wall behind the counter displayed all sixteen flavors of milk shakes available. The square floor tiles were red and white, creating a checkerboard pattern. Along the counter were thick, red, plastic upholstered stools. Mirror tiles ran across the back wall and compact Seeburg 1000 tabletop juke boxes were at the counter and each of the tables. Someone was wishing the winter away: Frankie Ford's *Sea Cruise* was playing and sailing sound through the little restaurant.

Annie and Alex sat at a corner table, set apart from the others and away from the cold drafts of the opening and closing aluminum and glass doors.

"Just coffee, Annie? Anything else?"

"No, thanks. I'm not hungry at all. Just coffee is fine."

A young waitress dressed in white, and wearing pink teardrop eyeglasses with sequined corners, sauntered over to their table. She held out her order pad as if it were the offering basket at Sunday services. She stood in the classic waitress-hand-on-hip pose.

Alex ordered. "Two coffees, that's all, thank you."

She made a wide gesture toward the counter, "Like it says on the sign over there, sir. There is a one-dollar minimum order at the tables. Coffee is just a dime."

Annie quipped, "Two ten-cent coffees and an eighty-cent glass of your best water. How's that?"

The young woman twitched her forehead and blinked twice, rapidly. "Sure. I can do that," and she was gone.

They sat looking out the window and didn't speak. Their coffees arrived along with a tall soda fountain glass full of water with a lemon wedge stuck on the rim and a maraschino cherry lying on the bottom.

Annie smiled at the young woman, "That's perfect. Just what we wanted. Thank you very much." She and Alex watched as the waitress made her way back behind the counter.

"Well, Annie ... after the morning we just had, how would you describe your first experience with an attorney?"

"I think Meriwether is a pompous oaf who smokes too much, and he should hire an assistant or secretary with a pleasant disposition and a personality. And that poor canary. He should find a new home for that frightened bird."

"Other than that, what do you think?"

Annie spoke in a serious tone. "Did you sign any Statement of Parenthood in 1953, Alex?" She looked across the table directly into her husband's eyes.

"No. I did not. I wasn't there. I told you: all this is news to me. But like Meriwether said, it's a moot point provided I do not object. Somehow, Katy had someone sign that statement. I don't know how she did it, but the result is clear. Unless I raise a stink and deny it, I'm the father of both children in the eyes of the law. It's unsettling but considering our current circumstance and all the possible outcomes, the result is beneficial to us. And more importantly, to the twins."

Annie listened intently. Their eyes were unwavering, locked.

"I believe you, Alex. I believe you."

They continued to talk quietly to one another, reaffirmed their commitment to the twin sisters, and jointly concluded they made the right decision concerning the birth certificates naming Alex as the girls' birth father. The way things were stacking up, it was for the best. It was, without a doubt, more conducive for the desired outcome; the final result being Alex and Annie assuming full parental guardianship of the children without a drawn-out custody or probate hearing in the courts.

One more time, Alex went through the time-line of his bond with Katy back in Japan. Annie agreed that when the dates were considered, it was obvious Alex was the father of the twins. Now, since Katy was no longer living, it would be impossible to determine how Alex's name was entered on the birth certificates in the first place. It was pointless to ponder why.

Alex became reflective, leaned closer across the table, and spoke quietly, almost in a whisper. "Annie, back in Japan, when I was intimate with Katy, I was careful. We were careful. I mean, I used a *Trojan.* Always."

Annie's lips curled at the corners. "They aren't perfect, Alex. You know that. There are lots of rubber babies born every day. It doesn't matter, either. It's settled … we have two daughters." They were silent. Alex nodded in agreement.

About halfway through her cup of coffee, Annie likened their situation to that of jumping into the cold water of your favorite childhood swimming hole in early June. Your senses are startled at first, your body undergoes a temperature shock, and you suddenly have a new, refreshed awareness of your being. Gradually, you become accustomed to your new surroundings, your body adjusts to the temperature change, and you actually begin to enjoy the experience.

"See what I mean, Alex? Sometimes you just need to take off your shoes and socks and jump right in. You will learn to love it."

Alex took a sip of coffee, and spoke positively, "You're right, Honey. Absolutely right."

The conversation then drifted toward speculation and into curious wonder. It took a few guesses before they could agree and remember that the sisters were named Sarah and Karen. Their anticipation was building and impossible to restrain. They shared a tempestuous impatience to meet the children.

Alex left two dollars on the table, and they started out the door and down the street toward the law office of Reginald G. Meriwether, Esquire.

They walked up the steps, opened the heavy door, walked directly through the foyer, through the anteroom, into the office and shut the door behind them. Alex repositioned the two chairs, moved them even closer together and they sat down.

"Come Softly To Me."

Thursday afternoon, January 7, 1960

They were seated perhaps thirty seconds when the office door opened and the portly woman with the purple dress and black cotton stockings stuck her head into the room.

"Here we are. Mister and Missus Throckmorton, you're back. My husband will be with you directly. He got back from his lunch at the diner five minutes ago." Her head disappeared behind the door as it closed with a solid thud.

Annie whispered, "See that, Alex? A perfect husband and wife team: a lawyer and his secretary."

"And it seems like we made the right choice by walking past the diner down to the soda shop."

"Yep."

For the next few minutes, they sat in silence, waiting impatiently for the next chapter of their Rochester experience to unfold. Their immediate future appeared as bits and pieces of a thousand-piece jigsaw puzzle that had been dumped on a table in front of them. Two children just became the newest pieces that needed to find their place in the picture.

126

The white porcelain doorknob twisted abruptly; the door opened and shut with a thump. The lawyer walked into the room and yet again maneuvered his cumbersome frame into the big leather chair behind his desk. It could have resembled the throne of a king, if only it would have had some gold ornamentation.

He methodically lit a cigarette, as if it were a ceremony. "Well, during our break, I was able to contact Emily Rutherford, the Rutherford wife, the custodian and inform her that you have arrived and will, indeed, be assuming custody of the children. She, of course, was very curious as to your nature and ability to provide for the children. Not that she has a say in the matter, but she is understandably concerned, and I was able to put her mind to rest. You are financially sound? Am I correct, Mister Throckmorton?"

Alex was taken aback and answered immediately, excitedly, "Absolutely. You can contact my bank, *Cotton States National*, if need be."

Not more than a half second later, Annie added, "We are quite financially secure, Mister Meriwether."

"Fine. Fine. That's not an issue. It was a question that perhaps I should not have asked. It was Emily Rutherford's question, that's all. She had expressed her concern."

He cleared his throat and began again, "You brought your birth certificate, Mister Throckmorton, or a photo-static copy and you have a driver's license with you for identification purposes?"

Annie and Alex were growing impatient with the tedious procedure and its slow-moving legal pace. It was reflected in Alexander's answer. "Yes, we both brought copies of our birth certificates and we both have our driver's license."

A long ash fell off Meriwether's cigarette and onto his vest. "Fine, fine. But I only need yours ... Alexander."

He leaned back in the chair, brushed the fallen ashes, and further punished the buttons on his vest and shirt. "Well, I can tell you what I expect will happen tomorrow. I should be able to finish all this up in the morning, what with the necessary affidavits, filing, notary and such. Miss Dobbs' estate consists of what remains of her personal property, clothing, furniture, household goods, some tangible jewelry items and a trust for the children. The trust is for their care, as deemed proper by their guardian, in this case, you, Mister Throckmorton. I will transfer the trust and you will sign the Assignment of Executor. There is no real estate, no real property involved ... she sold her home in Brighton right before her hospitalization. If you so desire, you can continue my services for the proper dispensation of her goods, such as furniture, clothing and household items, or further assign them as you so determine. There is some small indebtedness that remains and some medical expenses still outstanding, but seemingly inconsequential in the scope of the estate. The tangible portion, the trust, is just under five thousand dollars. There are also some Eastman Kodak shares of common stock in the children's names. At the time of her death, Miss Dobbs still had modest assets of her own combined with that of her deceased parents, considering her extended ill health." He rolled the cigarette between his thumb and forefinger and continued. "All things considered; I expect that you will be able to leave here on Saturday with your two daughters. Am I wrong to believe that would be satisfactory with you, Mister and Missus Throckmorton? May I refer to you as Alexander, and, and ...?"

Annie interjected, "Annie. Maryanne to be precise."

The attorney put the cigarette back to his lips, deeply inhaled enough to fill both lungs, and held the smoke within his chest long enough for his eyes to bulge as he exhaled. "Fine. Fine. Alexander and Maryanne, it is, then. Well, then, together we can work toward that Saturday goal on the horizon. Saturday.

In the meantime, all you folks have to do is enjoy yourself. And of course, you will want to meet the children. You can never predict how these initial interactions will work out. I mean, emotionally. I do know, Alexander and Maryanne, that Katherine spoke to the children prior to her passing and they had something of an understanding of the way things were to evolve. Let me say it this way: about as much understanding as six-year-old girls can muster."

Alex and Annie were leaning forward in their chairs, hanging on every word the lawyer spoke. He took another drag on the cigarette, crushed it into the over-flowing ashtray and exhaled a gray cloud from deep within him. The lawyer's tobacco exhaust stung Annie's eyes.

He continued, "You will find that they are two very special girls. Very well behaved, polite, intelligent, respectful, and they both know how to express themselves. Great talkers. Great language skills, not like mine."

He feigned a little chuckle and brought a thin, worn, kerchief out of his jacket pocket. He blinked and wiped the cloth over his red eyes. Annie watched carefully as he daubed them one more time.

"Katherine Dobbs told her daughters that they were going to get a *Daddy* for Christmas. She had faith in me, that I would be able to contact you, Mister Throckmorton ... Alexander. As she grew weaker, she expressed to me that she also held deep faith in you, Alexander, and that you would welcome the girls into your life. I know personally that those girls really look forward to meeting you, Alexander. They genuinely do. I will give you the Rutherford's telephone number and, if you so desire, you could call them and arrange a meeting, maybe this evening, if that would be convenient for you. Missus Rutherford is expecting your call sometime today."

Annie squeezed her husband's hand and let out a sigh of anticipation. Alex put his other hand directly over hers.

Alex spoke with an understandable crack in his voice. "Yes, let's do that."

The next few minutes moved by as slowly as pouring blackjack molasses right out of the Frigidaire. The attorney wrote down the telephone number and asked Alex to return to his office before five o'clock with the copy of his birth certificate. They made a verbal appointment with the attorney for the next day, Friday, at eleven in the morning. Reginald Meriwether said that he expected all the paperwork to be finished and ready to sign at that time.

There were quick handshakes, goodbyes and nodding heads. Alexander and Maryanne Throckmorton left 25 Main Street East with their heads in the clouds and stars in their eyes.

Inside the Packard, they actually had to catch their breath. Alex sat holding his ring of keys in his right hand. Annie had her purse on her lap. Their hearts beat at the pace of lovemaking and their emotions were peaked in ecstasy as high as Mount McKinley. They stared out the windshield, their eyes fixed somewhere down the street.

It took awhile, but they grudgingly broke away from their heartfelt bliss to continue tackling the matters at hand.

"Alex, I think we should drive to the Holiday Inn, check in and call that Rutherford lady. What do you think?"

"Yes. Yes. That's what we'll do. I was just thinking it would be wonderful if we could spend an hour or two with the girls and even get a chance to talk with the Rutherfords. Maybe they know more about what went on in Katy's life."

"I can't wait to meet the girls, Alex ... our girls."

"Look At Little Sister."

Thursday, late afternoon, January 7, 1960.

After check-in and bringing in their bags, Alex immediately telephoned the Rutherford household. During a short and cordial conversation, a seven o'clock *meet and greet* was arranged with concise directions to the home on nearby Erie Station Road. Excitedly, Annie and Alex decided to shower and change clothes. In less than an hour, they would meet Emily Rutherford, her husband Carl and the new members of their family: their daughters, sisters Karen and Sarah. First impressions are important, but somehow this first impression would be, without a doubt, one of the most important of their lives. The aphorism goes *"clothes do not the person make."* However, regardless of if it's going to a job interview, popping in at a party, or even attending church on Sunday, so many critical stares and visual judgments are made based on how you look.

Inside room 41 of the Henrietta Holiday Inn, Alex hurriedly got out of the shower. Annie had just finished dressing and was fixing her hair. She wore a green tartan plaid, fully pleated, skirt and a beige lace-trimmed blouse. Their thoughts were dancing the jitterbug, bouncing and travelling at the speed of light from anticipation, to wonder, to nervousness and back to just plain impatience. There was very little talk or conversation since they brought their luggage from the car into the room.

Alex straightened his tie and tucked his shirttails inside his slacks. Standing next to Annie at the large mirror above the dresser, he ran a comb through his black hair and put his wallet and keys into his pockets.

"I don't think I've been this jazzed-up since the day we were married, Annie." He sat on the bottom edge of the bed, slipped into and tied his *Florsheim* oxblood oxfords.

His wife turned away from the dresser, stood close and directly in front of him. Alex rose and she tenderly kissed him. "We are going to do just fine, Alex. Be yourself. Be your kind and caring self. And I'll be me. That will throw them for a loop!" He held her and kissed her back.

"Thanks, Hon. You're right, we will do just fine." He put on his wool sport jacket and helped Annie with her coat. They decided to proceed directly to the Rutherford home without stopping for dinner, agreeing that they were too excited to sit still for any meal, of any size.

Although it was a mere four miles to the house on Erie Station Road, the trip was nearly as unnerving as driving in a Buffalo blizzard. At their destination, they found a saltbox home, two stories tall with a flat façade, sloping down to one floor at the rear. It was neat, with butter yellow paint over clapboard siding. Maple shade trees, in their winter nakedness, were scattered over the property on a half-acre lot. The house sat back from the road, at the end of a cracked and pitted concrete drive. A powder blue 1956 *Pontiac Catalina* and an older *Chevrolet Styleline* sat near the house. Visible from the road, inside the home, behind tall windows and sheer curtains, table lamps were lit, gently glowing in the darkening twilight. The curtains on two windows wiggled and parted, each with the face of a curious little girl; peering out at the cream yellow Packard coming down the driveway.

"Goodness, gracious, Alex. Do you see that?" They both felt heart-stirring, warming, emotion. Quite impossible to explain, it tickled from deep inside.

Three wood steps led up to a small, covered entryway stoop at the side door. Annie took the steps ahead of her husband, the door opening as she reached the last one. Emily Rutherford, a lean woman of perhaps forty, welcomed them inside. She had light brown hair, with tight curls a poodle would envy. Her smile pleasantly complemented her cheerful, floral print housedress. In the kitchen was a long, white pine, trestle table with lengthwise benches along each side and two straight back, Shaker-style chairs at the ends. A sturdy wagon-wheel light fixture hung from the ceiling directly above the large table. In a doorway at the far side of the room, five children huddled together with a smiling Carl Rutherford standing behind them. He wore a faded blue denim shirt, with *Carl* embroidered over the pocket and tan *Williamson-Dickie* work trousers. Alex and Annie's eyes went to the children and easily spotted the twin sisters, standing close and near the wall. Their eyes locked on the twins. Annie's heart left her chest and traveled across the expanse of the kitchen. She instantaneously fell in love. Alexander experienced tidal waves of emotion crashing within his chest. He saw two beautiful, innocent girls reflecting the likeness of their mother, a lover from his past.

Emily Rutherford walked to Alex and extended her right hand, grasped his, and drew him into a hug. "Welcome, Alexander. Welcome." She quickly moved to Annie and did the same. Motioning toward the doorway, "This is my husband, Carl. He's actually ready to leave for work."

No one changed position in the room. Nine complete strangers, four adults and five children, were presented with the gigantic task of immediate familiarity at a very personal level. There were some casual nods and innocuous whispers of *"hello, pleased to meet you"* between Carl, Annie, and Alex.

Annie's off-the-cuff personality awoke. "Goodness, we have a house full! And it looks like you have plenty of room for everyone. Your home looks and feels very welcoming and warm."

Emily eagerly accepted the chance to escape the awkward task of forced friendliness. "How about we all sit, have some apple pie and ice cream, and get to know each other? What do you think, kids? Come on, now, everybody sit down. Except Carl, he's going to miss out on all the fun. He's leaving for work." Annie noticed that Emily twice mentioned that her husband was ready to leave for his job.

The children slowly, cautiously, edged forward into the kitchen. Carl worked his way through the five children and moved to Alex and Annie, still standing near the entry door. He greeted them and immediately excused himself. "I'm behind schedule. But I really wanted to put a face to your names. It seems crude, doesn't it? But I really did. I am sure I will see you two again before you leave." He took a half step closer and whispered to them, "You have two of the most wonderful little girls in the world." He picked up the grey round-top metal lunch bucket off the edge of the counter, gave his wife a peck on the cheek, and was out the door.

"Carl works at the shipping docks, over at *Kodak*. He works nights and I work the dayshift in production. He's running a little bit late tonight. It works out fine, the hours I mean, with the both of us working. The kids are never alone here; my mom and dad live right next door. Come on, kids, sit down at the table. Nancy, you can help and set some dessert plates around, OK?"

Her eldest daughter started toward the cupboards and answered, "Yes, Mommy." Emily's two other children crossed to the bench and sat down. The twins had been standing, holding hands, with a cautious, sensitive smile.

Annie offered to help, Emily graciously refused, and said, "You sit down over there with your husband, get acquainted and introduce yourself to the girls and my kids. I'll put on a pot. You'll have coffee, right?" She didn't wait for an answer and didn't get one.

Alex and his wife were in a different world. Annie had her gaze fixed on Sarah and Karen. The twins were as identical as twins can be. In Annie's eyes, any remaining questions about

134

their fatherhood were negated beyond any doubt. Annie's eyes moved quickly as she studied their earlobes, noses, foreheads, and chins. To Annie, their features clearly revealed that they were Alexander's children. Both girls were blue-eyed, blonde brunettes.

Alex stood drowned in emotion. His eyes disagreed with Annie's and told him the twins were Katy's girls. He went down to one knee and as on cue; his daughters sprang across the kitchen floor to their father. They ran to his open arms and were wrapped inside his cuddle. At that moment, nothing else mattered in the universe. Three souls were joined as one, locked within a private slice of time reserved just for them. Annie, already having fallen in love with Karen and Sarah, fell deeper in love with her husband and wiped aside a tear with her forefinger. She was not alone with her damp expression of emotion. Alex blinked his wet eyes. The girls buried themselves into his arms. He kissed the tops of their heads and spoke in a wavering voice, quietly stuttering in joy, "Let's go sit down and have a piece of pie. And you can help me figure out who is Karen and who is Sarah. And you can tell me all about your favorite things and what you like to play with. And I can tell you all about your new home in Florida."

Alex sat on the empty bench, with a daughter on each side and an arm around each. Annie took a chair at the end of the table.

The young girl sitting to Alexander's right started, "I'm Karen. My eyes are just a little bit bluer. But if you're far away, you can't tell. And I'm older, too. I was borned first."

"And I'm Sarah, and I'm the one with the new front tooth! You can tell if I smile. It's bigger than my other ones." She looked up at her father and down the table at Annie. "Mommy said you were coming for Christmas, and we were going to have a daddy. You're a little bit late. But that's OK. Is that our new mommy down there?"

Alex looked at his wife and each of his daughters. "Yes, it is. And I'm sorry we are late. We were terribly busy, and we came as soon as we could. And you are right, Sarah. That is your new mommy."

Annie beamed. Her heart opened wide.

"Hushabye."

Thursday evening, January 7, 1960

Time flew by at jet speed. Apple pie, ice cream and two pots of coffee were only passing diversions. The sisters, Sarah and Karen Dodd, had boundless curiosity and limitless energy. They were excitedly involved with Alex and Annie, hanging on every word and listening intently to every conversation, regardless of direct concern to them. It was unavoidable; a time or two they acknowledged the passing of their mother, Katherine. Their subtle melancholy, when noticed by an adult, would dissipate and vanish once the subject was changed.

After the initial excitement passed and the food was all gone, everyone moved from the spacious kitchen to the living room. A Christmas tree was still standing in the corner, a bed sheet partially covering the floor underneath. Fallen pine needles and small bits of aluminum tinsel were everywhere. Scattered nearby, a box of *Tinker Toys*, a *Candyland* board game, dolls and a folding paperboard dollhouse created a playground on the carpeted floor. Emily and Carl Rutherford had three children of their own: Nancy, the eldest, William and Wanda. They were born about a year apart and ranged in age from six to eight. Mixed with the twin sisters, the gang of five created what could become a very volatile combination of active youngsters. Little William's decision to use a doll's toy baby bottle as a hammer to assemble various Tinker Toy parts was the only problem that needed to be defused.

The cuckoo clock's annoying little carved bird emerged from hiding. He got everyone's attention by noisily announcing nine o'clock. Together, as one, the children let out a moan.

Emily ended it with, "It's bedtime kids! We all know it. You can show our guests how grown up you are. So come over and say, 'good night', brush your teeth, put on your pajamas, go to bed, say your prayers, and go to sleep."

She quietly invited Alex and Annie to stay a while longer after the children went to bed. She suggested that they could imbibe a beer or mixed drink, and she could enlighten them with anything she knew about Katy's life.

Like an assembly line, all three Rutherford children walked to the couch, gave mechanical kisses and said *good night* to Annie, Alex and their mother before scurrying out of the room and down the hall. Sarah and Karen Dobbs were last in line, undoubtedly on purpose. They gave their goodnight wishes and kiss to Emily. Quite often, children can work around delicate little troubles by themselves, without any adult intervention whatsoever. Sarah stood directly in front of Alex and Karen in front of Annie.

"Goodnight, Daddy."

"Goodnight, Mommy."

Little kisses followed, they switched positions and repeated. What happened next could be best described as a mob hug. If all the love in the world could ever be jammed and stuck together like a massive, gooey, gigantic popcorn ball, there was one right there, right then, on Erie Station Road in Henrietta, New York.

Alex was the first to pull back from the sticky mass of emotion. "Brush your teeth and put on your pajamas like

Miss Emily said, and then me and Mommy will come in and tuck you in. How's that?"

There was "Okay, Daddy" in unison and Karen spoke up, "This is the latest, biggest, and bestest Christmas present ever in the whole wide world!"

Emily felt proud, and rightfully so. Annie watched the girls leave the room with her heart and soul refreshed, renewed, reborn, and bubbling over with compassionate love. At that moment, there was nothing else in Rochester, New York that was more important.

Alex wiped his eyes on his shirtsleeve. "I sure didn't see that one coming, Annie girl. No way would I ever predict what just happened here. I'm amazed. Simply amazed."

"The girls are wonderful, Alex. We are blessed."

Emily became reflective and wiped a tear, "Well, it's obvious you got two very special girls there. No doubt about it. Katy raised her kids right and she would be proud as all get-out of them if she were still here. She sure would."

Alex stood and straightened his frame. Annie rose also and took him by the hand. "I don't think we will ever forget this, Alex. Ever."

Emily stood, took two steps toward the kitchen, turned, and asked, "How about a drink ... anyone?"

"A beer is good. How about you, Annie?"

"A soda pop will do. Or juice. Anything, really."

They watched Emily disappear into the kitchen and held hands. At that particular twinkling of time, they were the richest people on Earth. They were swimming in an ocean of love. Their emotional vertigo was unwittingly interrupted when Emily returned to the room. Her house slippers shuffled along the floor with a muffled whooshing sound, the soles collecting static electricity along the way. She set a

138

stubby bottle of *Genesee* beer, a can of *Nehi* grape soda, and two glasses on the coffee table. She left the room for a moment and came back with a mixed drink in her hand, "After you tuck in Karen and Sarah, we can start some serious tongue-wagging."

An oil-fired boiler sucked in a gigantic breath of air, clanged and groaned in the basement, echoing the ruckus through the cast iron radiators. Alex and Annie broke their embrace and started toward the hallway to tuck their daughters in bed for the very first time. Emily spoke up, "They're in the second room on the left. We leave the doors open a crack."

The girls were in one double bed, lying on their backs, covers to their chins, feigning slumber. Alex and Annie stopped at bedside, gazing down at them. Karen peeked. Then Sarah, "Are you going to be here when we wake up tomorrow?" Kisses, *goodnights*, and little hugs ensued. Alex answered, "Not in the morning. Mommy and I have some more business in the city, and then we'll be back. Right after school."

They lingered by the bedside for another moment before they moved quietly toward the door. Alex said, "See you tomorrow, girls." Annie whispered one more *goodnight* over her shoulder. Holding hands, they walked back to the living room and the sofa. Emily was comfortably seated in the halfway position of a brown, corduroy-upholstered *Barca-lounger* recliner, with her mixed drink at the side table.

"It sure is nice to have a bit of peace and quiet, put your feet up and relax, isn't it?"

Annie poured some soda from the can into her glass. "Well, I say you certainly deserve a break whenever you can get one. You have a house full of kids to take care of and that cannot be easy."

"You will discover that it's a labor of love, Annie. It truly is. Hard work, yes, but it is wonderfully rewarding when you just take a step back now and then and look at the world around you as a whole pie and not just a crooked, broken slice."

Over the course of the next two hours, Emily disclosed much of her shared experience with Katherine Dobbs. Their friendship began as employees of *Eastman Kodak*. The sprawling two-thousand-acre industrial complex on the Northwest side of Rochester, *Kodak Park*, was home to the design, manufacturing, warehousing, research, and shipping of one of the world's largest and most profitable corporations. George Eastman believed in people. One of his most significant quotes gave a unique insight at his worldview: *"A good reputation is measured by how much you can improve the lives of others - customers, employees, and community."* To prevent anything from going wrong at the first levels, he gave his employees almost unbelievable benefits. Not just excellent pensions, he made available doctors, dentists, optometrists, drug stores, dispensaries, restaurants and pre-school childcare on site at Kodak Park. Dinners could be had for a few dollars and medical care at nominal cost. The employees were treated extremely well. There were over fifty thousand people working at Kodak Park, Rochester in 1960 - an almost unbelievable total.

Katy Dobbs and Emily Rutherford first met at the Kodak Children's Nursery Center and realized they had many things in common. Their pre-school children came under the care of Kodak while they worked. As their friendship grew, they began to share rides to and from work, an occasional dinner at Emily's home, and they even joined a Saturday afternoon women's bowling league at Kodak Park. Their lives meshed. The women lived in close proximity and as the children left pre-school, they attended Jefferson Road Elementary.

Katherine worked on product design and, understandably, never could share much of her work. Emily worked on the assembly line, on either shutters, gear drives, or film doors. The women boasted that their friendship was based on *"diapers, finger-paint and doo-doo"*, with an occasional bottle of beer, whiskey sour, and game of bowling.

Emily began, "I guess I'll start when she returned to civilian life after her Navy discharge. She came back home to Syracuse and did not seek employment, given her pregnancy. Her mother passed away just after the twins were born, in late July of 1953. From what, I don't know. I think Katy was tormented by that, too. She expressed how sorry she was about the so-called burden she put on her parents concerning her status as an unwed mother and everything. Then, as it so often happens, more problems came. Shortly after her mother's passing, Katy's father became senile and started losing his mind and memory. How Katy stood up to all that, I don't know. I don't think he could be left alone. You have to admire her courage, you know, and it's funny how things work out sometimes. Before she enlisted in the Navy, Katy got a bachelor's degree from Cornell. She needed to find employment, and answered a vaguely worded want ad in the Syracuse paper, the *Post-Standard*, for industrial design. It turned out to be a job here at Kodak. That was it. She was hired, moved to Rochester with her father and bought an old farmhouse with an acre of land on the GI bill, just up the road in Brighton, on South Winton. She had to hire a live-in nurse to help with her father. And like I said, he could not be left alone. Finally, she had to put her dad in a facility about three, maybe four, years ago, before he passed away. Katy used to say *'eat, drink, and be merry; tomorrow you'll cry'*. She inherited a chunk from her parents and ended up using it, and a lot of her paycheck, some of her Kodak stock and more, for all the bills from her father's care. Katy had spunk, she did.

She was a brave woman. And she loved her kids to the moon and back."

Emily began to tear up again, stood, and walked to the bathroom. Alex and Annie could hear her sobbing and blowing her nose. The commode flushed with a loud, rude, gurgle. She returned holding a wad of toilet tissue in her hand.

Between sniffles, Emily went on, "Katherine did not speak very much of the twins' father until last summer, when she got the bad news about her cancer. And when she began mentioning the girls' father by name, Alexander, she admitted that she had deep feelings for you, but she felt the Navy and her life ambitions stood in the way of a lasting relationship. The doctors said the disease started in her breast and was painfully spreading to her bones. When the hospital ended her Radium treatments in September, her foremost concern was the welfare of her children. She struggled hard with the decision to contact you, Alex. Although Katy never mentioned your name to the girls, she was deeply tormented by the decisions she made in 1952 and '53. She had stopped working in June, as soon as she got the news from her doctor. Carl and I began looking after Karen and Sarah at the beginning of August.

"It wasn't until October when she ultimately decided to attempt contacting you. I believe she was encouraged by an argument I made about her honesty and feelings about you, Alex. I told her that a man who was good enough to share her bed should be good enough to share in the lives of her children, and she should not be afraid to let you into their lives. That was perhaps the strongest statement I ever made to her, but I think I struck a nerve. No offense intended, Alex, but me, well, I didn't know you, and was taking stabs in the dark, so I hope you don't take it the wrong way. She held a high opinion of your character and I told her she should trust that assessment. Her initial decision not to inform you of her pregnancy back in 1952 was, without doubt, haunting her for the past seven years. She clung to a kind of selfish pride, maybe, that she could handle things on her own. I think maybe the cancer was the thing that caused her to suddenly become concerned about the girls growing up without a mother or father. Anyway, when she first went to the lawyer, she spilled the beans and told him to try and find you. Near the end, Meriwether would come right to *Strong Memorial* hospital, sit at her bedside consoling her, making out her will, and helping her arrange things. I think that was beyond golden, thoughtful, and caring for a lawyer to do that. I had never heard of, or seen, a lawyer in a hospital before. She was relieved beyond words when he told her not to worry and that he would be successful in contacting you. But I think I'm being awfully long-winded here."

Emily began to weep, brought a hankie from inside her blouse and went on, "The day she passed away, just before Christmas, I fibbed and told her that the lawyer informed me that he found you in Texas and that you were on your way. She died with her mind at ease. About a week earlier, she asked me to thank you. Some of her last words were *'tell Alexander that I loved him, and ask him to forgive me'*.

"The saddest, tragic, heart-wrenching part was that she didn't dare to see her girls at the end."

Annie and Alex sat nearly motionless on the sofa, hanging on every word Emily spoke. She took a drink from the tall glass, filled her lungs with breath and slowly exhaled. "I really don't know everything about Katy's past, just the stuff she shared with me." She gathered her emotions, wiped her eyes yet again, and swirled the drink inside the glass. Melting ice cubes tinkled.

A moment of silence later, Emily rose from the recliner, and walked to the bathroom. Alex and Annie could hear her sobbing and blowing her nose. The commode flushed with a loud, rude, gurgle. She returned holding a wad of toilet tissue in her hand.

"When Katy asked me and Carl to watch the kids for her and wait for you to come, I was so proud that she thought of me in that way. She was a good person, Alexander and Annie. She really was. And considerate and thoughtful. She even set aside money for me to use for the children. Katy was a gem."

It took more than just a few minutes for Emily to regain her composure. Annie began to shed tears of her own and pulled a kerchief out of her purse. A flood of emotion is like a river overrunning its banks. It takes time for it to recede.

Annie wiped away her tears and spoke first. "You have been a great help in all of this, Emily. Thank you so much. Alexander and I will be forever grateful for all you have done."

Emily wiped her eyes again and sniffled. After the noisy cuckoo clock made eleven annoying squawks, Emily said "I'm so glad that it all of this worked out. When do you plan to leave for Florida?"

Alexander answered, "Tomorrow is Friday, and I believe that we'll be able to wrap things up with the attorney. So, we will be heading back on Saturday, if that's all right with you and Carl, and it doesn't interfere with anything that perhaps you may have already planned."

"No, no. we have nothing planned. So that's good. Saturday is good. But I'm going to miss those two kids, I'll tell you … excuse me … Carl and I were wondering … how long have you two been married?"

Annie immediately piped up, "Six years this coming June. Since 1954."

There were a few seconds of silence before Emily added, "I don't know why I asked that. I hope that wasn't rude of me."

Alexander assured her, "No, no, Emily. That was a perfectly kosher question, but I'll tell you what ... tomorrow evening ... Friday evening … perhaps Carl could take the night off … how about you and Carl pick a good place to eat ... and Annie and I can treat you and the kids to a meal at a nice restaurant somewhere before we head out on Saturday morning. What do you say?"

"Sure. Carl can swap a shift and get the night off. And Grandma can babysit the kids. So, that would be nice. But tomorrow, after work, I'll have to get Karen's and Sarah's things together. They don't have a whole heck of a lot, so it should fit in two or three boxes. Plus, a box of toys, of course. I can have it all ready for when you leave on Saturday. Karen and Sarah have been on a couple of car trips, and they always behaved good in the car, even with four kids in the back and Nancy, our eldest, up front with Carl and me. In and out of the car, the girls are good girls … gems."

Emily's voice cracked; she seemed exhausted. The visit was over. They decided that Alex would call tomorrow, and they could meet up before dinner right back there on Erie Station Road.

It was cold outside; the sky was coal-black with brilliant stars. The snow crunched under foot. Alex used the backside of his pocket comb to scrape the frost off the Packard's windshield. Annie sat in the front seat, her overcoat pulled up over her nose, warming herself with her breath.

Alex turned the key in the ignition and the engine reluctantly, slowly, turned over. After a click, a groan, and another click, the engine started. Alex let the motor run for a minute or two before setting the transmission into drive. The snow and ice groaned in frigid protest under the weight of the car as it slowly traveled down the driveway, out to the street, and on the way back to the motel.

The headlights cast reflections like diamonds off the snow crystals. There was a frozen halo around the moon. Cold, sharp needles of frosty pain from the steering wheel stung deep into Alex's fingers.

They didn't talk on the way back to the Holiday Inn. Annie remained huddled up in the front seat, holding her coat up over her nose, keeping her warm breath inside the garment. When Alex parked the car, they rapidly walked to their room. Ice crystals formed and fell from their breath. Their noses were numbed and cheeks stung from the frigid air. The cold was that brutal.

"Among My Souvenirs."

Friday morning, January 8, 1960

It took a while to fall asleep that night and when they did, it was a restless slumber. It wasn't troubled sleep; they simply were captured by thoughts of things to come. They had a lot on their plate.

They got up early and by seven-thirty, they were enjoying a hearty breakfast at the in-house, beef-themed restaurant, the *Steer In.* Annie was conservative with a cheese omelet, while Alex indulged in steak, eggs and home fries.

Back in their room, Alex occasionally peeked up from the pages of the *Rochester Courier* and caught glimpses of *Huckleberry Hound* on the color television. After Annie finished her shower, Alex took his turn under the hot torrents of Lake Ontario water. Squeaky clean, with a fresh shave, and feeling frisky, he lured Annie back under the covers. He often teased her and called such impromptu rapture *the horizontal waltz.* After their impassioned dance between the sheets, they lay on the bed, their heads propped up by pillows.

"Look at that, Alex. The curtains are dancing the vertical waltz!"

The light green draperies covering the window were drifting and swaying with the waves of heat rising from the natural gas space heater underneath the sill.

"As nice as this is, Annie, we best ignore the dancers. We need to get up and get moving. There's a lot ahead of us today, and not the least, a lawyer. And I suppose I should make a few telephone calls back home, just to check on things."

Their eleven o'clock appointment with Reginald Meriwether was still two hours away. Alex called his partner Louis but did not mention the twin six-year-old girls who had unexpectedly entered his life. Rather, he decided it was enough to simply explain that he was named as a beneficiary in the estate of someone he knew during his enlistment in the Navy. He and Annie agreed it was perhaps best not to say anything, to anyone, until they were actually on their way back home. Things at the shop were normal and moving along without any problems. This close to the holidays, business was understandably slow. As the conversation was ending, Louis jokingly made an off-the-cuff remark that carried a sting of irony. "The last time you were away on a road trip, Alex, and called me long distance, you came home with a wife. What are you bringing back with you this time?"

Alex appreciated the ironic humor. "I haven't made up my mind yet, buddy. But I'll tell you what … it will be something good. A real surprise … I guarantee it."

Next, Alex telephoned Renaldo, and informed him that he and Annie should arrive back on the ranch either Tuesday or Wednesday of the following week. Everything back on the ranch was going well and Coko had continued to accustom herself to the herd. The only issue was a bucked shin on Cassandra that Doc Adams had wrapped two days earlier. Renaldo said he also started to bring in some alfalfa.

Still, with an hour and a half before their date with the lawyer, they decided to drive to East Main Street and stop in at *Sixteen Reasons* again, for some coffee and a pastry. They were uncontrollably anxious, with simply no escape. Their wandering thoughts were relentless, despite their attempted diversions, either between the sheets, or with *New York Bell*.

Overnight and early morning snow left about an inch of clean, white, powder covering the dirty piles along the streets and storefronts. The street crews were busy, spreading a salt and sand mixture that created wet pavement. They parked directly in front of the small eatery. As Annie exited the car, a snowplow rumbled past, with diesel smoke erupting lazily into the air, splashing slush, sand and salt onto the opposite side of the Packard. Alex was already on the backside of the car and missed the filthy shower of wintertime debris. "Did you see that, Alex?! That was one gigantic truck with a gigantic snowplow. I didn't know there was such a thing as an *Oshkosh* truck! A big bright orange-yellow Oshkosh! I'll have to remember and tell that to Beth. Golly, the hood on that thing was as big as a parking lot!"

"They probably need those big trucks here, Annie; considering all the snow they get coming at them from across Lake Erie and down off Lake Ontario. They make them right in Oshkosh, but this is the first time I ever saw one outside of Wisconsin and Michigan. My grandfather, Dominik, Nora's father worked at the Oshkosh plant. They make seriously big trucks."

They sat at the same table they occupied the day before. The waitress who recited the *'one dollar minimum'* speech recognized them and gave a warm, welcoming, smile. Alex

148

and Annie ordered hot malted chocolate, topped with whipped cream, and a cheese Danish. As she cut the pastry with the side of her fork, Annie excitedly uncovered another change coming to their lives. She brought the conversation directly into the alterations that would be necessary to their home. The realization of the changing dynamic of their family structure appeared front and center. They would be returning home with two school-age children plus the coming attraction Annie carried within her belly. Suddenly, home remodeling stood in the forefront. Their two-bedroom, cottage style home would need to be altered to fit three more souls. New furniture would be required: twin beds, a crib, and a youth bed in the not-too-distant future. Excitement rushed in and replaced their nervous anticipation.

At once, Alex solved the living space issue. "Well, at one time, I was thinking about extending the house to where the carport is. And I guess that's what we'll do, Annie. And I'll have Sectional Homes come again and put up a detached garage out toward the barns."

Annie spoke as the thoughts came to her. "First thing, we will need to get the girls signed up for school. Maybe the girls will ride the same bus as Benjamin, but he's only in kindergarten. I guess we'll find out."

As the clock approached ten forty-five, Alex left four dollars on the table and helped Annie into her green woolen coat. "We may as well just walk down to his office. It's just a half a block. But I was thinking, and I hope we don't get blasted with snow before it comes time for us to drive back home. But worse comes to worse, I can always just buy a set of snow tires."

"That's one thing I don't miss about Appleton, Alex. The stinking snow. I mean, when you live there you just accept it and it becomes a way of life. But now that I know I do not have to live that way, I have no desire to go back. No way.

And this trip up here has been a strong reminder of how nice it is not to struggle with the white junk. And besides, my toes get cold. I absolutely hate it. I would not go back."

As they walked out the door and started down the sidewalk, he put his arm around her waist. "I'm hanging on to you, Annie. I'm not going to let you go back to Wisconsin any time soon. Or ever. You are not going to escape my clutches."

She playfully pushed her hip into him. "I am not going anywhere without my husband. Not anywhere without you."

Number twenty-five Main Street East was at their feet. As they took the steps, Alex spoke matter-of-factly, "You know, now that our family is suddenly growing by leaps and bounds, we should consider trading in the Packard and getting one of those *Chrysler Town and Country* station wagons that are as big as the Queen Mary." He held the door open for his wife.

"I don't think so. Three kids will fit in the Patrician's back seat just fine. And besides, the Packard's got a great radio."

Inside, they stomped the snow off their shoes and hung up their coats in the foyer. The stale smell of cigarettes and full ashtrays drifted across the waiting room. Alex checked his breast pocket for his birth certificate. He was holding Annie's hand and gave it a gentle squeeze. The office door opened with a click and a muffled clunk. Reginald Meriwether's form almost filled the doorway. "Come on in, folks, and we'll get this all settled and in order." He moved his frame into the office and held the door open. Alexander and Maryanne sat in the two chairs directly in front of his imposing desk. There were three small stacks of papers neatly placed in the center of his desk. Two ink pens sat near the edge, close to, and in front of Alex and Annie's chairs. Both green-shaded desk lamps were lit, and a cigarette sat smoldering in the over-full ashtray. Annie had wondered if the lawyer ever took the time to empty it.

150

After the obligatory shallow greetings, the attorney got down to business. He began with the explanation of the Deed of Assent, Testamentary Letters, Probate Inventory and finally the Probate Clearance. They all required signatures by Alex, the attorney and a notary, Edna Hicks, a small elderly woman, who sat in a straight-back chair quietly to the side of the lawyer.

The first collection of papers was explained as Alexander's assumption of the role of Executor, his agreement to the estate inventory, his subsequent surrender, and release of, the Probate Clearance back to the attorney. There was no real property involved, and the bulk of Katherine's furniture was bequeathed to Emily or had been sold with the old farmhouse on South Winton Road. The attorney placed the first stack of papers, signed and notarized, on the desk directly in front of Annie.

"For this next item, Alexander, I would advise you to actually go to the bank today. It's the passbook savings account that Katherine established for her, for your, daughters. It became a Totten Trust with her passing, and now it's back to a simple savings account with the transfer. Of course, Katherine intended that the funds are for the girls, and under your administration. There is just under five thousand dollars in this account, earning I think, one percent interest. Frankly, I would ask the bank, *Community Savings Bank of Rochester*, to either wire the funds to your bank in Florida or ask if you could close the account and take it with you. That's your decision. There's an office just around the block on Westfall Street. All you need is this Affidavit of Assumption and your identification." Meriwether set that pile sideways, directly on top of the first.

"Next, we have thirteen, one-hundred-block, Kodak common stock certificates in the girls' names. They are redeemable only by the owners, the girls, upon their twenty-first birthday, or as early as their eighteenth birthday, should they marry by that age. These belong to the young ladies, and I would take care that they are kept in a bank box. Kodak has an excellent investment history." Those were piled on top of the bank papers and sideways again.

"And finally, Alexander, here are the girls' birth certificates. We have already been over this, in detail, haven't we?"

"Yes, sir. We have. My wife and I understand perfectly."

"Good, then. Here they are, as amended and dated June 23, 1954, signed by Katherine, and the attending physician, as doctor ... looks like ... Lawrence Fitzsimmons, and with the seal of *Syracuse General Hospital*. Date of birth is listed as June 21, 1953, at 10:00 PM. And, an Affidavit of Paternity, dated April 14, 1954, signed by you, Alexander, and the hospital's Custodian of Records. Do we agree with that, Alexander?"

Annie nodded quickly to her husband. "Yes, and I agree. We both agree. And we will make some photo static copies." There was a tone of urgency in her voice.

"One other thing, Alexander. In New York State, the law allows parents to determine the family name of their children. The girls' birth certificates list them as Karen and Sarah Dobbs, with their parentage listed separately. Check with your law in Florida, but I believe you can just start using the family name *Throckmorton* and use *Dobbs* as a middle name, or drop it altogether, if you desire. It happens a lot. It's just that sometime in the future, it will make things easier for you and your daughters. It's better to prevent problems before they ever get a chance to begin, whenever you can. Do you understand what I am saying?"

Annie and Alex shared a quick glance. With a little head bob to Annie, Alex said, "Yes, we understand. Thanks for explaining that. We will check on that in Florida." They were both eager to get this paper party over with.

Reginald Meriwether let out a sigh, folded his pudgy, pink, hands across his midsection and moaned a near thunderous, "Yes! We have finished and all is well, both in Rochester and in Florida. Thank you very much, Mister and Missus Throckmorton. It has been a pleasure, albeit a conclusion to a very sad and tragic circumstance. I am pleased it turned out well for everyone, especially concerning the two innocents involved, Sarah and Karen, the little sweethearts. From the time I was first acquainted with Katherine, I can tell you that she exhibited only the best, honorable and decent qualities."

Edna, the gray-haired notary, sat motionless, with no expression, just an impish, droll smile. She had small reading spectacles sitting at the end of her nose.

"So, when are you leaving for Florida, Alex, Annie?"

Annie took the opportunity to speak. "We are hoping for tomorrow."

"Good, good. What kind of a place do you have down there, Alexander? What line of work are you in?"

"We live on a decent-sized ranch north of Pensacola, in a town called Chumuckla, maybe five miles from the Alabama state line. Well actually, I'm an engine mechanic, but I am able to spend most of my time running our quarter horse ranch. We have a nice herd started. I own and operate an engine and machine shop with my partner, an Air Force veteran. He manages the place, and Annie helps with the book-keeping."

Without acknowledging what Alex just said, the attorney deftly nodded, pursed his lips and twisted his wristwatch to check the time. "Well. See that? It's just after noon and we're done. I will contact you, Alexander, if need be, but I doubt it will come to that. I believe we have everything all in order. Edna, here, will give you an envelope for all your papers. Make sure to guard them until you get home. I have copies, but to avoid any problems, it is always best to have the originals."

He opened his desk drawer, took something out, and sidestepped from behind the desk. With one hand, he gave Alex his calling card and offered a handshake with the other. He stood shaking Alex's hand vigorously. "Good job, well done. That's my card if you ever need to call me for any reason, whether it's past, present, or future business. It has been a pleasant experience dealing with you and your wife, Alexander."

Edna was putting a stack of papers into a large brown envelope with an oversized flap, and strings attached. She closed the flap, tied the strings around the envelope and handed it to Annie. With the wrapped papers in her hands, she was able to avoid Reginald's sweaty grasp. She nodded at him and spoke in an even tone, "It has been an enjoyable experience. A lot easier than I expected from a lawyer."

Meriwether let out an uncomfortable grunt and said, "It's been my pleasure, Maryanne. Good luck with your new family."

Alex saw a chance to escape and encouraged his wife to join him, "Well, I think we should get over to the bank, Annie. Where is it again, Mister Meriwether?" Alex had his arm around Annie's shoulders, protecting her from capture by the legal system.

"It's right around the corner, just up the street past the deli, on Westfall Street. Community Savings Bank of Rochester. You can't miss it."

Alex and Annie started out the door. Annie turned and gave a small wave, "Bye, now." As they passed through the anteroom and into the foyer, a sense of satisfaction and finality came over them. Annie switched the brown folio of papers from one hand to the other, sliding her arms into her coat, while Alex held it for her.

He wrapped the scarf around his neck and tucked it into his overcoat. "Well, that went well. It went a lot faster than I would have guessed. All we need to do now is visit the bank." He closed the heavy wood door behind them and looked back at the two-story brick building. "We're on our way back home, Annie. One more night."

Walking close, they started down the block toward the bank. The gray skies were clearing, and patches of blue appeared between fluffy, snow-white clouds. "I'm anxious to go home, Alex. I know these things take time, and I'm not complaining. I'm tired of it, I guess. You know how something can stick in your head, and it won't go away, like a song? Well, all I can think of is Jack Benny calling for that butler of his, *'Oh, Rochester!'* And Rochester answers, in that pitchy, raspy gravel voice of his, he knows what's coming, he always does, and he says,*' Yes, Mister Benny!'* I think it's time to go home, Alex."

Inside the bank, they found themselves sitting at the front side of yet another desk, facing a round-faced, balding man in his fifties. The brass nameplate on the desk read: Howard J. Pippine, Assistant Asset Manager. He wore a blue, pin-stripe vest, with shirt sleeves rolled up to the elbow and a deep red kerchief protruding from the vest pocket. Alex had placed all the required documents on the desk and wondered why the man needed to ask so many redundant questions. "The Affidavit of Assumption is there, the account book and my identification are there, as is my driver's license. And the girl's birth certificates, too."

The bank clerk's chair made a horrendous squeaking, scratching sound across the granite floor as he pushed back from the desk. "I'll be right back. I need to bring over Miss Meriwether, my supervisor."

Annie looked to Alex and whispered, "Alex! What is this? Another Meriwether?! And this guy cannot make any decisions without checking with the boss? And his little nameplate says he's a manager! Unbelievable."

Alex shook his head. "I agree. But, then again, even the sign on his desk says he's only the *assistant manager* of assets."

A tall, buxom woman returned with Howard Pippine. Her ample hips were tightly packed into a deep maroon cotton dress. "Hello." She leaned over the desk, her pendulous breasts undulating and fighting the confines of her dress. She shifted the papers, picked up the Assumption Affidavit and set it back down, and turned toward Alex and Annie. "I'm Eleanor Meriwether, the Bank Manager. Everything is fine here; all in order." She looked over her shoulder, "You can close this account for cash, Howard." Then back to Alex and Annie, "Or perhaps you would like us to transfer the funds to your bank, Mister Throckmorton?"

"Let's transfer the funds if we can, so my wife and I are not carrying the cash around. My bank is Cotton States, in Pensacola, Florida."

She smiled broadly, "Cotton States ... yes, I have dealt with them before. Good, we'll contact your bank, create an account and send a bank check to Florida for you. Looking at the paperwork, I assume you just left my father's office, Reginald Meriwether, the attorney?" Her deep red lips formed a forced, superficial smile.

Alex and Annie nodded together and shared a quick glance. Annie's eyes twinkled. Alex's lip curled upward, "It's a small world, isn't it? At least here in Rochester." He looked over to his wife and he *knew* she was thinking about Jack Benny.

156

There were perhaps fifteen more minutes of inane questions, suppositions, telephone calls and obvious assumptions before Karen and Sarah Dobbs had their own accounts in Florida. When Alex and Annie were able to leave the bank, they did so without looking back and walked directly toward the Packard, a half-block away.

"How about we look for a place to grab a lunch, Annie?"

She firmly held the folio of papers in one hand and her purse in the other. Alex unlocked the car door, and held it open for his wife. She gingerly stepped over the small ridge of curbside snow, slipped, and awkwardly settled into the front seat, the papers still safely in her grasp. Alex walked around the front of the car to the driver's side. The engine came to life with the first turn of the key.

"We can drive around and find a place nearby. Some place simple, Alex. I'm not too hungry and we're going out tonight, too. But right now, I could celebrate with only one glass of champagne. Just one glass. We've earned it today."

"Come Go With Me."

Friday afternoon, January 8, 1960

On the corner of West Henrietta and Ontario Street, a large, square, black sign with a crisp white border hung out over the sidewalk. It was an attention-getter. Tall neon letters of bright crimson read: *Snap Shots*. Underneath, smaller and in green neon: *Restaurant and Lounge.* The large building was slate gray, the color of exposed negative film, with sharp white trim around the windows and doors. The exterior was clean, with sidewalks clear of snow and slush. The place appeared as an album page, waiting for photographs to be stuck in place. The clever design drew Alexander to pull the Packard into the blacktop parking lot. It was a four-story wood structure with clapboard siding. In days past, it could very well have been a boarding house or hotel. A black cast-iron fire escape zigzagged down the side of the building to the parking lot. On the opposite corner was a large single-story building, the home of the *Fire Ball* bowling alley.

Snap Shots' entrance door was cut directly into the corner of the building, with two rows of glass block surrounding the frame. Multi-colored lights behind the block created a soft diffused glow all around the door. The street level windows each brandished neon beer signage. Inside, the room was divided by a half wall. A dining room full of tables covered in white linen on one side and a bar, with booths and smaller tables on the other. A blackboard easel and hostess podium stood at the dining room side. A folded sign sat atop the podium, advising that the dining room opens at 4:00 PM. A young woman was writing the daily specials on the chalkboard as Alex and Annie entered.

"Good afternoon! Welcome to Snap Shots ... please have a seat anywhere in the lounge and I'll be right with you folks."

Recessed lighting in the black ceiling and miniature floodlights in the corners mimicked the atmosphere of a photography studio. Two interior walls were gigantic collages of large, black and white portrait and landscape prints. Above the swinging door leading to the kitchen, an illuminated sign in red letters displayed the words: *Dark Room*. Like the dining room, the tables in the lounge were also covered with crisp, white tablecloths. There was a half dozen occupied tables with two or more patrons and one with four men wearing department store suits, miss-matched ties and wrinkled slacks. There were two men and a woman at the bar, separated by a half dozen empty stools. The bartender was bald, with a halo of thin hair running across the back of his head to just over the top of his ears. Black garters were between the elbow and shoulder of his buttoned, long sleeved, white shirt. A flickering black and white television

158

sat atop a shelf at the far corner of the bar. It was tuned to a Peter Lawford movie, *The Thin Man,* with the sound turned off.

Annie had brought the folio of papers into the restaurant, unwilling to part with them. Alex's eyes quickly surveyed the room, and he decided on the supposed privacy of a booth, situated next to the partition wall. Votive candles twinkled on the tables inside translucent, red, tear-shaped globes.

The waitress wore a black rayon dress, with an above-the-knee hemline, a snow white, half-moon apron and a white lace headband. Her pleasant, beaming disposition welcomed Alex and Annie to an obviously efficient establishment. The interior atmosphere of Snap Shots was equally as impressive as the building's exterior.

A relaxed lunch was the welcome break they needed. They ordered the Friday special of beer battered haddock, French fries and coleslaw. Alex ordered a *Christian Brothers* brandy and Annie asked for a glass of *Great Western* New York champagne. The waitress praised their selections. "Excellent choice ... you see, the sparkling wine as well as the brandy cuts through the thick tempura of the battered fish and the weight of the fried food. Not many people realize that. Like I said: excellent choice." When the server left the tableside, Annie let out a little giggle.

"See that, Alex? I'm one of those high-class wine connoisseurs and I had to take a trip to Rochester to find out."

Before their meals arrived, they raised their glasses in a few quiet toasts and quickly looked through the papers in the folio. For the first time, they looked closely at the birth certificates of Karen and Sarah Dobbs, particularly, the signature of *A. Throckmorton.*

"It's obvious that is not your signature, Alex. But like the lawyer said, it's meaningless unless we make a stink about it.

It doesn't add up to a hill of beans. All that matters is that the girls are your daughters, our daughters now."

They leisurely finished their meals and drinks. Gradually, additional customers filled the lounge, more wait staff came on duty and the restaurant got noisier. Their lunch time tête-à-tête was an enjoyable, tranquil reprieve.

They left Snap Shots eagerly anticipated the coming evening with the Rutherfords and their daughters. So much had happened and so much more lay ahead. It was a quick ride back to the Henrietta Holiday Inn. The afternoon skies cleared to light blue with a few white puffs of cloud. The cold gray skies disappeared briefly so it felt warmer than it actually was. The sunshine warmed and enlightened their spirits to the maximum extent possible for early January in upstate New York. As soon as they got back inside their room, Alex telephoned Carl Rutherford.

"Little Darling."
Friday evening, January 8, 1960

When Alex telephoned, Carl suggested that they have dinner right there at the Holiday Inn, at the in-house restaurant. The motel eatery had a good reputation of service and food quality; it was certainly convenient for Annie and Alex and close for Carl and Emily. They arranged to meet at six o'clock and Alexander reiterated that he would pick up the tab.

They showered and changed into fresh sets of clothes. Annie teased her husband that this could very well be the last time she wore one of her tight-fitting skirts for six months or more and she may even quit shaving her legs. Alex was straightening his tie at the mirror and watching her. Annie's giggle revealed her fib. Their excitement was bubbling over. Hopefully, this would be their last night in Rochester, and tomorrow they could be on their way back to Florida. Together, they decided to forego any visit to Niagara Falls. The combination of winter weather, the sudden, unforeseen presence of two children in their lives, and the urge to get them home in Florida made the decision easy. Annie mentioned she noticed that there were several picture postcards of the Falls at the motel desk. "We can buy a couple of those, Alex. I'll send one to Beth and one to Mama."

Inside the Steer In, Alex and Annie sat waiting, together, alone. They sat next to one another, waiting at one large round table, with a setting for ten. The hanging ceiling fixtures were chandeliers, with cut glass teardrops. The flatware, water glasses and butter plates sparkled on the maroon tablecloth. Although they had already met the girls, they sat in almost unbearably hungry anticipation. "I think Karen and Sarah have already accepted us, Alex, don't you?" She was running her fingers up and down the sides of her glass of ginger ale. Her eyes looked deep into his.

He reached and took her hand. "You already know the answer to that, Annie girl. Of course, they do. They have accepted both of us. Sure, it has been a big deal for them, but children adjust a heck of a lot easier and quicker than we adults do. You remember they already referred to you as their *new mommy*."

"I hope I can live up to the part. I mean, I'm new at this. I don't want to mess anything up."

Alex spoke with a tone of confidence. "You won't mess anything up. You're going to be a wonderful mommy and a wonderful mother. No doubt about it."

Annie took a deep breath, held it a moment and exhaled slowly. "I'm just nervous, Alex. That's all. Thanks."

The sound of a young girl's voice from across the dining room drew their attention. "There they are, Karen! There's Mommy and Daddy!" The twins sprang toward them; Alex and Annie stood from the table, went to their knees and welcomed the girls with open arms. Four souls joined in a mass hug on the floor of the Holiday Inn's restaurant. The doubts Annie had a few moments earlier, melted with the warmth of Karen and Sarah Dobbs' arms around her. Carl, Emily and their three children sat around the table.

Annie whispered to Alex, "When I stand up, see if my skirt is all right. I'm afraid that I may have ripped a seam or the zipper ... and stand close, just in case I did."

Alex immediately responded, in an excited tone, undoubtedly, to avoid suspicion, "Sure thing! Is anybody hungry?" As he stood, he checked Annie's taut skirt. Not quite as animated, he gave Annie the message, whispering in her ear, "Everything looks fine to me. Really fine," offered his hand to Annie as she stood, and gave her a reassuring nod.

Together, Alex, Annie and the twins made their way to the table. The children worked out the seating arrangement. Annie and Alex would sit together with Karen on Annie's right and Sarah on Alex's left. Sarah told her sister, "We can switch seats for dessert."

During the meal, all five youngsters behaved like the minister's children at a Communion dinner. They talked quietly among themselves. They were certainly making secret pacts, such as planning the next dollhouse tea party. Dinnertime progressed without any spilt milk, dropped spaghetti, or tipped applesauce. The adults relished the somewhat rare opportunity to carry on conversations without refereeing a childish squabble. They all noticed how well the children were behaving. It was a pleasant mealtime.

Emily confessed that she and her husband Carl had both taken the day off. They had used vacation days to get things in

162

order and help prepare for the twins' trip to Florida. She collected Karen and Sarah's immunization records, their latest school progress reports and their kindergarten assessments from last year. Their clothing was nearly all packed and ready to go, along with their toys and dolls. She added that the girls made a point that they would travel in the car with their dolls in their arms. Emily said she bought the girls a half dozen *Little Golden Books* and a copy of *Little Black Sambo.*

Carl explained that both girls had accepted their new situation remarkably well and were excited about the trip to Florida. He revealed how overjoyed the girls were when the news arrived that their *daddy* was coming. Katherine Dobbs was convinced that if Alex was found, her daughters would have a home with their father. Carl explained, "I don't think I have ever seen a woman express such confidence in a man; let alone a man she left behind and had not seen in years. Katy had faith. And after Karen and Sarah found out you were coming, I never knew two happier children ever, not ever, in my entire life. Me and Emily are so glad things worked out this well. We really are. But you have to tell us about your place in Florida. Are you right near the Navy base there in Pensacola, or what?"

Emily caught that part of the conversation. There was eager curiosity. "Yeah. Tell the girls about their new home in Florida."

"Go ahead, Annie. Tell everyone about Straight Eight Farm." The children's chatter stopped. All eyes turned to Annie.

"Well, first of all, we live on a horse ranch. And ..."

She was immediately interrupted by five super-charged curious children. "Horses? Are there ponies, too?" This was news to Emily and Carl Rutherford as well. Five excited children gave their full attention to Annie.

"Yep, we have horses and every now and then we have baby horses, too. Right now, we have five big horses and two smaller ones, sort of like teenagers, almost big, but not quite. And we have a dog, too. He's big, friendly, likes to chase squirrels and his name is Clarence. And down at the end of the driveway, we have neighbors with two young boys, Tommy and Ben, and they are three and five years old. And we have neighbors who live and work right there on the ranch with us and they have a little boy, too, and his name is Johnny. So, Sarah and Karen, there are kids for you to play with. I am sure you will love it in Florida. And you are going to have a baby brother or sister next summer, because Daddy and I are having a baby."

The magic dust was sprinkled twice around. Little girls and ponies; that simply translates into *Wonderland Forever*. A baby brother or sister ... well, that means unlimited *Fun House* tickets. The next five minutes were nothing less than supervised pandemonium. Hopes, dreams, promises, desires, expectations, enthusiasm, excitement, all the essential ingredients of childhood delirium bubbled around the big table. The only thing missing was a troupe of circus clowns.

Emily and Carl were, without a doubt, a little overwhelmed also. They got all this new information at the same time as the children. In between all the verbal buzz, a waitress appeared carrying her own aura of curious wonder at all the commotion. Annie ordered ice cream for all the children, drink refills and another ginger ale for herself. By the time the desserts arrived, some calm had returned to that particular section of the restaurant.

Annie promised riding lessons and naming rights for the next new foals born on the ranch. And, of course, an open invitation to Emily, Carl, and their children for a visit. The standard adult reply of *'we'll see'* fell on the deaf ears of the Rutherford children.

164

Alex and Carl started in on their own little back-and-forth. They were still essentially strangers, having met only for a few moments on Thursday, just as Carl was leaving for work. Alex gave Carl a brief history of his time in the Navy, his romantic endearment with Katherine Dobbs, his marriage and life so far with Annie. Carl grew up on the family dairy farm down the road in Chili, New York and held a farm deferment from the Korean draft. After the war ended, he secured employment at the warehouse and shipping dock of Kodak, where he met his wife, Emily. He confessed that neither he nor his wife were ever outside of New York State, and he just might take the opportunity to visit Florida some day.

That left an opening for Alex to mention that he would actually need to add at least one more room to his cottage-style, two-bedroom home. "Sure, I have a horse ranch, but not a ranch-size house."

Carl's curiosity was piqued. "Tell me, how did you get started with horses?"

"When I got out of the Navy, I used the GI Bill, bought the farm and opened an engine works and machine shop. Later, on my own, and after my mother passed, my inheritance enabled me to start with the purchase of a brood mare and it just grew from there. I was fortunate that my first horses, a stallion and that brood mare we bought, paired up as fast and friendly as they did. Things have worked out very well. I've been fortunate. That's the best way to describe it. The engine shop took off, and now with some solid Navy contracts, we are in great shape. I have been lucky, I suppose. And I have good people around me. And a fantastic wife, too. She's my pillar of support. My Annie."

Carl poured the last of his Genesee beer into his glass. "Yessir. Women are important. No doubt about that. Emily has always worked right alongside me."

After hearing her name mentioned, Emily asked, "So what time do you folks plan on heading out tomorrow?"

"Oh, goodness, I don't know. What do you think, Alex? Nine, ten o'clock? Would that be all right, Emily?"

Emily looked at the children, over to her husband, and back to Annie. "I think ten o'clock would be great. That way, I can make a good breakfast for the girls, we can get everything ready, and all the kids will have a chance to say good-bye. The weatherman said he didn't see any storms on the way, so that's a good thing. But it's going to get cold tonight; well below zero they say. So, let's go with ten o'clock, then." She picked up her glass of Royal Crown cola and finished it.

A half minute of relative silence ended when Carl spoke up. He glanced at his wristwatch. "Okay, kids. Let's get our coats on and head home. We are going to have a busy day tomorrow."

A fracas of arms, elbows, coat sleeves, scarves, and mittens ensued. Alex lifted his daughters one after the other, hugged them and offered them to Annie for her kisses. He promised, "See you girls tomorrow and we'll head for home." He caught their waitress standing off to the side, watching the group good-byes. He nodded and acknowledged her glance, "We'll be right back, Miss. My wife and I are just going to walk our girls to the door."

The group of nine walked out of the restaurant, through the motel lobby, in a beeline to the double glass and aluminum doors. There were a few more goodbyes, hugs and one or two handshakes before Alex and Annie stood alone, waving out the window. The black sky was dotted with the winter twinkle of starlight. He put his arm around Annie, and they stood looking into the frigid darkness of the winter night.

"You know, Annie, it's nice knowing that we do not have to go out in that cold air, to a cold car and drive for miles before we hit the hay for the night. That's the one big plus about staying right at the motel for dinner."

Annie nudged him and playfully pushed him with her hip. "There you go, again, Alex; talking about getting me into the sack!"

He landed a kiss on her lips and looked down into her eyes. "All right if we have a drink in the lounge before we leave?"

"Sure. I got room for another ginger ale."

She slid her arm through his elbow and together they headed back inside the Steer In. Alex spotted their waitress and motioned to her as they walked toward the bar. Annie's pumps were click-clacking across the parquet floor. They found seats near the end. He took his wife's hand as she stepped up onto the barstool, carefully positioned herself, sat, and hooked her heels over the bottom rung of the chair. He allowed his hand to secretly slide over her backside as she settled onto the stool.

She spoke quietly, "I really was scared earlier, Alex. When I bent over and hugged the girls, I mean. I really thought my skirt split right down the back."

Alex leaned into her and whispered, "This new material they use now, all this man-made fabric ... it really stretches."

She poked him with her elbow. "Oh, really? That's nice, Alex. Real nice. Thanks." A little giggle followed.

The dining room waitress brought the dinner check, set it on the bar and smiled, "I'll be back in a few minutes." The bartender stood across from them, also waiting.

"No, no, wait just a second." Alex pulled his wallet out of his rear pant pocket. He glanced at the total and brought out forty dollars. "Thank you. That's close enough. Thank you." He held onto his wallet, now being able to give his attention to the bartender. He nodded to him. then turned to his wife and asked, "What would you like, Honey? The usual?"

Annie twittered, "Yep. A glass of ginger ale."

"And I'll have a Jim Beam, no ice, and a decent bottle of beer. Something other than a Genesee. What else do you have?"

"How about a *Molson*? It's a Canadian beer: Molson Canadian."

"Fine. A Molson, then." Alex paid the barman with a worn two-dollar bill, a single, and a fifty-cent piece.

There was subdued piped-in music in the background. It was barely discernable above the muffled bar buzz, whispers, laughs, promises, invitations, and clinking glass. Their eyes traveled across the bar, into the darkened booths and the bar-side tables. The bartender returned, and with a gentle thud and a tinkle of coin, set their drinks and change on the bar. "Thank you, sir."

Alex lifted his glass of whiskey to his wife. "Tomorrow we are going home, Annie girl. Thanks for standing with me. Thank you for your love and trust. Really. You have proven your love and trust time and time again. The last couple of days have been compelling."

"We got through it together, didn't we, Alex? Everything went smooth. It was a lot easier than I had first anticipated while we were sitting in that lawyer Meriwether's office. The girls are wonderful and the Rutherfords were so nice. Now that I think about it, this whole ordeal must have been tough for Emily. I mean, she lost her close friend Katy, and she has taken care of those two girls as if they were her own, not knowing when or if, you would show up. She did a marvelous job, taking care of the girls from the time Katy got real sick right up until it all was settled. Emily's got a heart of gold, I think. She sure was a good friend. Without doubt, she is a good person ... a caring, loving person. I suppose Katy had to know that, too."

"Shuffle Off To Buffalo."

Saturday morning, January 9, 1960

Alex was up early, just as the sun was coming up, and intended to get the oil changed in the Packard at the *Amoco* service station across the street from the motel. It was bone-cold in Rochester that morning, eight below zero. The air was dry, ice crystals immediately formed and dissipated on his exhaled breath. The Packard's straight eight turned over grudgingly but would not start. A few electronic clicks meant one thing: the problem was either the points, coil, or distributor cap; maybe all three. Adding to his frustration was the fact that all the ignition parts were new, replaced just before he left home the previous week. The aggravation of a car problem this early in the day and this far away from home was only accentuated by the extreme cold and his desire to get the Packard headed back down the road to Florida. With his head under the hood, his breath freezing mid-air and fingers stinging in the cold, he removed the distributor cap, rotor and points. Blowing warmth into his hands, he put the preciously stubborn parts into his coat pockets. He lowered the hood slowly, and let it close with a clunk, the sheet metal groaning in cold discomfort. Three tractor-trailers sat on the far side of the parking lot, running at idle, with long plumes of blue-gray exhaust drifting out of their stacks and toward the heavens. Under the canopy of the motel entrance, a Monroe county sheriff patrol car was also running, spewing out grey puffs of exhaust into the frigid air. As Alex entered the lobby, his toes began to painfully ache inside his oxfords. He felt his cheeks becoming crimson red with the prickly sensation brought on by below-zero temperatures. Through the lobby and down the hall, he couldn't get inside their room soon enough. In her pink robe, Annie peeked out from the bathroom.

"Annie, I'm ready to go home. This is simply too damn cold for me. I have to tell you: I sure don't miss these cold temperatures." He set the parts on the bed and took off his overcoat. "I need to warm up and dry off these ignition parts. Then I'll try to start the car again."

He was watching his wife at the dresser mirror, brushing her hair. "Do you know what? We're not dressed for this climate. We forgot what winter is like up here ... cold and miserable." He sat on the bed, kicked off his shoes and rubbed his stocking feet, trying to get some circulation warming his toes. "I'm ready for Florida, Annie. I'm ready to hit the road. I'm ready to shuffle off, right past Buffalo, and drive to any point south of the Mason-Dixon Line." He stuck his hands under his armpits, warming his fingers. "I could kick myself for not bringing any gloves. My fingers are freezing off."

With a wry, teasing, little grin, Annie looked at her husband in the mirror, pursed her lips, and sent him a pretend kiss. "If we jump back in bed, under the covers, I bet I could help warm up those hands of yours."

He smiled at the thought. "As much as I would enjoy that, Annie, I have to take a rain check ... up here I guess it's called a *snow check*. I need to get the car started. But first, I need to warm up, so I am going to take a long hot shower and change; then, dry off these ignition parts and try to get the Packard fired up. Then we'll have breakfast, pick up the girls, hit the highway and head south. We have a busy day ahead of us." He walked to the dresser, put his arms around her, gave her a gentle little kiss on the neck and whispered, "Love you."

Annie shivered, and exclaimed, "Goodness, you're cold!"

170

She murmured and watched him in the mirror as he started toward the bathroom. "You better take a hot shower! You're a walking icicle!

"I'll turn on the television, Alex, and see if I can catch a weather forecast on the local news." The door shut and she heard the shower come on.

After his shower, Alex sat at the small round table by the window, taking bits of newspaper and pulling them through the contacts of the ignition points. He could see the entire motel parking lot through the frosty window. Four cars sat idling with their hoods stuck high into the frigid air, mimicking an ancient Inca sacrifice to the internal combustion engine. Wafts of exhaust spread upward and dissipated into tiny clouds of fumes and frozen mist. Parked next to the Packard was a maroon 1958 *Cadillac Eldorado*. Alex was wiping the inside of the distributor cap with toilet tissue, keeping his eyes on the Caddy. There was a fellow dressed in a hooded fur-lined parka, boots and leather gloves with his head leaning into the engine compartment. Like his Packard, the dried, white road salt made the Cadillac appear as it was frosted, or dipped, in confectioner's sugar.

Realizing the opportunity that was presenting itself, he set the parts carefully onto the bed, hurriedly put on his coat, and shoes, and went directly out the door without saying a word to Annie. He was on a personal mission of mercy. The primary objective was being able to leave Rochester. Annie watched her husband approach the man who was dressed like an Eskimo. Both men began a very animated conversation with pointing fingers, nodding heads, and waving arms. Annie assumed there were swear words mixed in. Within a matter of seconds, both Alex and the Eskimo had their heads and hands under the hood of the Packard. Shortly, with the driver's-side door wide open, Alex sat behind the wheel and a plume of grey exhaust billowed from the back end of the

Patrician, signaling the start of the engine. Annie sighed. Relief was felt both inside room 41 of the Holiday Inn and inside the car as well. There were now five cars idling with open hoods in the Holiday Inn parking lot. Alexander sat for a few moments, worked the accelerator pedal, and watched the dashboard gauges. When the engine warmed and began to run smoothly, he set the heater fan on low and opened the defrost vents.

He walked across the lot back to the motel room, removed his overcoat and grabbed the bedspread. He set his frame into the chair, covered himself with the quilt and again tried to warm his frigid fingers under his armpits. "It's bone-busting cold out there, Annie." He watched and waited as Annie got dressed in her warmest outerwear. She decided on slacks.

The plan was to have breakfast just down the street at the Olympic, and afterwards, drive to the Rutherford home on Erie Station Road. He decided to let the Packard idle while they were at the restaurant. He could delay the engine oil change until tomorrow or the next day.

FOUR: A NEW FAMILY - GOING HOME

"One More For The Road."

Saturday afternoon, January 9, 1960

The Rutherford family anticipated that Annie and Alex would not be making an extended visit that Saturday morning. Karen And Sarah were fully dressed in their winter wear, and right inside the entrance to the home, the twins' clothes and toys were inside cardboard boxes, packed and ready to go. The contents of each of the six boxes were written in black crayon on the folded top flaps. When they arrived, Emily took Annie to the side and whispered, "I think it's best if we just get the girls' things into your car and say a simple and quick *good-bye*. My own kids became quite emotional earlier this morning." Annie nodded in agreement and the subject was put to rest.

Carl said the same thing to Alex as they loaded up the trunk of the Packard. When they finished, everyone was standing in the hall. The Rutherford children were trying hard to fight their emotion, obviously with parental encouragement and admonition. Quick, heartfelt hugs erupted between the five children: handshakes and stoic embraces within the circle of four adults. Emily mentioned to Annie that she also packed a few pieces of Katy's costume jewelry, a portrait of Katy and the twins, and two photograph albums into the boxes. "There wasn't much else. Anything she had of value, she sold either to help with her father's stay at Chestnut Ridge old folks' infirmary, or whatever Kodak didn't cover for her own doctor and hospital bills over the last year."

As delicate as final good-byes can be, this was particularly difficult for the Rutherfords. It was also uncomfortably sentimental for Alex and Annie. Two distinctly different forces were tugging at one another in Henrietta, New York that morning. The joy of a new love entering one life and the melancholy of separation from another are difficult elements to mix. Alex forced the issue with one simple statement; short, sweet, and right on point, he announced, "Let's hit the road, girls."

With that, four bodies settled into the Packard. The cream Patrician was ready for the trip: a full tank of Amoco High Test, a trunk loaded with toys, clothing, photographs, and two sisters in the back seat with their dolls and books. Alex hung his arm over the seat, turned his frame, strained his neck, and alternately looked at his daughters and the driveway, as he backed the four-door sedan toward Erie Station Road. Through the windshield, Annie waved to the Rutherford family shivering in the cold, standing on the porch, just outside the front door, and waving back. Within fifteen minutes, four *Goodyear* super-wide whitewall tires were rolling the Packard down the New York State Thruway toward Pennsylvania, and points south. The eleven o'clock *CBS Radio* newscast ended with the local weather. The sub-zero temperatures of the early morning were expected to moderate to the low twenties, with bitter assistance from a cloudless sky and bright sunshine. Annie jokingly called it a *Tropical Heat Wave.* Alex knew better, however, he was happy to have his Ray-Ban sunglasses in the glove box. The snow-covered countryside was blinding bright. He was hoping to make it past Cleveland and perhaps as far as Columbus, Ohio. He knew his wife traveled well and hoped his two daughters would be able to withstand the long ride without trouble. Regardless, he realized it would be necessary to make additional stops, if only to relieve boredom.

Two hours later, between Buffalo, New York and Erie, Pennsylvania, lunchtime was fast approaching. Underneath the long hood, the big engine purred in a smooth, sweet rumble. Annie easily found a Top 40 powerhouse on the radio, *1520 WKBW, Buffalo.* Dave 'Baby' Cortez' *The Happy Organ* filled the inside of the Packard. Alex raised his eyes to the rearview mirror and gazed at the two young girls in the back seat. They were looking out the windows, bobbing their heads to the rock and roll beat on the radio. He nudged Annie with his elbow and gave his head a nod toward the girls. She got the silent message and turned her head slowly.

Sarah let her opinion be known, "I like the music this car plays, Daddy!"

Karen excitedly echoed, "Me, too, Daddy!"

The newness of their new family sharpened Alex and Annie's senses. That one little word, *daddy*, caused a tug on their emotions that was felt deep within their hearts. Of all the things that occurred over the past three days, that morning's events in Rochester would be remembered forever. After Karen and Sarah Dobbs' belongings were finally loaded into the trunk of the Packard, and the girls said goodbye to the Rutherford family, the reality of it all began to slowly swirl around Alex and Annie. When the twin sisters had settled into the back seat of the car and waved out the back window, the whirlpool of emotion grew. The house on Erie Station Road disappeared behind them in the frozen air and the only life in the universe was seated inside the cream yellow Patrician. The realization that their lives had been radically altered struck home. Everything: the hours they spent with the lawyer, the letter from Katherine Dobbs, their initial meeting with Karen and Sarah, the family dinner at the Holiday Inn, all combined, could not come close to the emotions they were feeling now.

It was real now. Their daughters' presence in their lives was no longer a fleeting possibility, a concept, or an abstract thought. They were real. The life path of Alexander and Maryanne was forever altered by unforeseen circumstances. Four lives were conjoined, molded together by the actions of two people, seven and a half years earlier and half a world away. Lives were wound together by the corkscrew turns of fate itself.

And like the seemingly endless ribbons of black asphalt and poured concrete that lay ahead of them, the final outcome, the ultimate destination, lay somewhere just beyond the horizon. The previous night in bed, under the warm blankets of the Holiday Inn, Annie told her husband: "The best roadmap is love. The best route is to follow the faith of those you love and those who love you."

In Erie, the parking lot of Howard Johnson's restaurant drew them in for an encore visit. It was the first meal they would share alone and together, as a family.

Sarah had a question. "Do you think they have spaghetti?"

"Put Your Head On My Shoulder."

Sunday morning, January 10, 1960
Cincinnati, Ohio

The day before, they were able to travel just over four hundred miles and went as far as Columbus, Ohio. Already, there had been many lessons learned and old habits altered. Annie and Alex were unexpectedly given new life roles as parents. The night before was the first time they secured a motel room with two beds. They were able to unwind for about a half hour with the melodies of the *Lawrence Welk Show* before it was bedtime. Immediately afterward, they discovered that *Ipana* was not the favorite toothpaste, and nighttime prayers are mandatory. Annie and Alex sat on the edge of their bed as the girls, almost in unison, prayed for *Mommy in Heaven* and asked blessings for *our Mommy and Daddy here now*. Lives were altered during the preceding week: sideways, backward, forward, up, down, and every which way to Sunday.

176

A mere five hundred miles away from Rochester meant a temperature swing of forty degrees. They awoke to warmer temperatures, brilliant sunshine, and two young girls eager to get on the way to Florida. A *Standard Oil* service station sat adjacent to the *Columbus Family Restaurant* and *Snooze Inn Motel*. Alex dropped off Annie and the girls, fueled up the Packard, arranged for the postponed oil change and a car wash. A clean car seems to run smoother than a dirty one. Perhaps the road salt, grime, and the brutal cold of winter can hinder the spark in the cylinders, the oil in the crankcase, and the very essence of a gasoline engine.

After breakfast and back on the road again, Annie sat in the back seat with the girls, one on each side. She read several of the Little Golden Books with them, starting with *The Little Red Hen* and ending with the *Animals of Farmer Jones*. Alex felt an inexplicable tingle within him when he glanced at Annie, Karen and Sarah in the rearview mirror. His wife was embellishing the little stories with explanations, descriptions and comments of her own. Annie discovered that the girls knew quite a few of the words. They had started first grade only four months ago, and already could read simple sentences.

For a few moments, he allowed his thoughts to drift back to Sasebo, Japan, and the months spent with Lieutenant Katherine Dobbs. Had Katy hadn't kept her secret, Maryanne Dahl would still be in Appleton, Wisconsin.

Glancing at his family in the mirror, he was deeply enamored with his wife and the decisions that they have made together.

Alex had altered the route home on the suggestion of a filling station attendant in Cleveland. On the trip north, he stayed close to US Route 19 and the new sections of Interstate 75. This time, the fellow in Cleveland suggested he drive further west on US Route 42 and US 25 from Columbus. The advice was golden. On the outskirts of Cincinnati, a brand-new

Interstate 71 stretched out ahead of them. It meant a fast, smooth, and safe ride through Kentucky, Tennessee and the new Interstate 65 into Alabama. Alex held Nashville as the destination for the day. An overnight there and they could easily finish the trip through Alabama south on US 31 and arrive in Chumuckla on Monday. The Packard seemed to purr, longing for the carport at Straight Eight Farm. The chrome cormorant on the hood held its wings high and was proudly winging its way due South.

They stopped for lunch in Elizabethtown, Kentucky, half an hour from Louisville. *The Super Chicken* restaurant presented the twins' first experience with deep fried chicken, French fries and *Mountain Dew*. It was a good one; their meals disappeared with only sticky fingers and catsup splatter as the leftovers. Conveniently, a *J.C. Penney* department store was located in the shopping plaza directly behind the restaurant. The previous night, after Karen and Sarah were asleep and they were getting ready for bed, Alex mentioned to Annie a shopping trip was required. He realized that pajamas were a modest requirement for Annie and himself, and it would be necessary to stop somewhere to purchase a pair. The girls could also use a pair of Keds and new pajamas themselves. They purchased two pair of flannel, animal-print pajamas with feet attached for the girls. The new parents light-heartedly arguably complained that they both suffered from cold feet and never had the chance to own a pair. When Alex asked if the girls thought he should get feet pajamas too, Karen spoke matter-of-factly, "They don't make daddy pee-jays with feet or mommy pee-jays with feet. There is no such thing." Little golden moments like that were making Alex and Annie keenly aware of new feelings. The night before, during their pillow talk, they shared how their emotional attachment to the girls had strengthened since their meeting and was continually growing stronger. The unconditional love, the totality of commitment and the pure innocence of

Karen and Sarah were enriching their lives beyond expectation. Annie and Alex became able to discern who was who by a few little nuances. Karen had a giggle of her own and Sarah's smile created its own special dimples. But if they remained quiet and stoic, it was impossible still. Annie explained that she had confidence she could correctly identify them before too long and the sisters would not be the *Doublemint gum* twins forever. Alex wasn't so sure.

After lunch and J.C. Penney, Alex gassed up the car and headed south again. It was half past one and Nashville was less than a hundred and fifty miles down the road. The brand-new pavement stretched over rolling hills toward the southern horizon. They would be able to get to bed early that night and get a good night's rest before the last leg of their road trip. The *Galvin* dashboard radio was tuned to *650 WSM*, Nashville. Webb Pierce was lamenting, *"I Ain't Never."* Alex checked the backseat in the mirror. Annie's eyes were closed, with her head off-kilter and leaning to one side. Karen had her head on Annie's lap and Sarah leaned on her shoulder. Alex turned the volume low. Rolling down the new Interstate, the miles were flying by. The tires hummed.

"Tallahassee Lassie."

Monday afternoon, January 11, 1960
Santa Rosa County, Florida

The previous day they drove as far as Franklin, Tennessee, about half an hour beyond Nashville. Their arrival at the *West End Motel* was early enough to enjoy a quiet, unhurried meal at the *Rusty Rooster* restaurant next door. *The Ed Sullivan Show* and *The Dinah Shore Chevrolet Showcase* provided the evening's entertainment within the cramped quarters of the motel room. The children realized they would be travelling to, and arriving at their new home the next day, and were understandably anxious and fidgety. The *"how much longer will it be until we get there"* question was asked innumerable times. Annie answered each time with golden patience. Despite the excitement, they fell asleep quickly and slept throughout the night. At first light, however, they were firing on all cylinders and ready to go.

They made excellent time through Alabama, even though the only completed sections of Interstate 65 were twenty or fifty-mile sections around the cities of Birmingham and Montgomery. The old US Route 31 ran straight, smooth, and true, enabling good travel to Florida. The southern sun pushed the temperature up into the mid-sixty-degree range. The twins asked Annie why there wasn't any snow, and whatever could the children do without making snowballs or snowmen. They had genuine concern about the reality of *no snow*. Annie reassured them there was plenty to do without the cold white stuff. "For example, you can blow bubbles, fly a kite, play with a squirt gun, or ride a bicycle just about anytime you like."

An urgent question came from the back seat. "Are you going to buy all those things for us, Daddy?"

Sarah immediately announced her main concern, "How about Santa? How does he get around without snow?"

Annie smiled and answered both questions. "You girls are going to get a lot of new things, but it is all going to take a little bit of time. For one thing, I know we need to go shopping tomorrow for groceries. And Santa, well, he has wheels on his sleigh when he flies around down here. I have seen them myself."

Karen and Sarah's personalities opened up. With every mile, the girls were becoming more and more comfortable with Annie and Alex. Their mannerisms and expressions of emotion became more open and fearless. Annie and Alex were deeply affected by Sarah and Karen's curiosity, innocence, honesty, and their unquestioning, undoubting trust and love.

Annie and Alex both knew that the questions the girls would ask were only beginning. Plenty more would follow, all with countless consequences, answers, solutions and conclusions. Inside the Packard were four lives that were abruptly joined together just four days earlier with decisive life-long effects on each of them.

When they crossed the Alabama-Florida state line, Alex announced they were only twenty miles from home. With germane irony, Freddie ('Boom Boom') Cannon was wailing *Tallahassee Lassie* on the radio. The girls were antsy, curious and attentive. They moved forward to the end of the seat, hanging with both hands to the back of the front seat and glaring out the windshield.

Karen gave her observation, "All I see is grass! Where are all the houses where people live?"

Annie turned halfway around. "You will see some houses pretty soon. And of course, there is grass, and lots of it. That's what the horses eat, you know: grass, hay and some oats." She turned her attention back to Alex. "We need to stop at the EZ Shop for some milk, Alex. And some bread, too. Anything else you can think of?"

"That should just about do it, Annie. At least for tonight. If we think of anything else, we can pick it up. I know tomorrow we'll be busy; that's for sure. We will certainly have some more shopping to do."

As they traveled down the road, heading for home and their looming lifestyle change, Alex and Annie discussed plans for the next day. A top priority was the purchase of beds, bedding and certainly, a cupboard full of child-friendly foods. The sleeping arrangements for the first night would be made later, when the time came, with any of the girls' concerns taken into consideration. The next few days would be full of introductions, discovery and exploration. A trip to the Milton school offices will also be high on the to-do list.

Just ahead, Louis and Hedy's home was coming into view. Annie pointed toward the house, "Our neighbors and friends live right there, girls. They have the two young boys I told you about. One is five and the other one is almost four, so they are younger than you, but they are good boys and fun to play with. And that building right there is where Daddy and I work. That's the business we own with Louis and Hedy."

Karen and Sarah strained and pulled themselves forward on the back of the seat once again and looked intently out the windows. They were searching for things that were more important. "Where's the horses?"

Alexander slowed the Packard, turned into the driveway and gave his trademark greeting of two short honks on the horn as he drove past the shop. "Here we are, girls. We're home. Keep watching, and you will see the horse barn and out-buildings. And then our house ... real soon."

Karen had to ask, "How come you beeped the horn, back there, Daddy?"

Annie turned around and answered, "That's what your Daddy does when he comes home. It's a signal. He always beeps the horn two times. When you hear that, then you know your Daddy is home."

Annie rolled her window down, stuck out her arm and pointed again, just as Alex tapped the Packard's horn another two times. "That yellow house, there, is where Renaldo, Theresa and their little boy Johnny live. And right up here ... right there ... the white house with the big porch and the swing ... and the blue trim ... that's our house. That's our house, girls."

The twins moved their heads side-to-side, eyes wide open, looking in each direction, and catching as much as they could.

"I see the horses, Karen. I see the horses!"

At the moment Alex put the car into 'park', Annie turned around and smiled at the two beaming faces in the back seat. "Do you girls want to walk over to the pasture and look at the horses?" She didn't have to wait for an answer. Both rear doors opened, two lively youngsters sprung to Annie, reached out and each took a hand. Alex opened the trunk and stood beside the car, watching them walk toward the barn and paddock. When they reached the fence, Annie helped the girls, one by one, to a seat on the top rail. With her arms around their waists, she pointed to the horses with her fingers. Alex could hear her identify each one by name for the twins. They immediately picked their favorite: Poko, the new filly. Clarence, the Bluetick, stood close, his tail wagging excitedly and shoved his head onto Annie's legs. It appeared that the sisters would settle into their new lifestyle easily and quickly.

Renaldo appeared from around the corner of the barn, driving the Ford 9N tractor and towing the hay wagon. He spotted Annie and the girls, gave them a tip of his straw-colored Stetson and parked next to the Packard. He looked curiously toward Annie and greeted Alex. "Happy to see you home, Mister Alex! Everything is fine here, patrón: the horses, everything. We have company, I see."

Alex realized this was only the beginning of the explanations and introductions. "Renaldo, come on over with me and I will introduce you to the newest additions to our family." Walking toward Annie, Karen, and Sarah, Alex could not explain it, but a new sensation came over him. He was extremely proud of all three of them. He had a beaming smile. His chest was churning with emotion.

"I Want To Walk You Home."

Tuesday, January 12, 1960
Straight Eight Farm, Chumuckla, Florida

After the Packard was unpacked and all the suitcases, cardboard boxes and paper sacks unloaded, the entire evening was spent showing the girls around the house, the farm and introducing them to Louis, Hedy, Renaldo, Teresa and the three young boys. Alex and Annie later admitted to each other that their homecoming was the most stressful part of the entire trip. The reason was quite clear: introductions needed to be followed by factual explanations, and there was no simple explanation. The cold, hard facts, and plain truth can be demandingly burdensome.

When bedtime came, it was welcomed by everyone, and especially appreciated by Annie and Alex. Sarah and Karen Dobbs spent the first night in their new home sleeping in Alex and Annie's bed. Annie was relegated to the couch and Alex set up a makeshift bed on the floor next to her. He used chair cushions and the seat pad from the porch swing, in much the same manner as they did on their first night together six years ago, before they were married. It was good to be home, and everyone slept well. Karen was the first one up and stood quietly in the living room next to the sofa where Annie lay half-asleep. She opened her eyes. "What's the matter, Sweetie? Are you all right? Is everything okay?" Alex awoke and sat up on his bed of chair cushions.

"I forgot where the bathroom is." Her sister Sarah appeared in the doorway. Annie smiled and escorted the girls down the hall.

In a few minutes, she returned and sat next to Alex. They smiled and shared a kiss. "I'll start breakfast, Alex. Pancakes should work. You can do what you need to do in the barn, and we'll eat in about a half hour. Hot coffee and hotcakes."

They sat for a moment longer, held hands and wore contented smiles. The girls finished in the bathroom, peeked into the parlor and scurried back to bed. They didn't speak.

Alex broke the stillness, stood and pulled his trousers right over his pajamas. He slipped on his boots and denim jacket, gave Annie another kiss on the cheek and was out the door. She didn't know exactly what prompted her recollection, but Annie remembered Dinah Shore singing *There'll Be Some Changes Made*. She rose from Alex's makeshift bed, put the chair cushions back and folded the bed linens. She was very happy.

Half an hour later, they were all seated around the Formica-top kitchen table. No one took note of the fact they were sharing their first meal as a family, at home, together. Everything was new for everyone. Every experience was fresh and shiny. Every moment was a pleasure of innocence.

Prompted by the pancake breakfast that Annie put together, the sisters discussed the story of *Little Black Sambo*. After some clarification from Alex, it was decided that it was quite impossible for tigers to turn into butter, no matter how fast they ran around a tree. Annie assured the girls that the butter she used for the pancakes was purchased at the grocery store, just like the *Log Cabin* pancake syrup. There was no *melted tiger* involved. There were a lot of giggles and laughter that morning. Alex and Annie shared several private glances, each realizing and appreciating the new treasures they had.

After breakfast, the girls helped Annie compile a shopping list to replace the butter and several other items deemed necessary for the continuity of life according to six-year-olds. Some of the things that made the list were *Peter Pan* peanut butter, *Welch's* grape jelly, *Trix* cereal, *Bosco* chocolate syrup, *Chef Boy-Ar-Dee* spaghetti and *Jell-O* dessert mix. Annie wrote it all down and commented to Alex, "We see this stuff on TV and don't pay any attention to it. But the kids do, don't they? I mean, this is amazing, Alex. The kids know all this from television commercials!"

As if to prove a point, Sarah added, "We're supposed to pay attention, right? And they even say that *Trix are for kids*."

Alex looked across the table to Annie, and they shared another smile. "You're right, Sarah. It's always good to pay attention."

Annie put the finished shopping list into her purse along with the twin's birth certificates, immunization cards, school reports and her checkbook. Alex surveyed the bedroom that the girls would be using, measured the windows and got a general idea of the room's size. By nine o'clock, they were on the road again, but for local trips only this time. The plan was to stop first at the Santa Rosa School District offices in Milton, then *Estes Furniture, Horne's Department Store* and, finally, the Piggly Wiggly market.

The Santa Rosa School District Superintendent, Roger Morgenfeld, reluctantly agreed that Sarah and Karen could delay the start of school until the following Monday. Alex and Annie asked for the brief delay to help the children become accustomed to their new situation and new home. They would take a ten-minute bus ride to Chumuckla Elementary, in Jay, just down the road from home. The twins were enrolled as Sarah Elizabeth and Karen Ann Throckmorton. The girls remained very still, attentive and quiet in the polished rock maple chairs of the administration office, their hands folded on their laps, patiently sitting and waiting as various forms were filled out. Annie kept an eye on the girls, glancing at them occasionally and giving them a warm smile every so often. When everyone was out of the building, in the parking lot and walking toward the Packard, Karen spoke up, "You see, Sarah, we got a brand-new last name now because we have a daddy. We have Daddy's name now."

Annie took the opportunity to elaborate and turn the name change into a positive development. "You are right, Karen. You and Sarah have a new last name, but you still have your other name, *Dobbs*. It's still there, and it will always be there. You both got a new name, that's all. Dobbs is still there, it's just in the middle. You have an extra middle name."

The new name was not a concern to the sisters. Sarah proved the point, "You need to teach us how to spell and write *Throckmorton*, Mommy."

It was immediately clear to Annie that her apprehension was not warranted. "We'll do that when we get home. It's easy to learn." Annie opened and held the back door of the Packard for the girls. They eagerly climbed into the back seat, ready for the next adventure. The twins were keenly aware that new beds, blankets and a visit to the grocery store were on the list of purchases and events to come.

Estes Furniture promised late afternoon delivery of two twin beds, mattresses, two three-drawer dressers and an oval area rug. Bed linens, blankets, pillows and red gingham tieback curtains from Horne's were packed inside the trunk along with the bags of groceries from Piggly Wiggly. The food store was the high point of the trip for the girls. They giggled at the name and fell in love with the pig caricature. The morning flew by and after burgers and fries at *Freddie's Drive In*, it was time to head for home.

FIVE: A KODAK PHOTO WORTH 1000 WORDS

"Sea Of Love."

Sunday, January 17, 1960

The biggest chunk of the past week's experiences was a wondrous time of unconditional love and boundless trust. The pristine innocence and youthful curiosity of Karen and Sarah completely captivated Alex and Annie. Their hearts were warmed soul deep. On the home front, Annie and Alex were struggling with twin identification. Sarah had the new front tooth, Karen had the deeper dimples, but without a wide smile, there was no obvious distinction between them. Doctor Heinemann explained to Annie that birth parents have an edge when it comes to twins and she and Alex would require a little more time to tell the girls apart. Until that time came, Annie decided not to dress them in conventional 'twin clothing', and daily inform Alex which twin wore what.

On the downside, home and away from home, there were occasions when their lives seemed to be under an emotional medieval siege or onslaught; complete with brutal Mongol hoards bearing burning torches, waves of arrows and hurtling projectiles from trebuchets. Annie and Alex were peppered with endless questions and introductions, from not only the people closest to them, but also casual acquaintances like Henry the mailman, Pete the grocer and even Roscoe the gas jockey at the *Texaco* station. At times, the questions bordered on interrogation. The twins remained unflappable and paid little or no attention to the bevy of especially nosey adults poking into their lives.

There were plenty of little accomplishments over the next few days. Alex painted the girls' bedroom a rose mauve with sage green on the chair rail and trim. The green gingham curtains and the multi-colored area rug that Annie bought gave the room a warm glow. She enlisted the twin's help to clean and varnish a wooden tack box from the barn. It had become too small for its original purpose and was recycled into a toy chest. Alex threw two lengths of braided hemp rope over a large extended branch of the Live Oak in the front yard. He fashioned a seat out of a piece of 2 x 10 lumber as the girls curiously watched him hang their first swing. Annie gave swinging lessons interwoven with periods of childish laughter and full-blown giggle sessions. It was also discovered that much of the clothing the girls brought with them from New York was either too small or unsuitable for Florida. Snowsuits, galoshes, and parkas are not often seen in Santa Clara County. Annie made several trips to Horne's, supplementing the girls' dresser drawers and closet. On Friday evening, when the stores were open until six, Alex and Annie drove to Pensacola with the twins.

Sitting just outside the gates of the Naval Air Station, *Simon's Sporting Goods* offered a wide selection of outdoor diversions. Hiking, camping, baseball, tennis, and football were not what the girls considered high priority. Their father had something else in mind, but children possess an uncanny ability to cut through the fluff of a well-planned surprise. Somehow, the twins knew exactly what Alex had planned. He had to fulfill Annie's promise that instead of making snowmen in New York, they could ride a bicycle at any time in Florida. Sarah boldly spoke up, "Are you going to buy us bikes, Daddy?"

Two *Huffy Convertibles*, with training wheels and rear steps, were loaded into the trunk. With only one-color scheme, red and white, the identification issue needed to be solved. Long colorful tassels, plastic streamers, were attached to the handlebar grips. Karen selected bright pink and Sarah picked out purple ones. Of course, Alex added round chrome bicycle bells. Life was grand. With two new Huffys sticking out of the Packard's trunk, the twins were so impatient to try their new bicycles that they declined a stop at the *Mister Swiss* soft-serve custard stand on the way home. By the time they got back to the ranch, it was dark, and Alex turned on the white porcelain, reflector-dome, yard light over the barn door. After a little assistance, both girls were cycling freely on the gravel and sand driveway. Clarence followed close behind them, with an occasional yip and yap. The bells were ringing and the streamers flying. Life was a celebration; bedtime came all too soon.

When Alex would be at the shop, in the fields, or yard with Renaldo, Annie spent hours with the twins that first week. They read stories, created countless pieces of Frigidaire art, played Candyland and Pik-Up-Stix. Outside, Annie scratched a new hopscotch pattern onto the driveway almost daily. Karen and Sarah enthusiastically managed to put several miles on their new Huffy Convertibles. In the side yard, the girls discovered the wondrously mysterious, round, silver gazing globe neatly perched in the center of a raised bed that fills with Black-eyed Susan blossoms during spring and summer. Annie showed Sarah and Karen their distorted reflections and how the entire world appeared before them within the mirrored circle of infinity. The sisters were mesmerized even more when Annie promised, "At night, in the summertime, you can see the Moon, the Milky Way and every star that twinkles in the whole wide universe."

On Wednesday afternoon, during a rain shower, Annie brought out one of the photograph albums Emily Rutherford packed with the girls' belongings. The sisters excitedly sat on the sofa beside Annie. The matte black pages were full of snapshots neatly arranged and affixed to the book with little black adhesive corners. Underneath each photo, there was a brief description of whom, when and where it was. Written with a fountain pen in white ink, the handwriting was clear and steady. Each page was neatly presented and even impressive. Many of the photographs did not include the twins and consisted of work-related snapshots taken at the Kodak facilities.

Seeing images of their mother, it wasn't long before Karen and Sarah became emotional. Annie decided to look at the pictures some other time, either alone or with her husband. She promptly closed the album and put it away. Oreos and milk calmed the storm.

Annie called her sister in Green Bay, Wisconsin, early on Tuesday morning, two days after they returned from New York. Beth acknowledged that she was waiting for the call and was antsy with curiosity.

"Well, Beth, our trip to Rochester, New York ended up like this; Alex and I got a whole new family. Just like that Jell-O instant pudding that they advertise on TV; empty the box, pour in the milk, heat it up, and *voila*! Instant family. I mean, I just find out that I'm pregnant, and wham-oh! Instant family." Annie explained it all in detail, and her sister hung on every word. "But, after all is said and done, I would not change anything. I have to say, Beth, these two sisters are the most charming, loveable, warm and caring kids on the face of the Earth. I love them to bits. And Alex proved how big of a man he is. He accepted those two girls without question."

The conversation lasted for two cups of coffee. She eventually garnered the nerve to ask for Beth's advice. "How should I handle this with Mama?"

"The only thing to do is shoot right from the hip, Sister mine. You know Mama will, so be prepared to dodge those bullets. So you just need to be honest, and don't hold anything back. What's the use? Let it all out. Stand your ground, Annie. You already know how Mama is going to react. She's going to come at you with both barrels. You know what's coming … so you can either fight fire with fire, or just stand there helplessly and duck every shot she takes. Personally, I would wear armor plate and let all the nasty comments fall to the floor, kick them to the side and ignore them. But maybe Mama will surprise you, and actually listen and be nice."

"You and I both know that ain't going to happen, Beth. But you are right. She's our mother, and she has to know. I got to tell her; there's no way to get around that. If I weren't pregnant, I'd pour myself a stiff drink before that telephone call. It's a darn shame that I am an adult, and I am still scared to death of what my mother might say. It's just not right. And after I call her, she will call you and run me over the coals all over again. I know she will."

Beth tried to calm her sister's nerves. "Sister, whatever Mama says will not change your love for Alex or the girls. Remember that. Mama has made that bed of hers countless times over the years and she continues to sleep in it. She must be comfortable with herself. Just be thankful you make your own bed now. Tell her the news, and let it be. You know all this already, Annie. You don't need my opinion."

She was right. "Thanks, Beth." After Annie hung up the telephone, she made peanut butter and jelly sandwiches for lunch. Just being around Karen and Sarah, watching them kick their feet under the kitchen table, make their plans for the afternoon and laugh about what they did earlier in the morning, lifted Annie's spirit like a kite.

After lunch, Annie made the dreaded call to Vermont. Just under three minutes later, it was over. When Annie hung up the ivory wall telephone, a wry smile appeared, and she nodded in self-affirmation. The conversation was like a macabre passage from an Edgar Allen Poe story. She sat at the kitchen table and looked out at the girls riding their bicycles. Watching the girls, Annie knew it would not be long before the training wheels would be coming off. After talking with her mother, Annie's thoughts were going in every direction. The conversation pulled a cloak of melancholy over her usually sunny disposition. She thought

192

of a back-and-forth gab session she had with her grandfather, Sven Dahl, many, many summers ago on his farm back in Fond du Lac, Wisconsin. She asked why the grass was so green next to the silos on the pasture side of the cowbarn. Annie will never forget his answer: *"Bullshit, Maryanne, bullshit."* Remembering Grandpa Dahl's unvarnished honesty, she nodded in affirmation and acknowledged that her grandfather was absolutely correct. So many of the answers to life's deepest mysteries are quite obvious. Annie's spirit got the lift it needed just by watching Karen and Sarah racing around the yard on their new bicycles. Annie poured a glass of orange juice, turned on the radio and sat on the sofa, watching the twins.

Later that same day, after dinner, Alexander telephoned his father in Jacksonville. Jovita relayed the message that he was still at work and was putting in long hours on the job lately. Alex thought nothing of it at the time, but after he hung up, he questioned it with Annie. "Do you think he could be back in Cuba, Annie? I mean, Castro is raising cane in Havana. The whole place is still in chaos. Some say it's going to Hell in a hand basket without any outside help."

"I doubt it, Alex. He said he was done travelling."

As it turned out, two hours later his father returned his call. Nicholas explained that he had been very busy at work for the last few months. Alex did not ask any questions, but instead, he let the cat out of the bag. "You are a grandfather, Old Man, and sooner than you expected. Two girls. You have twin granddaughters, six and a half years old."

Alex then began a concise account of their trip to New York. He detailed the reason why, explained his romantic union with a Navy lieutenant named Katherine Dobbs from Syracuse, and the surprising ultimate result of an immediately larger family. Alex did not embellish the story and gave only a bare-bones outline. His father listened and did not interrupt as Alex dropped his load of bricks. After the news, there was an understandable moment of silence. Nicholas roughly cleared his throat over the phone. "No shit? Really?"

Alex pictured his father standing motionless, holding the telephone, agape and thunderstruck.

"I'm happy for you and Annie, Alex. I am so glad this tragic incident turned out so well. It is utterly amazing how things can happen so many miles away, so many years in the past, and end up changing your life. This world is getting smaller with every day that passes. Things happen and create results that we just never see coming. We are blind-sided so often in life. It's incredible."

The telephone call was short on two fronts: length of conversation and expression of emotion. Nicholas made plans with Alex for the upcoming weekend, January 23 and 24. Nicholas, Joey and the kids would arrive on Saturday, spend the night at the *Tuck Inn*, and leave on Sunday. His father said he looked forward to meeting the twins and he would call to confirm the trip. Alex put the receiver down and walked with Annie to the sofa.

"That was a strange conversation, Annie girl. The Old Man didn't get enthusiastic like I thought he might have. His reaction was simply matter-of-fact." They sat in silence for a few minutes, holding hands.

"Maybe your father wasn't overly excited, but I am sure your conversation with him was not anything like the one I had with my mother, Alex. It was a dandy. It was like tiptoeing across a bed of hot coals. I knew what to expect, but my mother never ceases to amaze me."

It was Sunday night and Allen Funt's *Candid Camera* was on the television. Alex put his arm around Annie. It was her turn to be reflective. "It seems like the only one who got emotional and happy about our baby news was my sister

Beth. I mean, you just said that your father didn't seem overwhelmed by the news of our two inherited children. I know my mother certainly was not. You and I both know how she is. That woman is a grizzly bear. She can virtually eat her young with words."

"Maybe it has something to do with age, Annie."

Annie thought about what Grandpa Dahl would say, *"Bullshit."* She kept it to herself, gritted her teeth and shook her head. "It has nothing to do with age, Alex. It's a complete, total, disconnect from reality. It's a withdrawal from love and affection. That's what it is. Plain and simple."

"My Heart Is An Open Book."

Friday afternoon, January 22, 1960

Annie was resting on the sofa with one of Katy Dobbs' photograph albums on her lap. She had spent the better part of her afternoon looking through one of the two albums that Emily Rutherford had given them. Her thoughts drifted away, and her gaze wandered outdoors. She placed a protective hand over the life in her belly. She could see about half the herd through the windows. She set her glass of orange juice on the end table and allowed her imagination to drift out to the pasture. It was a glorious day; blue skies, bright sun and April temperatures. The windows were open, allowing the warm breeze to push the sounds of calling mockingbirds into the front room. From Pensacola's top-forty radio station, Hank Ballard was telling the world it was *Finger Poppin' Time*. While Annie was home and not doing the accounts at the shop, she always listened to either the living-room Philco radio, or the *RCA* in the kitchen. Music filled the silent little cracks in her daily life.

Annie glanced over to the bold brass clock on the buffet, and back down to the photo album. The girls would be home from school before too long, coming up the driveway with Alexander, packed in the front seat of the '55 Chevy pickup. When they got off the school bus, the girls walked to the engine shop and met their father. They started a brand-new pattern that so far, was working out well. Annie got up from the couch and put the book of photos away in the buffet drawer on top of the twin's birth certificates. She set it in the drawer carefully, on top of everything else and left it open to the pages where she had left off.

She walked to the kitchen and finished preparations for dinner. There was meatloaf in the oven and a pot of potatoes bubbling on the back burner. She stood at the stove, stirring a pan of gravy made from the meatloaf drippings. She was far away, lost in her thoughts. Annie was quite unaware of her swaying gyrations to the music. She was even tapping her stirring spoon to Wilbert Harrison's *Kansas City*.

The screen door squeaked open. Karen and Sarah rushed into the house ahead of Alex. In perfect harmony, the twins announced, "We're home, Mommy!" and scurried into the kitchen. Alex held onto the brass handle and let the door close quietly. The girls plopped their notebooks, *Annie Oakley* and *Sky King* lunch boxes on the table, and flung their arms around Annie's thighs. Alex entered the kitchen yards behind his eager daughters.

"I could smell your world-famous meatloaf from the steps."

"You guessed it ... now, everybody, get washed up, and we can have dinner. Alex, please turn off the radio in the parlor for me. Thanks."

He walked over to his wife, placed a hand on her hip and landed a gentle kiss on her lips, "Will do, Annie girl."

The girls had good appetites, were not fussy eaters, and did not protest the presence of any food. They were accustomed to condensed or even powdered milk in New York, but Annie easily effected the conversion to farm fresh milk. She mixed the evaporated concoction with Milton Dairy's whole milk. Gradually, over a five-day period, she was able to eliminate the twin's preference for the watered-down taste of the canned or boxed catastrophes.

During the meal, Annie's thoughts continued to wander away from the kitchen. The meatloaf, gravy, mashed potatoes, and *Del Monte* creamed corn she prepared for dinner was about as All-American as anyone could get. Complete with the blue gingham tablecloth, *Sears-Roebuck* ironstone dinnerware and *Oneida* stainless cutlery, the meal could be a cover story in next month's *McCall's*. She glanced around the table at her husband, Karen, and Sarah. She smiled, gently placed her left hand on her belly and re-loaded her fork with creamed corn. Annie was content and held self-confirmation that life was grand on Straight Eight Farm. She was determined to do everything in her power to keep it that way. Nothing would ever spoil this piece of Paradise. Annie would not allow it.

The girls readily gave Annie whatever help they could after family meals; obviously, a behavior pattern they had acquired from their mother. They assisted in small ways, stacking or storing clean dishes, glasses and utensils, all while managing not to get too far under foot. Annie washed and Alex dried. Karen and Sarah considered themselves an important part of the team.

When they finished up, Alex went out to the barn for evening chores: mucking stalls, turnout, and cleaning water buckets. It was a labor of love. This evening there was a little more labor than usual. Tonight's unseasonable forecast of cold weather meant that more food needed to be available to the horses. Alex and Reynaldo took bales of timothy and pans of oats out to pasture. Poko would spend the night in the stall.

Annie reminded the girls that it was Friday, and *Walt Disney Presents* would be on television. "After TV, you girls need to take your baths and get to bed. Tomorrow, your Grandpa and Grandma are coming. And that means you will get to meet Roberta and Hector. It will be a fun day, girls!"

Friday also meant the weekend homework project for Miss Anderson's first grade class. This week's subject matter was farm animals, giving the girls a bit of an advantage. Annie brought out a few sheets of white typing paper, normally used for invoicing at the shop, and the big *forty-eight* box of *Crayola* crayons. It was a foregone conclusion that the twins would be drawing horses and a Bluetick coonhound. Annie folded the tablecloth and cleared the table. The young artists were at work for nearly an hour and a half.

A pattern of life was developing. The young girls effectively altered two adult lives, smoothly molding Annie and Alex into parenting roles in the abbreviated time constraint of two weeks. Their willingness to help, buoyant personalities and cheerful disposition made the shift appear effortless. The lives of Karen and Sarah were suddenly plunged into Alex and Annie's world by unpredictable and fickle circumstance. The consequence was a harmonious family unit born of unquestioning love.

Alex finished *horsing around*, as he called it, took his shower, switched on the *Huntley Brinkley Report* and got comfortable in his recliner. He had a bottle of Viking lager on the end table. Annie sat thumbing through her Redbook magazine and both girls were in the tub enjoying all the fun that a *Calgon* bubble bath brings. Annie closed the magazine and dropped it into the rack next to her chair. "When I was helping the girls with their schoolwork, I told them that we are having company tomorrow, your father and Joey. I had a little bit of a problem calling Joey *grandma*, but I managed to get the word out. I mean, she's nearly our age, Alex. And what are Roberta and Hector? Golly, Alex ... Karen and

Sarah have an aunt and an uncle younger than they are! So, I just referred to them by name. Do you think that's all right?"

Alex got up, walked over to the television and turned the volume all the way down. He spoke as he settled back into the chair. "I think that's perfect, Annie. You handled it exactly the way I would have. Kids don't really hang too much on a name or a title. It's important who grandpa and grandma are, but titles don't matter. Look at all the kids who refer to their grandmothers as *nanna, granny, grammy, mimi,* whatever. And grandfathers can be *pappy, umpa, papa, gramps*, anything. Karen and Sarah just need to know who they are. They can give them whatever title they want. And think about this *Twilight Zone* brain teaser, Annie: Roberta and Hector are my sister and brother. I am still not able to wrap my mind around that."

Annie nodded and Alex continued, "Anyway ... I got some good news today. We may even need to hire another mechanic because we are going to be busy. The Navy accepted the bid we submitted to them back in October and awarded us the contract for refurbishing some Patrol Torpedo, PT boat engines ... left over from the World War. I cannot imagine what they plan on doing with them and I really don't want to know. Those speedboats saw limited duty in Korea ... but get this, Annie: they have Packard engines. Big old V-12 Packards, 1200 horsepower each. I was just a kid when I first heard those big Packards roar in a boat race on the Detroit River. Me and the Old Man had fun that day. What a quirk of fate. Now I'm going to be working on that engine."

Annie was thoughtful, pensive. Alex detected her reflective mood. There was something on her mind, as if she was planning a surprise party. Alex knew his birthday was coming up in a few months; that had to be what was going on.

Annie's eyes moved around the room and over to her husband. "It's baffling how things happen sometimes, isn't it?" She stood, reached over and gently placed her hand on Alex's shoulder. "I'm going to get the girls out of the tub and into their pajamas. Then we can all watch Disney."

Alex got up from his recliner and turned the television volume up a notch. He took a drink of beer and continued to watch the nightly news. The Russians were once again test-launching long-range ballistic missiles, the US Space Program launched a monkey into orbit from Cape Canaveral and Senator John Fitzgerald Kennedy of Massachusetts, a Roman Catholic, said he was running for President. All was well with the world.

The girls scurried into the parlor just as *"goodnight, Chet; goodnight, David"* closed the nightly newscast. Their fuzzy pink slippers swished across the wood floor and onto the oval rug. Drying their hair in bath towels, Karen and Sarah plopped themselves onto the sofa. Annie sat between the girls, holding a hairbrush and waited patiently for them to finish. She had rolled up the shirtsleeves and pant legs of the girls' oversized *Peter Pan* pajamas. The big brass clock on the buffet brashly resonated eight o'clock. The unmistakable Disney theme song magically drew all eyes to the twenty-three-inch black and white screen. That night they aired a repeat of *The Story of Donald Duck*.

Alex would take an occasional peek up at the cartoon duck as he glanced through the *Pensacola News Journal* sports pages. He was looking for coverage of the Detroit Lions, Tigers, or Red Wings. There wasn't any, and seldom was. His hometown teams simply did not generate much print in any Florida newspaper, and ice hockey was completely unknown. After the sports pages, the want ads were the next best thing.

During Disney, Annie finished brushing out the twin's hair. She gave them a "mama bear" hug at the end of the show and followed them to the bedroom. After bedside prayers, Annie tucked the girls in, gave each one a little kiss and clicked on the night light. She and Alex decided that next week, they would begin Sunday school at First Presbyterian. When Karen asked what Annie and Alex would do while they were at class, it forced Annie to commit herself and husband to "big people's church". Children have the ability to effect change without direct intention. She stood at the partially closed door for a minute, watching them. She waited patiently until their active little bodies settled down. In a few minutes, she returned to the parlor, walked to the buffet table and brought out the photo album. She slid the twin's birth certificates behind the open pages of the book. Alex watched with curiosity. "Are we going to look at some photographs, Honey?"

She held the book under her arm, with a finger between the pages, marking her place. She sat on the sofa. "Yeah. Come on over and sit down. I found something this afternoon … something very interesting … something that will surprise you. It knocked my socks off when I found it today."

Alexander walked to the Admiral and switched it off. There was the usual small electric pop and snap, followed by the dissipating static and crackling of the cooling vacuum tubes. He took a spot next to his wife on the divan. They settled into the sofa. "What do we have here, Annie?" She reached to the adjacent table lamp, turned it on, and opened the album while holding it in place on her lap.

She turned to her husband and began, "I discovered something today that ... I think you will agree, is pretty darn interesting, so look closely. You can see that Katy neatly wrote a complete description under each photograph. She wrote down who it was, when it was and even where it was. She took very good pictures, too. But I suppose that's understandable. She worked for Kodak."

Alex leaned forward on the sofa and looked closer at the album. "I see that. It looks pretty thorough." Annie did not need to say any more. She did not need to point to a specific picture. Alex found it by himself. There was funeral parlor silence. There were three rows of pictures on each page and, as Annie detailed, each one was clearly labeled in white, handwritten script. On the right-hand page, in the second row, at the right end, was the photograph that captured all their attention. Alex blinked, leaned in and looked even closer. Annie watched her husband and waited for his reaction. His gaze was fixed on the picture. His pulse quickened, he blinked rapidly and quickly shifted his eyes from the photograph to his wife. They briefly looked at each other. Alex then shifted his attention back to the snapshot, shook his head and muttered under his breath. "Judas Priest. Judas H. Priest."

Pictured was a mixed group of several people around a large table with champagne glasses raised for a toast. It was covered in a white tablecloth, with flowers and hors d'oeuvres. In the middle of the photograph, and closest to the camera, stood a shapely, smiling, young woman wearing a ruffled white blouse under a snappy vest. She was grouped in front, with two men dressed in suit coats and ties. What must have been cameras, lenses, or camera parts sat behind them and beyond, down the length of the table. Directly underneath the snapshot, on the buffered black album page was written in white:

3-54, Nick T, me, Ted G, Research Park Party

Alex knew the woman in the foreground to be Katherine Dobbs. The identity of the man standing immediately to her right was obvious to both Annie and Alex. There was no doubt. It was Nicholas Throckmorton.

"I don't have to explain this to you, do I, Alex?"

He swallowed hard. He was speechless.

"When I first saw that picture Alex, my heart stopped, and my eyes locked into place. I couldn't look at anything else. I stared at that photograph until my eyes burned. My scalp tingled. It took a while for me to snap out of it. It was like I was hypnotized like they do on them TV shows. And after I broke free of my trance, I looked through the album again. Then, I quickly looked through the other book. That's the only picture of your father I could find, Alex. Your father has some explaining to do tomorrow. Don't you think? And hang onto your hat, I'm not finished yet. Not by a long shot."

Annie turned the page, pulled an address book from between the pages and handed it to her husband. "Remember this, Alex? This is your father's address and telephone number in Jacksonville. He wrote it down for me, years ago, when we first met. Do you remember that? It was the first time he and Joey were here, back in '55. It's right here in our address book and it's in your father's handwriting. Look how he wrote his name, with those curly-Q's. Take a good look at that and then I'll show you something else."

Without skipping a beat, Annie's fingers flashed through the pages of the photo album and brought out the Affidavit of Paternity. "I thought there was something fishy about your signature on this paper, Alex. Now I know. I want you to look closely at that signature ... now ... take a good, long look at your father's handwriting in the address book."

Alex was barely breathing, as if he had the wind knocked out of him. He held the birth document in one hand and the address book in the other. He looked at the book, the affidavit, and back to the address book again. He bit his lip and shook his head. Again, he uttered, "Judas Priest" and sat back into the sofa.

He looked at Annie. "This is unbelievable, Annie, unbelievable. This is akin to a *Ripley's Believe It Or Not* feature in the newspaper. Yeah, believe it or not!"

He did not say a word but got up from the sofa and went into the kitchen. He brought Annie a half glass of Rhine wine and set it on the end table next to her. Alex carried an empty glass to the buffet cabinet and poured three fingers of Old Crow. For the next five minutes, they sat without uttering a word. Annie sipped, and Alex swallowed.

"Well, Annie, there is one thing we know for sure. My skin was crawling for a minute there. I got the creeps. My head started to spin, and I was imagining a giant calendar and figuring out dates, months, and years. But, given the timeline, the Old Man cannot be the girls' father. I'm the father, without a doubt. What he was doing in Rochester in March of 1954, how the hell he knew Kate and how he signed that certificate of birth paper, are questions he will have to answer tomorrow. Just when I thought that things were getting all settled down ... and there weren't any more surprises ... then this party only got wilder, Annie. And here I am, dumb enough to believe that we were finished with all this crap."

"Your father has kept a lot of secrets from you over the years, Alex ... a lot of deep secrets. Lord only knows how many there were or if there are any more that he's keeping."

Alex's thoughts began spinning at light speed. "You know, Annie, now we know. Now I understand why he got so quiet when I told him we went to New York and came back with two kids. He knew. He knew it all along, and he didn't say a damn word. Not a single damn word. Not one. I wonder if we didn't find this picture, would he have ever said anything to us? That's the question I need to ask him. I am going to ask him flat out: when does the secret become more important than the family? He treated you and me like dirt ... like the horseshit I scrape off my boots. I mean, a secret like that; a secret about two little, innocent girls and he didn't say a damn thing. To me, that's just too damn much."

"That's the *Sixty-Four-Thousand Dollar Question*, Alex: 'When is the secret more important than the family?' They could have your father guest star on the next episode of that game show."

Annie had never seen her husband so agitated. He was flushed and looking forward, straight at the wall. "We cannot make a scene, Annie. We cannot make a scene in front of the girls. I will take him on the side and ask him in private. I have had it *up to here* with all his secrets, but I need to control myself. I need to be calm, cool and collected about this. I will get to the bottom of this. You can believe that. I will find out why." Alex finished his bourbon, walked over to the television and turned it on. Rod Serling was welcoming everyone to the *Twilight Zone*.

Alexander did not turn up the volume. He didn't need to. Their heads were too busy in thought to hear the television anyway.

Annie put the album and papers carefully back into the buffet drawer and switched off one of the table lamps. They sat on the sofa, their stocking feet resting on the coffee table. Alex put his arm around his wife. She leaned into her husband. "When is this roller coaster ride going to end, Annie?"

"When we get off. But I think we should stay on. That's just the way life is, Alex. It's a crazy ride. Life's one crazy ride ... all the way to the end. We need to hang on, that's all."

"Rumble."

Saturday, January 23, 1960

Annie and Alex awoke the next morning knowing that the day would be nerve-racking and the time leading up to Nick and Joey's arrival would pass agonizingly slow. While they didn't expect a harsh confrontation, the revelation of intentionally kept secrets is always a bit more than just awkward. Nick was no stranger to secrets. Alex and Annie were no strangers to his deception.

They knew it would be a busy morning, full of questions from two impatient little girls. During breakfast, the girls were exuberant over the impending introduction of grandparents into their young lives. They had known no other.

Although the sun quickly washed away the overnight frost, the chilly temperature alone was reason enough for the children to stay indoors. Saturday morning television showcased children's programming almost exclusively. *Captain Kangaroo* was followed by the adventures of a young boy and his horse, *Fury*. Karen and Sarah were fans of the show long before their move to Florida. Every day since they had arrived on the farm, Alex and Annie introduced them to the horses and explained the daily care horses need on a ranch. The sisters learned early on that interacting with a real, live horse is quite a bit different from the ponies portrayed on television. They discovered that adult help is required nearly every step of the way. Although their patience had been tested now and again, they seemed to have some understanding of the problems they faced, such as size and availability. Alex had yet to purchase riding helmets or a children's saddle, so the girls were eagerly awaiting their next trip to a tack shop. Alex and Annie became deeply impressed with the twins' rapid grasp of several equine terms and practices.

Just as the table clock sounded the twelve brassy clangs of noon, Alex came in from outside, pried off his boots at the bootjack and walked down the hall to wash up. The noise brought Karen and Sarah into the front room to look out the windows, just to check and be certain no one arrived without notice.

Annie announced lunch and the girls scurried into the kitchen ahead of their father. Hot tomato soup and bologna sandwiches were on the kitchen table. All morning, the twins waited patiently and listened intently for a car to pull into the driveway. Karen asked a question with significant forethought. "What if Grandpa sneaks in real quiet, like Santa?"

Alex looked across the table to his wife. Annie had a constrained ironic smile when she answered, "There is nothing sneaky about your grandpa, Karen. We will know when he gets here. Daddy and I are good at that. Your grandpa can't trick us." Her answer was sufficiently reassuring. Alex was grinning at Annie's winsome remark.

The sisters put on their jackets and went outdoors after lunch, switching from bicycle to swing and back again. It was now Alex and Annie's turn to wait for a car to come up the driveway. Alex washed and Annie dried the lunch and breakfast dishes, taking turns peeking out the kitchen window at the girls and the driveway. Whenever Nicholas made the trip from Jacksonville, he left about four in the morning, putting his arrival at the ranch right around noon. An emerald-green Oldsmobile should be arriving at any time. They did not have a long wait. Alex pulled the plug on the sink and Annie folded and hung up the dishtowel.

It was then they heard a big V8 rumble to a stop and checked out the window to the driveway.

Karen and Sarah left their bikes in front of the barn and scurried to the porch. The twins stood close and curiously watched the two children in the back seat of the car. Roberta and Hector stretched their necks, pushed up their heads, and peered over the seats of the Oldsmobile coupe. Joey was the first out of the vehicle, and held the door open for her children. Nicholas exited the car and all four started toward the house. Karen and Sarah rushed into the house announcing, "They're here!" Outside, Joey held her children by the hand and led them up the steps. Nicholas held the screen door open and let his family enter ahead of him. Inside the parlor there were handshakes, hugs, nods and curious looks from one child to another. The sofa quickly filled up with Nicholas, Joey and a sleepy Hector. The youngest was struggling to keep his eyes open, clinging to his mother with arms around her neck. Karen and Sarah took turns with introductions, hugs, and kisses, which prompted Joey and Nicholas to affirm that the girls resembled their father. Curious stares and bashful smiles abounded. Alex and Annie remained standing, watching and witnessing the insertion of new relationships into the lives of Sarah and Karen. Jovita became *Grandma* and Nicholas was *Grandpa*. The twins were affectionate and gracious, yet understandably shy. When given the choice, children prefer the company of children to doting adults, regardless of family tree or kinship. It was not long before the twins and Roberta shuffled away, went down the hall and disappeared into the bedroom. The three girls were undoubtedly on doll patrol. Hector fell fast asleep on Joey's lap, allowing her to settle him into the sofa, cradling him against the back. Annie excused herself and went to the kitchen to start a pot of coffee.

Alex sat in his recliner, directly across from the sofa and began to plot his plan to pry for more information from his father. The required small talk about the trip from Jacksonville began. It didn't last long. In short order, Alexander was left standing at the station. Perhaps as an act of self-defense, Nicholas took command of the parlor parley.

"I need to have a serious talk with you and your wife, Alex. I need to come clean about a secret I have been keeping for someone. Someone that was once close to you. And a secret that perhaps will be a little disturbing to you and your Annie."

Alex did his best to hide his surprise. He was searching for words to deflect his shock and stall his father until Annie got back into the room. He started to ramble, "All right, but we have all day today and tomorrow for all that. I'll go and see if I can help Annie along. Are you hungry, Joey, Old Man? I could see if we have some snacks. I'm sure the girls would like cookies and milk anyhow ... and it looks like young Hector there is passed right out. The little guy is all tuckered out from the long car trip, I suppose."

Joey looked to her husband, and answered, "No, we're fine. We stopped for burgers about an hour ago. We're fine. Coffee is enough."

"Good enough, then. I'll go see if I can give Annie some help in the kitchen." Alex nodded and left the room. He couldn't believe that his father had taken the first step and was about to spill the beans. His thoughts were swirling in his brain at the speed of light. Doubts popped up about his father's motive. He wondered if, in fact, his father was talking about the same revelation that he and Annie discovered on their own, or some other deep, dark secret. Or perhaps his father had indeed turned over a new leaf and would be honest and forthright from this day forward. His father learned of Alex and Annie's sudden addition to the family exactly one week ago. Nicholas already had an entire week to think about his reaction; a week to ponder his honesty; a week to consider all the consequences a secret can create; a week to appraise the truth; and a week to consider his words.

Alex entered the kitchen and walked to his wife, who was standing at the window and gazing into the pasture. He stood close, and spoke in a whisper, "He's going to tell us, Annie. The Old Man said he has something to talk about."

Annie was motionless, her thoughts twirling in her brain like her husband's did just seconds earlier. "My goodness, Alex. Maybe he has changed. This is great. This is very good."

There was relief in the kitchen. A burden was lifted from their shoulders. Although the dark fog of doubt clouding Nicholas' character had dissipated, there was still a persistent, nagging mist of uncertainty over their perception of Nicholas.

Alex loaded the serving tray with cups, sugar and a half pint of *Half and Half*. Annie turned off the burner and grabbed the pot with an oven mitt. "It can trickle down in the front room, Alex. We're good to go. Let's get this show on the road."

Once inside the living room, Alex set the tray on the coffee table and Annie set the pot down, letting it rest atop her copy of Redbook. Hector was fast asleep, and the girls were quietly at play in the bedroom. Joey helped herself with a cup of black coffee and poured one for Annie.

Nicholas wasted no time. "Alex, Annie ... I have something to say, and I need you both to pay close attention. This is important … last Sunday, when you told that me you inherited two daughters, Alex, I already knew the whole story. I've known it for years.

"Years ago, the government was working with Kodak to develop cameras and high-speed film for use in both conventional and high-altitude aircraft. I was part of that project for a little less than a year. Several test flights were dispatched over the States, Alaska and Canada ... way up north to the *DEW* radar line and over the *Nike* and *Ajax* missile installations, and even over some of the banana republics in Central America. We tested the new equipment for about a year prior to my trip to Rochester in 1954 when we informed them of the kinks in the armor we discovered. It was in downtown Rochester at Kodak Park, which is actually a city within a city. It was there where I met a woman … the mother of those two girls in there. The mother of your daughters ... she worked for Kodak and her name was

Katherine Dobbs, but I'm positive that you already know that name."

Annie and Alex listened intently and did not let on that they had already discovered most of his story. They allowed Nicholas to continue with his tale uninterrupted.

"I was up there maybe for three days, and it was not until, I think, the second day that I actually met Miss Dobbs. It was at a party with the research team at Kodak, some civilian engineers, design people, military and defense people. It was one of them feel-good, let-me-shake-your-hand, nice-to-meet-you, champagne, congratulations, and chat-and-nibble parties. Long story short, when she found out my last name, she said that she served with a fellow sailor named Throckmorton in Japan during that Korea mess. And you can guess where that conversation went. She told me about your love affair, and about her battle with the flu and her rotation back stateside. She said that she was so distressed by it all that she never said goodbye or let you know the whole truth. And Kate, the poor kid was an emotional wreck, and I thought she was going right over the edge. I really did. At first, I thought it was all because of my last name that she was in such a stew. It was as if I was thrown up against a brick wall. And I suppose because of my personal embarrassment, selfishness and shame, I did not tell her that I was your father."

Alex and Annie had locked onto every word. Nicholas glanced around the room and continued, "I wanted to calm her down, and offered to buy her dinner that evening, and she accepted. It was nice, and maybe that's what prompted her to tell me the rest. I had no idea where or how that night would end up, but when she told me about her pregnancy and that she hid it from you, and the birth of your two daughters, she completely knocked my socks off. I've heard some bullshit stories during my life of deception Alex, but hers really floored me. My secrets were professional, but hers were personal. Very personal. She wanted her secret to be kept a secret. She was stand-up stubborn as an over-worked mule about it. It was the way she wanted it, and she was determined that was how it was going to be. She had feelings for you but did not want to rope you in or tie you down. Right or wrong, I promised her that I didn't know you from Adam and that I would forever keep her secret. That was then, this is now."

He was sitting at the edge of the sofa, his forearms on his knees, looking directly at his son. He pronounced his words perfectly, without hesitation or any noticeable or expressed emotion. He was the perfect picture of calm, cool, and collected.

"Anyway ... I did not say anything when you called last Sunday and I thought it best if I told you this story in person, Alex. I hope you and Annie can forgive me for not saying anything back in 1955. Kate asked me to respect her decision, and I did. For five years I kept quiet, Alex. Right or wrong. The unfortunate passing of Katherine Dobbs changed the lives of everyone she knew. Secrets might work for governments, but personal secrets can hurt personally ... hurt in both directions. I have learned that the hard way."

Annie and Alex each felt relief. There was no wrecking-ball confrontation. Nicholas paused his epic tale, took a second or two, glanced at the others in the room and asked for an ashtray. Annie stood and got one from the buffet drawer, carefully pushing the photograph album to the back and out of the way. Alex noticed. Annie set the ashtray on the coffee table and made eye contact with her husband. Alex smiled discreetly and gave her a nod of acknowledgement.

Nicholas lit another Pall Mall and continued. The ashtray was an opportunity Joey could not ignore. She put a match to one of her husband's cigarettes.

"Kate explained that when the twins were born, the hospital wouldn't let her add your name without a statement of paternity or a marriage license. She wanted to list you as the girls' father. I suggested that I could help. It was me. It was all my idea. I volunteered and signed that certificate, or affidavit, for Katherine, Alex. I did it at her request. Within a year of birth, they can be re-issued in New York without a notary. I told her I would sign it as *A. Throckmorton*. After all, I am a Throckmorton. So, I drove to the hospital in Syracuse, quickly showed my driver's license and Air Force ID, and sweet-talked the girl in the office. I signed the parentage paper as 'A. Throckmorton' and when I returned to Kodak, Rochester, I left it for Katherine Dobbs at Visitor Reception. I was gone that day and never spoke to Kate again. We never again had contact of any kind."

Alex spoke up, "She re-filed those birth certificates with my name, Old Man. I wondered how my name got on them." He gave his wife a glance and a nod. "Now we know, Annie."

Nicholas continued and clarified his reasoning for the decision he made in 1954. In a tone of self-verification he said, "All's well that ends well. It's over and done with. I'm happy it turned out the way it did for the girls." Alex remembered he heard those words before.

Annie looked to her husband. "We have two beautiful daughters. That's the single consequence, the happy ending that cannot be denied. I think we should leave it at that. The girls only need to know that their mother loved them, and now they have our love. All of our love ... everyone's."

Alex spoke with pride, "Well said, Annie. Well said."

The ardent tension had disappeared from the room. Nicholas sat back into the sofa. Joey finished her cigarette and followed Annie to the girls' bedroom to check the status of everything in *dolly-land*. Alex got up from his chair and poured two fingers of bourbon into two highball glasses.

Joey, Annie and the girls wandered back into the parlor, with dolls and stuffed animals in tow. Hector woke up and was pulling a very noisy *Fisher Price* wooden toy dog across the floor. It was decided that Nicholas and family would drive to the *Tuck Inn*, register and get settled. Alex, Annie and the girls would meet them about six o'clock for dinner at the *Beef and Bottle Steak House*, about a mile north of the motel. With a bit of youthful pleading, it was agreed that Roberta could stay behind with Karen and Sarah and take the trip to the restaurant with Alex and Annie.

Alex finished his glass of Old Crow and set it on the coffee table with a plunk.

"You spilled a whole pot of beans today, Old Man. You laid it all out on the table ... out there in the open for everyone to see. But if Kate was still alive today, her secret would still be with you, wouldn't it?"

Nicholas spoke to his son in a low, subdued voice. "Maybe. Maybe not. I had a whole week to work this out. As soon as you called and gave me the news, I knew I had to come clean." He leaned in closer to Alex and lowered his voice further. "And to tell the truth, I nearly forgot about Katherine Dobbs and her ... your ... daughters. Last week Sunday when you called, a rock-hard, frozen, forgotten avalanche of years-old confidential information came tumbling down on me from a mountain glacier of ice-cold secrets. It started to suffocate me. I thought about it long and hard, and I determined there was only one solution. I had to dig out from under the secret I was keeping. I couldn't continue to breathe otherwise. It wouldn't be fair to anyone if I kept it to myself any longer. I had to clear the air, once and for all time. I told you before Alex, I'm done with the cryptic mysteries and back-alley bullshit. This was the last one."

He finished his bourbon, set his glass on the coffee table and stood. Joey was waiting patiently, engaged in small talk with

Annie. Two-year old Hector was standing at his father's side, arms stretched upward. Nicholas obliged and lifted him up and into his arms. It was about time to fire up the Oldsmobile and drive down the road. Nicholas led his family into the hall, out to the porch and onto the driveway. He turned and nodded to Alex, Annie, and the girls. "See you folks about six."

As soon as the engine started, Karen, Sarah and Roberta were back in the house. Alex and Annie stood together on the porch, waved goodbye and watched them leave. He put his arm around his wife.

"That went a helluva lot better than I expected, Annie. I didn't see that coming. Not at all."

"Neither did I Alex. And I don't think it's necessary to tell him about the photograph we uncovered. It would lower the importance of his revelation. It took some courage to come out with all that he did. He knocked over everything he had bottled up and spilled it all out in front of us."

"I wonder how much Joey knew. I wonder if there's more."

"It doesn't matter, Alex. It just doesn't matter. Not now."

"As Time Goes By."

Seven and a half years later:
Monday evening, July 10, 1967
Straight Eight Farm, Chumuckla, Florida

Alex and Annie sat comfortably close on the old porch swing. Soft breezes directly from the gulf tempered the heat of the day and wafted silently across the sprawling veranda. A large five-blade, rattan ceiling fan churned the air around them. A Tupperware pitcher, full of fresh lemonade, and two tall frosty aluminum tumblers sat on the wicker side table. They looked out over their world, peacefully content with the way things were. This was a day of reflection, of reminiscing and full of endearing memories. A new, sea-foam green, 1966 Chrysler station wagon was parked under the carport where the Packard once was. They had gotten married just over thirteen years ago. As they looked back over those years, they relished their enduring love.

Annie gave birth to a hardy, seven-pound, and four-ounce baby boy on June 20, 1960. They baptized him Herbert, after Annie's father. Hedy and Teresa chipped in back then, watching Karen and Sarah while Alex visited his wife and newborn son in the hospital. She and little Herbert were to be released from Santa Rosa Hospital after four days, but an unforeseen problem had arisen, bringing Annie to the brink of mortality. She suffered a critical postpartum hemorrhage and significant blood loss, requiring an emergency hysterectomy and an additional four days in the hospital. Her condition was, at times, grave. The attending obstetrician was a post-war Austrian immigrant, short on good English, patient interaction and bed-side manner. He was a tall, thin man with long, slender fingers, unkempt hair and a thick Tyrolean accent. It was a time that tested Alexander's nerves, patience and better judgment.

He was at her bedside constantly and caught whatever sleep he could while sitting up, leaning a shoulder against the wall. On the second day of Annie's extended stay, the doctor was at her bedside with an attending nurse. Certainly, with good intentions and as an attempt to ease Alex's anxiety, the doctor made a grave mistake in prudence that touched off a firestorm of emotion. In his dense Germanic jargon, good, bad, or indifferent, the doctor tried to calm Alex, "Your wife will be fine. She is strong and women were made to suffer."

Alexander let loose a right jab that landed squarely on the doctor's forehead, buckling his knees and knocking him out. Alex was arrested for assault, charged and spent a Friday night in Milton County jail, along with a handful of drunks and assorted other Pensacola riff-raff. Hedy and Louis took shifts at Annie's bedside during her husband's ten-hour lock-up. The doctor and hospital later withdrew the assault charge, but the fracas on the Intensive Care floor was, on occasion, the subject of cocktail conversation among close friends and family. The description of the fight given on the court papers only fueled the fires of local gossip and giggles for years to come. The charge nurse's witness statement read: *the doctor was knocked to his knees and passed out from a pounding.*

Years earlier, the same doctor had attended the birth of Louis and Hedy's youngest son, Thomas. Speaking from personal experience, Hedy affirmed that the physician was quite inept at communication and even questioned his professionalism. As the years passed, that particular doctor and one other, left Santa Rosa Hospital amid rumors of a malpractice scandal and lawsuit.

Annie fully recovered from her ordeal, but the complications suffered at birth and the hysterectomy left her unable to bear any more children. Herbert proved to be a very good baby, and his childhood development progressed without a hitch. With brown hair and brown eyes, he grew strong quickly. Always alert, he was receptive to all the attention that his parents and sisters gave. He turned seven years old a month previous and has continued to accompany his father everywhere at every given chance. With a *Marshal Matt Dillon* six-shooter on his belt and child-sized *Stetson* hat, he protected the entire ranch. Alex and Annie would watch Herbie walk across the yard, toward the pasture and paddock, keeping the peace. They felt very secure.

Karen and Sarah adapted quickly to life in Florida after their sudden transplant seven years earlier. The transition was smooth, pleasant and problem-free. The ability of children to adapt to any situation, give unconditional love, trust beyond limitation, and quickly put aside emotional disruption, amazed Annie and Alex. The twins had turned fourteen, and have proved themselves to be two strong cogs in the Throckmorton wheel of life. That fall, Sarah and Karen would be first-time entrants in the *Tri-State Quarter Horse Show* in Dothan, Alabama. They were already counting the days until the show and looking forward to the following year, junior high, and Milton Marauder cheerleader tryouts. The girls and their activities kept the entire family busy. Just then, they were in the parlor, watching *The Monkees* going through their antics and singing *Daydream Believer* on the new RCA color television. Over their thirteen years together, Annie and Alex had witnessed rock and roll evolve from rhythm and blues to bubble gum pop, and beatnik folk to psychedelic noise.

For a period of about two months, in the early spring of 1961, Nicholas Throckmorton was working long hours and eventually left Jovita and Jacksonville. Joey locked up the bar, left Jacksonville behind and drove to Straight Eight Farm with her young children, Hector and Ramona. Jovita was a distraught, weak, and lonesome woman. She found solace in Annie's company. Families come together in times of trouble, and cramped quarters, mixed personalities and personal preferences are set aside. For the children, all the excitement created an unexpected holiday, despite the nervousness and apprehension of the adults around them.

Two days after Joey and the children arrived, the television and radio ran nearly non-stop coverage of an ongoing invasion of Cuba by exiled nationals. Although it was pure speculation, everyone suspected what Nicholas was up to. Jovita was angry beyond words and was burdened with suspicion. Her husband had promised her, as he did Alex and Annie, that his days of doing field work for the *Company* were over. It was a tumultuous time: questions without answers, uncertain outcomes, and wavering emotion.

After a week, Joey opened up. During her stay at the farm, Joey revealed that she, too, had plenty of secrets hidden in the back of the cupboard. Annie's precognition of years earlier proved to be true. Annie, Alex and Joey sat in the parlor with the children safe in bed, the windows open and warm April winds pushing the curtains into a drifting muslin ballet. Annie poured a bourbon for Alex and made two rum and colas: the *Cuba Libre* concoction that Joey was fond of.

Amid the tension and uncertainty, Joey began to tell her story. There were no aunt and uncle in Chicago, and she did not have a mother and father who owned a bar called *Fernando's Hideaway* in Jacksonville. It was part of a ruse she concocted by herself with the complaisant and compliant help of Nicholas. Her childhood was spent not in Cuba, but Puerto Rico, just as Teresa's had been. An aunt and uncle were in her past, but not in Chicago. They brought her to the United States in 1930 and settled in New Orleans, infusing her into the bawdy Storyville district along with gamblers, thugs, and prostitutes. Joey quit school in the ninth grade and began working in the kitchen of a small, squalid jazz club called the *Sweat Shop.* Joey's tale sounded real, but scripted.

Amidst the commotion and celebration around the Japanese surrender aboard the *USS Missouri* in 1945, she said she had seized an opportunity to leave the bars, brothels, and back rooms of the barrio far behind. An AWOL soldier from Fort Polk bought her a ticket on the *Panama Limited* express Pullman to Chicago and she did not look back. She began a new life, albeit as a barmaid, and was never a student at any university. In April of 1946, fate brought Nicholas briefly and passionately into her life. They parted as casual friends and traded a few letters back and forth up until the time Nicholas unexpectedly reappeared in Chicago in 1950. He explained that he just bought a bar in Jacksonville and had an immediate need to secure a barmaid. He then encouraged, teased and cajoled her to return with him to Florida. Annie interrupted Joey's tale and made a statement that affirmed her humorous, witty insight. "Goodness gracious, Alex! You Throckmorton men are alike! You uproot young women and bring them to Florida." That was the kind of lighthearted remark that endeared her to Alex.

Joey became a different person that evening in 1961, not only in her affinity with Alex and Annie, but also with herself. It seemed that she had told the truth and came clean, but Annie had her doubts. Jovita claimed to have pulled the plug on her past and apparently allowed her deceptions to disappear down the drain like so much dirty bath water. Like her husband before her, it seemed that she escaped a cold, iron-clad lock of secrecy. Annie and Alex were not astonished at her story, but recognized once again that when it comes to Joey and Nicholas, they could expect the unexpected.

In six days, Nicholas arrived back at the farm unannounced. No doubt it was an attempt to find his family, repair the cracks of mistrust and mend yet again all that was broken. Jovita walked with determination from the house and met him in the driveway. After an animated ten-minute discussion, complete with waving arms, loud voices, and shaking heads, they embraced. An apparent cease-fire, armistice, and truce were called. Nicholas explained his absence was merely due to an unexpected and overwhelming workload that required the full attention of all available personnel. He claimed he never left the country but had spent the past three weeks behind a desk in a building with no windows. Immediately after dinner, and without ceremony, Joey, Nicholas and their two children left Straight Eight Farm and returned to Jacksonville.

The disastrous *Bay Of Pigs* invasion was history. Angry and embarrassed, John F. Kennedy vowed to "splinter the CIA into a thousand pieces and scatter it to the wind." That of course, never happened but as things developed, Nicholas left government service two months later and then spent all his time at Fernando's with Joey. Regardless of his retirement, the mystique, misery and mayhem of international discord did not disappear from the news. Kennedy, Castro, and Khrushchev kept a firm hold on the headlines for months.

Everyone leaves a footprint on world history in some small way. The Packard V-12 engines built in 1950s Detroit that Alexander refurbished in 1960 were reinstalled in PT boats that patrolled off the coast of Vietnam, keeping a watchful eye on Viet Cong activity and troop movements. Cameras that were developed by Kodak engineers and designers like Katherine Dobbs, and field-tested by pilots like Nicholas, were found inside an American U-2 spy plane shot down by the Russians in May 1960. Despite the Cuban missile crisis, the French failure in Indochina, the Kennedy assassination, and all the tension of the Cold War, Nicholas put his years of hard living, hard travelling and clandestine employment behind him. After his retirement, the world continued to withstand tensions between nations and survived countless crises. Nicholas watched from the sidelines and somehow, the sun still managed to rise in the East. He was content working behind his bar in Jacksonville, drawing a modest government pension and enjoying life with his darling Jovita and their children.

Annie's sister, Beth, her husband Bobby and three children, Becky, George, and Bobby Junior came for a visit during the hot summer of 1962. It was a week of reminiscing, updates and good company. Although they talked on the telephone, there were always stories that would go untold until face-to-face contact occurred. It was a heart-warming experience for Annie to see her sister again. Beth and Bobby's children had a fantastic time exploring the farm and the horses. George spent hours in the machine shop, curious about mechanics and enjoyed the slick characteristics of oil and grease on his hands.

Annie telephoned her mother about once a month and continued to endure Irene's maternal castigations and absence of humility. Although infrequent, there were times of warmth and endearment. Annie offered to send a check to cover her mother's airfare but had not received a positive response. Annie still hoped that someday her mother would telephone her and graciously accept the invitation. However, she realized that day could be somewhere way beyond the *Twilight Zone*.

A lot of water had passed under the bridge since Alex and Annie met, fell in love, married and began their life together in 1954. United, they grew their love, started a successful business, built a loving family, and witnessed drastic changes in the world.

Alex tenderly placed his right arm over Annie's shoulder. She leaned into him, as she always did. She fits into him, as if she were molded to him, and able to merge into one body. Her left hand and forearm rested on his thigh. The porch swing oscillated in a smooth, gentle to-and-fro. The high stratus clouds were the painter's canvas for a glorious pink and carmine sunset. In the magnolias and tulip trees, the katydids began their distinctive, chipping evening calls. It was bewitching, alluring and deeply intimate. All of this effected a private, personal paradise: a bubble, a slice of time, exclusively for two people on a wooden swing.

Alex whispered in her ear and asked his wife to close her eyes. He reached into his shirt pocket, and in one flowing motion, slid a custom diamond solitaire onto her finger. It was Annie's thirty-fifth birthday.

Fade to Black. The story continues with:

A BRIDGE TO CROSS

THE BOOK MUSIC:

(Music contemporary to the story.)

1.	My Happiness	Connie Francis
2.	I'm Sorry	Brenda Lee
3.	Singing The Blues	Marty Robbins
4.	Let Me Go Lover	Joan Webber
5.	Don't	Elvis Presley
6.	Problems	The Everly Brothers
7.	Dream Lover	Bobby Darin
8.	Loose Talk	Carl Smith
9.	The Tennessee Stud	Jimmie Driftwood
10.	Auld Lang Syne	Guy Lombardo
11.	Rocket 88	Jackie Brentson
12.	What's New	Frank Sinatra
13.	Fever	Peggy Lee
14.	Primrose Lane	Jerry Wallace
15.	A Lover's Question	Clyde McPhatter
16.	Too Much	Elvis Presley
17.	I Wonder Why	Dion & The Bellmonts

POST SCRIPT:

The title spring:

(From Chapter Five, "As Time Goes By") *The high stratus clouds were the painter's canvas for a glorious pink and carmine sunset. In the magnolia and tulip trees, **the katydids** began their distinctive, chipping evening calls. It was bewitching, alluring and deeply intimate. All of this **effected** a private, personal paradise: a bubble, a slice of time, exclusively for two people on a wooden swing.*

~ And after all, it is all about what Katy did. ~

This novel contains 100% recycled alphabetic symbols and post-consumer thought.

"Thank you!"

It Is Written in Stone

6½ x 15 inch
Carved Fieldstone
Crafted in Pigeon Forge, Tennessee, USA
at
The Sandman's Workshop

Kilroy was here.

Made in the USA
Monee, IL
09 June 2025

6e70a9e1-3af0-451b-8904-dc12e2220ca9R01